PRAISE FOR
Plain Jane: A Novel

"Well-researched . . . Henry's courtship of Jane has its romantic and affecting moments, and their interpersonal relationship is key."
—*Library Journal*

"Intriguing . . . Enables the reader a fascinating glimpse at royalty in the early sixteenth century."
—*Midwest Book Review*

"Wonderful! Beautifully written with a sensitive, thoughtful portrayal of the one wife to give Henry a son, this story grabbed me immediately . . . For a private journey through Henry VIII's court and personal life, *Plain Jane* should not be missed."
—*Romance Reviews Today*

"Gardner continues to bring the lives of remarkable women to life in historically compelling and compassionate novels in the style of Jean Plaidy and Thomas Costain. For those who've studied their history, this is a welcome addition to their knowledge; for those who haven't, it's a must read."
—*Romantic Times*

"A wonderfully told story . . . The reader will run the gauntlet of emotions as they read *Plain Jane*. From fiery Anne Boleyn's downfall to Jane finally taking the crown, the reader will get a bird's-eye view . . . [*Plain Jane*] delivers a heartwarming love story that will capture the reader's attention and not let go until the end."
—*Love Romances & More*

PRAISE FOR
A Lady Raised High: A Novel of Anne Boleyn

"An interesting historical look at the legendary Anne Boleyn . . . Readers will appreciate the tidbits of history . . . A well-written account of the relationship that changed England."
—*Midwest Book Review*

"A fitting continuation to the story of Henry's wives . . . Ms. Gardner has once again brought the Tudors and all of their foibles into light . . . Good dialogue, well-rounded characters, and a unique look at the court through the eyes of a young woman."
—*Romance Reviews Today*

continued . . .

"A remarkable story rich in historical background . . . The tragic life of Anne Boleyn is surely an enthralling tale. I give this high marks for historical background and recommend it to all lovers of Tudor history."

—*The Best Reviews*

"A thoroughly interesting read . . . Ms. Gardner ingeniously uses Frances as her medium through which the entire court of Henry VIII is given a more human characterization. Anne, in particular, is characterized as full of love, intelligence, and spirit with the flaws innate to all humans . . . Frances's voice is poignant and moving, and she's the perfect counterpoint to use in relating such a controversial time in England's history . . . This is a definite must for anyone who's a fan of historical romance."

—*Fresh Fiction*

"[A] satisfying historical drama . . . The novel offers a nicely paced view of life with the royals, complete with masques, political machinations, and courtly love."

—*Bookloons*

"With a spectacular history playing itself [out] in the background, this author delivers a powerful story that will either have the reader yelling at the injustice of Anne's fate or applauding in her demise. If you enjoy a story set in King Henry VIII's time and the story of Anne Boleyn's rise and fall from grace, then *A Lady Raised High* will surely grab your attention. Run to grab this excellent book to read on a lazy afternoon."

—*Love Romances & More*

Praise for
The Spanish Bride: A Novel of Catherine of Aragon

"Intriguing."

—*Midwest Book Review*

"English historical readers will treasure this deep look at Henry's first wife."

—*BookCrossing*

"For an excellent trip back in time, pick up *The Spanish Bride*."

—*Romance Reviews Today*

Titles by Laurien Gardner

THE SPANISH BRIDE: A NOVEL OF CATHERINE OF ARAGON

A LADY RAISED HIGH: A NOVEL OF ANNE BOLEYN

PLAIN JANE: A NOVEL OF JANE SEYMOUR

Plain Jane

A NOVEL OF JANE SEYMOUR

LAURIEN GARDNER

BERKLEY BOOKS, NEW YORK

THE BERKLEY PUBLISHING GROUP
Published by the Penguin Group
Penguin Group (USA) Inc.
375 Hudson Street, New York, New York 10014, USA
Penguin Group (Canada), 90 Eglinton Avenue East, Suite 700, Toronto, Ontario M4P 2Y3, Canada
(a division of Pearson Penguin Canada Inc.)
Penguin Books Ltd., 80 Strand, London WC2R 0RL, England
Penguin Group Ireland, 25 St. Stephen's Green, Dublin 2, Ireland (a division of Penguin Books Ltd.)
Penguin Group (Australia), 250 Camberwell Road, Camberwell, Victoria 3124, Australia
(a division of Pearson Australia Group Pty. Ltd.)
Penguin Books India Pvt. Ltd., 11 Community Centre, Panchsheel Park, New Delhi—110 017, India
Penguin Group (NZ), 67 Apollo Drive, Rosedale, North Shore 0632, New Zealand
(a division of Pearson New Zealand Ltd.)
Penguin Books (South Africa) (Pty.) Ltd., 24 Sturdee Avenue, Rosebank, Johannesburg 2196,
South Africa

Penguin Books Ltd., Registered Offices: 80 Strand, London WC2R 0RL, England

Copyright © 2006 by The Berkley Publishing Group.
Cover design by Erika Fusari.
Text design by Kristin del Rosario.

PRINTING HISTORY
Jove mass-market edition / July 2006
Berkley trade paperback edition / July 2008

Library of Congress Cataloging-in-Publication Data

Gardner, Laurien.
   Plain Jane / Laurien Gardner.
      p. cm.
   ISBN 978-0-425-22094-8 (trade pbk.)
   1. Jane Seymour, Queen, consort of Henry VIII, King of England, 1509?-1537—Fiction.   2. Great
Britain—History—Henry VIII, 1509-1547—Fiction.   3. Queens—Great Britain—Fiction.
4. England—Fiction.   I. Title.
   PR6107.A73P55 2008
   823'.92—dc22   2007050830

PRINTED IN THE UNITED STATES OF AMERICA

10 9 8 7 6 5 4 3 2

Plain Jane

The Phoenix in the Forest

October 1537,
Hampton Court Palace

JANE felt warm. Too warm. She pushed back at the heavy covers confining her slim body. Her fingers clutched feverishly at furs and finespun wool, seeking to free herself from the embrace of the enveloping softness that was making her burn.

Firm hands—the fingers cool against her skin—pushed the covers back.

Confined, bound, desperate, Jane tried to turn. The same hands, respectful and soothing, pushed her back. Another hand held her own—a large hand, enveloping but soft.

She closed her fingers hard upon it, and the hand clutched hers, feeling cold and moist against her parched skin. There was a sound, low and crackling, pervading all. Hail? No. Fire. It was the crackle of the fire.

The heat. Jane was burning. There was a fire. She would perish. Her mind conjured up images of a great conflagration, of fire eating walls and roofs and crawling, devouring, unforgiving, towards her in her bed.

"The heat," she whispered. "Burning."

"Jane," a voice said. A familiar voice.

The hand enveloping hers squeezed her fingers, and there was a great intake of breath, a ponderous sigh. Jane knew the sound of that sigh, she knew the voice, but she could not quite remember.

She fought to open her eyes. It felt as though twin weights rested on her eyelids, and all her efforts could only gain her a narrow sliver of light and vision. As if the world had become straightened, narrowed.

Turning her head slowly, she saw a large woman by her. Or rather, she saw the ample bosom of a woman rising and falling with deep breaths. It was covered in a rich red brocade surcoat. From that bosom cooing sounds emerged, the sort of noise a certain type of woman makes under her breath to calm babies, puppies, and invalids.

Jane didn't know who the woman was or why she was near. She turned her head away and saw at the foot of the bed two men in dark attire, their heads inclined. A faint whisper of Latin issued from them, soft-sweet in the heavy, closed-in atmosphere of the room.

It wafted in the air, crisp, familiar, and formal like incense at high Mass. Rolling her head further upon the pillow, Jane saw a roaring fire upon a deep, wide fireplace. *Too hot*, she thought. *Far too hot*. She smelled her own sweat tinged with the sharp tang of fever. She tried to speak, but no sound came from her parched lips.

The woman attending her raised her gently on one arm, supporting Jane against her bosom, the brocade rough against Jane's cheek.

Yet someone understood. A metal cup touched her lips. Sweet claret flowed upon her tongue and dripped down her throat. Jane swallowed. Again and again she swallowed with a sense of relief. She was released and fell back, gratefully, upon mounded pillows.

She managed to open her eyes a little further and allow her curious gaze to fix upon the tapestries on the wall, and the rich furnishings of the room. The bed was hung with heavy, intricately worked curtains that half obscured the two praying priests.

Where was she, and why were they praying? She could not remember anything at all, and her eyes dwelt wonderingly upon the great carved walnut bedstead above her head, far richer and costlier than any furniture she had ever had.

Why was she in such surroundings, and why was she so hot?

She felt as though a fire consumed her from the inside, as though the room were an oven within which they meant to roast her. The heat made her languid and slow and seemed to make her breathing difficult.

Her wondering gaze took in carvings up near the ceiling, gilded wood and inlays. A unicorn, a rose, and the motto, Bound to Serve and Obey.

Her gaze rested on it, fascinated, slow. It all felt so far away and strange, like the background of an obscure painting.

The hand holding hers squeezed, and she turned to look at it. It was a huge, powerful hand covered in a layer of fat. A massive signet ring shone upon the middle finger.

Jane recognized the ring and blinked at it in confusion. It was King Henry's ring.

The king. It is the king. She tried to rise. She must get up and prostrate herself before her sovereign.

But the woman in red held her down, and the king patted her hand with his free hand. "Jane, Jane," he said.

He spoke tenderly to her. The king was her friend.

Jane looked anxiously at the king's large face, his eyes fixed on her with peculiar kindness and concern. He squeezed her hand again. "Jane," he said. "You must live. And give me many sons."

Sons? The king was . . . her husband?

But it couldn't be. She'd known since she was nine that she would never be married. She wasn't beautiful enough for anyone to wish to marry her.

This was a dream. A strange dream. She must waken.

The sights, the sounds, the smell of her own sweat, the feel of oppressive heat all receded. There were images in her mind, and they overpowered all, shining clearer, brighter than anything outside. Her eyes fell closed.

"The queen, the queen," a woman's voice cried. "Someone help me."

But Jane did not hear. In her mind, she was a slight girl of nine running down a cool hallway at Wolf Hall, her family manor.

One

THE crisp, cool sunlight of autumn fell richly upon the stone walls of Wolf Hall in Wiltshire.

Filtered through the red and gold leaves of Savernake Forest, it lent a gilding patina, making the stolid stone building look like a rough common pebble that had been polished to look like a jewel.

The manor, traditional dwelling of the family that acted as guardians of the royal forest, bustled with the routine activity of a rural household. Grooms coming and going, maids tending to cleanliness and food preparation, entered and exited through various doors. At the kitchen door, a dozen hares were hung by their feet, waiting skinning and cleaning.

In the kitchen garden, a maid sang an old ballad while picking through the herb patch.

Three blond children, two boys and a girl, stood in front of the great detached barn at the side of the house. They were children of the Seymour family, the current owners of Wolf Hall.

Edward was twelve, Tom ten, and Jane nine. The boys had taken it into their heads to get their horses out for a run and, with the help of a young stableboy little older than they, were saddling them.

Jane stood a few steps away, looking on.

"If we had the king's permission," Tom said, "as he gives father twice a year, we could have a great hunt." Ruddy, bright-eyed, and stocky, he was fastening his saddle on sloppily, while smiling at the prospect of an imaginary sport. "We could hunt a deer. I bet I could bring down a buck with my bow."

His brother Edward, older and quieter, was also more careful and exact. He gave Tom a long, doubtful look. "We'll ride through the glades," he said.

"Jane, aren't you coming?" Tom asked as if only then realizing that his sister hadn't got her own horse and was making no move to saddle up.

The little girl shifted from foot to foot and edged away. Her threadbare pale green dress left her thin calves and slippered feet uncovered. "I don't know if—" she said. "I don't know if I rightly may." A slip of a child, with a cloud of spun-sugar hair and skin so pale that it appeared green in certain lights, she trained huge, eager eyes on her brothers, clearly longing for the sport and the race through the autumnal fields.

They always had a grand time while Tom shouted instructions as though they were all esquires on a royal hunt.

And she could almost feel the cool wind on her face, the horse beneath her, the excitement of racing out with the boys. The oldest daughter of the family, born after four sons of which Edward was the oldest surviving and Tom the youngest, she had grown up being treated as one of the boys.

Three years before, she would not have hesitated to saddle her own horse and go riding with her brothers, with no question to anyone. But the last three years had brought a change, as the nurse hired to look after Jane and her sisters had taken it into her head that Jane was growing wild and must be curbed.

She was a kindly, poor kinswoman, distantly related enough to have only a tenuous claim on the Seymours, but well brought up enough to know the rules. She paid great attention to propriety and behavior in those she pleased herself to call the young ladies.

Not that Jane minded, usually. The nurse, Anne, taught her embroidery and sewing, and Jane enjoyed the fine, demanding work and was good at it, learning designs quickly and executing them to perfection. But Anne was all too reluctant to let Jane go running with Edward and Tom.

And yet . . . And yet, Jane could almost feel the horse gathering speed beneath her, she could almost smell the spicy air of autumn amid the golden splendor of ripe crops and yellowing leaves.

"You should go ask your nurse, Jane," Edward said. "Mayhap she'll allow you to come with us."

"Why, only yesterday father said good riding and hunting were necessary accomplishments of any gentlewoman," Tom said. "I'll wager he wants you to acquire them right enough, Jane, if he expects you to marry well."

His boisterous words and encouraging smile defeated Jane's hesitation. She turned on her heel, headed into the house by the door nearest the stables, and ran down the long gallery that led to the family quarters.

The gallery was deep and narrow. On one side were portraits of her ancestors, going back to the thirteenth century, when the limning was done in paints that had faded and the figures represented distorted, the heads out of proportion, so that ancient Seymours and Esturmis looked not quite human but like those Titans and dwarves that ancient stories spoke of.

The Esturmi family had held this manor and the honor of keepers of the royal forest till a Seymour had married the last Esturmi and, with her hand, taken manor and honor.

Jane had heard all these stories from her older brothers, who'd heard them from her father, and every time she went through the gallery, no matter how fast she ran or how little she was thinking of house and ancestors, she got a sense of how long her people had been here and that the blood that ran in her veins was ancient and respectable.

That day she smiled a little at the long row of serious-faced men and at the occasional stern-faced woman, though her mind was wholly on her nurse, both anxious to reach her and dreading her response to Jane's request.

Nurse would be in Jane's room, or in Elizabeth's room at this time of the morning. She might very well wonder where Jane was. She might very well have already looked for the girl to set her at some mending task, or some other needlework. Or to sit her before her virginal, practicing the music at which Jane was wretched indeed.

The thought of how Nurse's lips would purse and how displeased she would look at Jane's lateness made Jane stop running and start walking, haltingly, down the hallway.

The house being made of stone, it was colder inside than out. Even the full heat of summer never penetrated the long gallery. And the windows that opened on the other side of the hall faced the wall of the great barn, too close by to allow direct sun in the house. Though glazed with panes divided by lead into small rectangles, the windows let in a hint of cold breeze through their imperfect jointures. Jane longed more than ever to be out in the sunlight of fall.

She didn't want to face Nurse, who might be displeased with Jane over her absence this morning so early. But neither did she want to go back and admit to Tom that she lacked the courage to ask. After all, though the nurse had authority over the girls, she was only a servant, and Tom would remind Jane of this in withering tones.

By the time Jane reached the end of the gallery she was walking slowly and halting often. Just then, from her right, her father's voice came, with a hint of stern reproach, "Jane, now."

Jane stopped and froze. She looked around wildly, thinking her father must be somewhere behind her and reproaching her. Perhaps the nurse had already gone to him?

But look as she might, she didn't see Sir John anywhere.

"Jane is so plain," her father's voice said, calmly, clearly, in the tone of someone who continues an interrupted conversation. "I doubt we can get her a marriage. Or at least a creditable one. Not on any dowry we can command."

Jane blinked. Her father was referring to her as too plain to marry? Why? And to whom would they marry her at nine, who would mind her looks? Looking around again, she realized the voice came from the barely open door of her mother's small sitting room where Jane usually went for her instruction in music.

Shocked by being called plain and by a hint of unconcealed disdain in her father's voice, Jane gaped and thought, *He's talking to mother. Mother will no doubt defend me. Mother always says it's the beauty of the soul that counts.*

"Jane is indeed plain," Jane's mother said, her voice containing no hint of offense or heated defense of her progeny. "And yet." She sighed. "You know plainer than she have got married before."

Jane's father made a sound in the back of his throat, a sound she knew full well from when John Seymour discussed the value of his ewes' wool or the price of lambs with their shepherds and thought the shepherds were far wrong.

"Aye, plainer have married," he said. "But not without a dowry. Not without some enticement to bring the young man to the altar. Come, come, Margery. Think of your daughter's face. Those protruding eyes, those thin lips, the receding chin—no, wife, we should thank the good Lord that Elizabeth and Dorothy are not as plain as Jane is. They will get good marriages, good husbands. But that leaves us still with Jane."

Jane's mother sighed. "Well then," she said, "it is a good thing that Jane is the oldest of the girls, and of a good, steady temper, too."

She paused for a moment, and Jane could picture her threading her needle in the interval, because Jane had never seen her mother hold any conversation without her hands being busy at some domestic task of sewing or embroidery.

"She'll help me till the others marry, and then we'll find the money for an offering to a convent and give her to the Church. Some small convents don't demand too much. And she can go in and spend the rest of her life decently, without remaining forever an old maid and a burden on her brothers as they go on to greater things."

"Well, and that's good enough," John said and sighed. "But how she should be born so plain when your beauty was reputed all over the countryside . . ."

His hint of reproach was ignored by his wife, who instead said in a firm voice, as if she were holding back comments about John's female ancestors, "Cousin Francis wants to take Tom with him to court. He says he could use a boy of such cleverness on his foreign missions."

"Francis Bryan?" John Seymour asked in a tone of great astonishment. "What a great opportunity for Tom, for Francis is a friend of the king himself."

"Yes, but . . . perhaps a little bawdy withal. And Tom is young."

John made a sound of dismissal at his wife's mention of their kinsman's less-than-reputable character. "Every male at court who is close to the king is reputed bawdy. It means nothing. A little too much drink, a bit of wenching now and then. It signifies nothing at all. Though to be sure, Tom is perhaps still full young . . ." His voice trailed off, as if he were thinking.

Jane became aware of herself where she stood in the hall. Her feet were cold in their thin slippers, and a breeze from some open door somewhere played the hem of her dress around her ankles. A thin dress and nothing much for the daughter of the manor to run around in, but her parents had never taken great pains over ensuring that Jane looked her best, and now Jane thought she understood why.

Her hands clutched at her skirt in distress, and her small teeth clamped on her lower lip. They thought her plain. Too plain to marry, too plain to display. Plain.

Her logical mind fastened on the list of faults her father had enumerated. She knew her own face well enough. In her room, she had a polished silver round she used as a mirror, and though Nurse had always discouraged her from contemplating herself in it, and Jane's mother talked of the demon of vanity hiding within mirrors, Jane had spent long enough in front of it while arranging her hair in the morning.

Thin and silk-soft, her hair shed all binds, all clips, all attempts at controlling it, and the family had too many daughters and too little money to afford her a skilled maid who could fashion her hair into something less than frightful. So the task fell to Jane herself, and while seeing to it, she had stared at her own features long enough.

Her chin did recede, and her lips were indeed thin, and her eyes did poke out a little, giving her an impression of perpetual surprise. She'd seen the way nearby landowners and her parents' friends would smile at her sisters and then let their gazes slide over Jane as if she didn't exist.

She'd heard—more in jest than in actual planning—several matches talked of for Elizabeth and even for little Dorothy, who was just learning to walk. But no landowner, no neighbor, no friend had ever joked about matching their likely lad to Jane.

Because she was plain. And yet her brothers, with much the same features, were not regarded as being less worthy. Everyone talked of how bright they were, and how far they would go in the world.

Jane let go of her skirt and lifted a hand to her hair in a desultory gesture. Her parents talked of sending Tom to court. And they'd always talked about how bright Edward was. Jane was bright, too—or at least she had a steady and capable mind. Why should that not count? Why would it be different for a girl?

And what fault was it of hers if God had made her plain? Surely all of the work of His hands was pleasing, no matter what form it took?

Jane shifted a little on the floor and frowned at the door of her mother's room, from which the sound of her parents' voices still issued. She was no longer attending to their conversation. She was no longer interested. She'd heard their opinion of her and their plans for her, and she was surprised and angry.

She did not want to be a nun. She wanted a family. She wanted a husband who'd look at her with the same love and desire she saw in her father's eyes when John Seymour looked at Margery.

"Jane?" It was Edward's voice from behind her, hesitant.

She turned to see her brother walking down the hallway towards her.

"Jane, have you asked? Can you ride with us?" he asked. "Only . . . Tom is anxious to leave. He says the ride will be at its best before the heat of noonday."

Jane realized she had been standing there long enough that she'd had time to ask her nurse for permission two or three times over. She felt the cold trails of tears down her face.

Oh, do not let her have to tell Edward what she had just heard. Not steady, unimaginative Edward, who would tell her that her parents were right and that she should be sensible about it all.

She covered her face so Edward wouldn't see her distress. She wanted neither sympathy nor mockery and, most of all, she did not want his sense and reason in this matter. There was nothing reasonable about this. It was a blight come upon her for no cause.

"Jane, what is wrong?" he said.

She could not stand to explain. Her face covered, she shook her head and ran away from him, down the hallway to her room.

Nurse was not there, the bed was carefully made as Jane had left it. Jane locked her door and flung herself, facedown upon her woolen blanket.

The tears came then, fast and unstoppable.

It wasn't just that she was plain, but that her parents thought so and that they thought her plainness and lack of grace would prevent her ever being anything in life, save perhaps a nun because the Lord didn't care how ill-favored His brides were.

"Jane?" Edward's hand knocked lightly on the door. "Jane, if you don't come, Tom and I will go. I can't hold him back much longer."

Jane wanted to reply, but she could not because her voice would drip with the unsteadiness of tears and shake, brittle with self-pity. She could not talk without giving away her distress, and Edward was a good person. If he heard her distress, he would demand a complete explanation, or worse, he would tell her parents.

She remained still, quiet. For a while, she was aware of his presence there, outside the door, and could imagine him, his hand raised to knock again but hesitating. Presently, she heard him walk away, headed for his ride through the morning-still glades.

And Jane would be left behind now, as she would be left behind in life. Always the one left at Wolf Hall until she became enough of an embarrassment that her parents would dispose of her to the cloister.

She cried she didn't know how long. It seemed to her that at some time someone tried the door—another of her brothers, or perhaps Elizabeth or even her nurse. Whoever it was asked no questions and made no sound beyond trying to open the door and leaving.

After a long time, Jane got up and looked at herself in the mirror. It was highly polished and gave her back her reflection with just a slight tinge of ghostly distortion. Her face was as her father had described it, save that her eyes were now rather swollen from crying and her hair, having come loose, made a pale halo around her unlovely face. None of which improved her appearance.

How strange it was that if a woman's face were her best weapon in the battle of life, she should have come to it armed with such paltry and insufficient weapons.

And yet, the intent, too-pale blue eyes that looked back at her from the mirror showed a more acute expression than she was used to seeing in people she met.

Jane had always been a good girl, quietly following her brothers, pacifying their quarrels, pleased enough to join in what they contrived for their own amusement. She had taken her mother's and nurse's impositions and done her best at her needlework and her music, though she didn't enjoy the latter very much.

Now, her pale eyes showed something like a fire of rebellion. Her small fists tightened on either side of her body.

Her father called her plain. And said that this made her fit for nothing but maybe the convent.

Well, let Jane be plain. The good Lord in His mercy had given her good and plentiful understanding, and that ought to be enough to make up for her plain face. She looked in the mirror, determined, intent.

Aye, she'd wager her good mind against any woman's prettiness, her understanding against any woman's wiles.

Looking at the pale blue eyes in the mirror, she vowed to herself that she would do better than any of her ambitious brothers or pretty sisters.

Two

✿

I T was summer. The brilliant, merciless sun glinted down from a molten-white sky and shone unforgivingly upon field and glade, upon town and village.

In London the sweating sickness raged. It was a peculiar malady where the seemingly healthy victim started sweating and felt faint and was dead within two hours. Women and men, children and adults seemed to melt in the intemperate sun of July and fell dead wherever they were standing.

Seventeen-year-old Jane had heard the stories, most of them told in great horror by noblemen fleeing the crowded cities in the hope of thus fleeing death. The sweating sickness was no respecter of persons. Unlike the plague, which took peasants by the dozens in their festering hovels but left the well-born near untouched, the sweating sickness took nobleman and peasant alike. It reached its fearful fingers even into the hallowed precinct of the royal court.

It was said that one of the ladies of Queen Catherine herself had fallen ill, and that King Henry was terrified of catching it.

And now it had reached into the Seymour family.

Jane stood outside, just within the shadow of Wolf Hall, staring out at the sun-dappled paths of the forest, and she felt like she would very much like to start walking and never stop.

The day before her youngest siblings, three-year-old Anthony and one-year-old Margery, had caught the sweating sickness.

Jane's mother had called on all her knowledge of herbs, and Jane had been summoned, too, to minister to them. But cold compresses and fanning, bleeding and tisanes had all been for nothing, and by nightfall both little Seymours lay dead.

They were now encoffined and resting in the chapel, to be buried before noontime, for this hot weather would not admit of a long mourning or a great vigil. Father James and John and Margery Seymour were in the chapel, too, praying for the repose of souls that, surely, had died unstained.

But Jane had got up from her pew at the back of the dim chapel and slid away between an Ave and a Pater Noster. She'd escaped the chapel for the well-lit hall and then from the hall she'd escaped outside, to the forest, whose trees started just past the great barn.

She felt unable to bear the confined atmosphere, the faint smell of corruption and death that seemed to her to escape from the chapel and penetrate the whole house.

And what she could stand least of all were her parents tear-marked countenances, their open crying for these young children, not yet much of anything on their own accounts. Perhaps it was that both her parents projected onto their babies what they wished to see. It was easy enough to do with young children, who were like wax to the adult molding mind.

Or perhaps it was that Anthony had been a clever, well-spoken child, already learning to read and knowing a little Latin. And Margery . . . Well, young Margery had been a pretty, round-faced babe with her mother's expressive dark blue eyes.

Pretty.

The word seemed a reproach to Jane. She knew she was being unkind, but she couldn't help but think that if it were she who lay in that chapel, waiting burial, there would be not a tear in her mother's eyes. Nor her father's.

Oh, they'd say the decent things and speak calmly of a great sorrow and a great loss. But in fact they would feel a burden had been lifted from them.

Jane looked up at the dark-green leaves on the trees and the glaring sky beyond. Already her sisters, Elizabeth and Dorothy, were never home. Always invited here, always going there, gracing various companies with their presences and doubtless fairly on the way to engaging many young gentlemen's hearts.

But Jane was here. No one ever asked her to go away, and her parents never requested that anyone take her, or show her off, or display her.

"Jane," she told herself in a low voice. "Your life shall be lived out here, at Wolf Hall, your days enclosed in the green cloister of the trees of Savernake Forest, at least until your parents find the money to shut you up in that more permanent cloister of a convent."

And suddenly her restlessness, her sense of being confined, was more than she could take. She must walk, or run, or die. She would go for a walk down a forest path. She'd tell no one.

If she asked her parents . . . if she told anyone she was going for a walk, they'd think her impious and unfeeling.

Oh, no, let her parents think her shut up in her room with

her crying, mewled up with her pain, but let her get out of here before she shouted truly impious things.

She went into her room for her hat, not the coif and headdress she would decently wear for company but a broadbrimmed straw hat of the sort that had come to Britain when the Roman Empire had occupied the isles and which, doubtless, would be around for another thousand years more. She often wore it while tending the garden at the back, which had, over time, become her responsibility, entire.

The hat would protect her fair skin from the unforgiving sun, but more important, unlike her headdress, it gave no indication of her being a lady of some quality. Oh, her dress was better than that of a peasant, but not much better than that of a merchant's daughter.

After all, new dresses were always needed for Elizabeth and Dorothy and even for little Margery, and Jane had to shift as she could by mending and refashioning hers. In this case it was a much-worn linen shift that had once belonged to her mother and that Jane had altered for herself.

With it on and the hat on her head, she looked like a woman without much to lose but her virtue. Which was good, for the paths of Savernake Forest were not wholly devoid of footpads, and normally she would have asked a servant or two to accompany and protect her.

But she did not intend to go very far and, dressed as she was, she did not think herself in much danger. As for her virtue, her plainness must be its shield.

She set forth quickly. There were, as usual, many people milling around the manor—servants and shepherds, a peddler or two come to show his wares to the kitchen staff, a few accustomed beggars, and the farmers who slept at the manor or the outbuildings during planting season, because the villages in which they lived were too far a walk to take after their day's work.

None of them stopped her, none of them questioned her. If any recognized her at all in her unassuming attire, they would have thought that she was on an errand for her mother. Jane had that reputation of a good, steady daughter, who never stirred but at her parents' order.

What other reputation would she have? No one looking at her could imagine her a wanton.

She walked down the first green path. There was in her mind a destination, a vague idea of where to go.

For years now, her walks had taken her to a place where the thick hedges formed a little refuge, a slight detour. There, the hedges, which in this part of the country surrounded every path, had grown into something like a loop, circling upon itself.

This hedge was between the forest and the fields and beyond it champion ground opened, tilled and fertile.

The circle it formed enclosed enough span of ground to create a good-sized room. It was carpeted in soft moss, due to a little rivulet of water that grew on the field side of the fence, and to the perpetual semidarkness of being enclosed by a man-tall hedge.

It could only be entered by a narrow opening, which Jane had found because she was following a small bird.

Her curiosity about the bird had led her to the perfect hideout, which most would imagine a mere thickening of the hedge.

Within it all was cool and green, and the only sounds ever heard were birdsong and the running brook. And the air was ever fragrant from the wild roses, pink and white—perhaps from the garden of some long-vanished cottage—which grew tangled in the hedges.

Jane had been accustomed to leaving her escort outside of it and going into the space confined by hedges on her own, and sitting alone and thinking of nothing much. It was a time when she could forget herself and the circumstances of her life, a time to just be, like those ephemeral, fast-withering roses.

Today she wished to go there and spend time thinking of how to escape her situation.

Well did she remember that day, so many years ago, when she'd stood before her mirror and promised herself that she would do better than all her siblings, that her plain face would not stop her achieving more than any of them. But since then, what had she done? She was seventeen. Had she been prettier, suitors would have been seeking her for two or three years now.

Had she been prettier, her mother would already have sought to place her in some local court, as attendant to some noble lady who could look after Jane and advance her prospects.

Edward and Tom, the companions of her childhood, were long since gone to London in search of their fortune. Edward was gentleman of the king's chamber, and Tom an envoy and aide to Sir Francis Bryan, indispensable—so that gentleman said—in diplomatic missions abroad. But Jane, despite her brave promises and all she'd told herself, had not gone anywhere. She remained here, circumscribed by her looks and her family's expectations for her.

The anger behind her thoughts quickened her steps, but she could think of no way to escape, nothing to do. While she was yet growing, she had dreamed that her features would somehow rearrange themselves with age and that she would wake up one day beautiful, like the caterpillar who, after long slumber, emerges as a butterfly.

But at seventeen her features were set for life, and she could no longer deceive herself. She kicked a small pebble hard and walked faster.

She could see, just ahead of her, where the path climbed slightly, and the trees thinned to the right, giving way to fields—a great expanse of champion ground now planted with green wheat, the stalks waving in the breeze, like the waves of a landlocked sea. There the hedge between path and forest curved. There Jane could already smell the heady scent of the summer roses.

She hastened forward, running a little, because here the path lost the shading provided by the tall trees, and once she got into her hideout she could sit down and be in cool shade once more.

She ran around the corner of the hedge and into the narrow opening that led to her sanctuary. And almost kicked a man who reclined on the moss-covered ground.

"Oh, I beg your pardon," she said, thinking he was surely a footpad and that this was the most ridiculous thing she'd ever done yet, apologizing to a footpad in this way. "I beg your pardon. I didn't see—"

"No, no, it is I who must beg—" He stood up, unfolding to a great height. A tall, ungraceful young man or older boy in the later stages of adolescence when the full adult height has been achieved but the body has yet to fill out and acquire the full adult proportions. "I should never have lain here like this, without cause," he said.

And Jane realized that if he were a footpad, he was the best-dressed footpad she'd ever seen and provided with the best horse of any footpad she'd ever known. The beast, white and high-legged, with something of the Spanish grace to it, stood a little while away, past the hedge, browsing on the grass of the nearby field just visible from this angle. At least Jane assumed it was the man's horse, for it was a strange beast to these parts, and it was unsaddled, while a saddle was flung on the ground nearby the young man, and he'd been resting his head upon it.

The man himself wore a rich, dark velvet doublet and fine hose and beneath it what were undoubtedly stockings of the finest silk. There was a pearl in his hat and another in his right ear. In all this splendor, it must be owned that he looked like a sow's ear that someone had tried, not very successfully, to make into a silk purse.

He was tall, and that was the best to be said for him. The praise ended there. His height, unsupported, left uncovered wobbly knees, prominent knuckles on his great, reddened hands, and a sharp Adam's apple on a too-thin neck.

His features were small, eyes and lips and cheeks all crowded in the center of his great square face, as though they feared giving offense. As if to compensate, his nose took up far more space than it should, protruding and making much of itself and quite appearing to rule over the rest of the face.

This should have made any other woman or eligible girl recoil, but it gave Jane an instant liking for him, a sense of belonging. He was as plain as she.

Not that it mattered much, she told herself, how a man looked. No. For men the yardstick was wholly different and had to do all with intelligence, pluck, and ambition, all of which she had, but went unheeded.

Still, she smiled at him, tilting her head back and allowing him an unstinting look at her features such as they were. "You will pardon me. It is not proper. I should not be out and about on my own, only I just came from Wolf Hall, and I—" She lowered her head, and curtsied, and started backing away, making as if to leave.

"I will go now," she said. "For my father and mother would be shocked to find me abroad like this, and were it not—" She curtsied again. She could see some feeling or other work itself through his large face. But expressions were hard to read on a man whose overriding look seemed to be of cringing in distress. "I shall go."

"Wait," he said, when her backing up had almost taken her out of the clearing. "Wait," in a tone of great urgency.

And then, while she stood there waiting, he visibly groped for words. "Wolf Hall," he said, at last. "Are you much acquainted with the family?"

"I am their eldest daughter, Jane," she said.

"Oh, Jane," he said, as if the name were perfectly original, so original in fact that he must repeat it to fix it in his mind. "I'd not . . . I'd not heard, that is . . ."

She supposed he was about to say he had not heard of her. Which she judged not. She did not know who he was or where from, but surely anyone speaking of the Seymours would mention pretty Elizabeth and lively Dorothy. Not Jane who usually hid at the back of the family group in any public gathering and had precious little to say for herself.

"I am William Dormer," he said. "Son of Sir Robert and Lady Jane Dormer."

It was Jane's turn to be surprised, though she recalled herself enough to make no sound of astonishment at his announcement but merely to curtsy again and lower her head.

The Dormers were by the way of being the well-regarded and most ancient family of the region. Unlike Jane's father who'd never held a title, Sir Robert Dormer was a knight, as had been his ancestors before him time out of memory. It was said they had come with the Norman conquest and stormed this region and held it for their seat.

Indeed, if the Seymours were to go to nearby Marlborough for some great religious ceremony, at the church they would be treated as no more than inconsequential local gentry.

The large pew and the place of honor were reserved there for the Dormers.

And the Dormers had many children, who were often heard of around the region for their intelligence, their acumen, their looks.

"I daresay you've never heard of me . . ." William said, and, before she could deny it, he laughed, a laughter that might have sounded foolish did it not resound with such great, echoing bitterness. "My mother would much rather I had been born the second son, I think. Or the third, certainly the fourth or the fifth, a boy she could have shut away in some monastery and forgotten about."

She looked up at him with sudden understanding and kinship.

He mistook her look for confusion, she was sure, because he said, "You see, all my brothers are handsome or clever or good hunters . . ." He shrugged. "I can match none of their accomplishments, and therefore I must go through life feeling the full weight of my parents' regret that I was born to them and that I am their heir."

He threw back his head and, for a moment, appeared if not handsome at least dignified. "So, you see, they sent me to a monastery, anyway, seeking to moderate my lack of accomplishments or ambition with learning. Perhaps it worked, but I find myself very out of place in society now."

There were many things that Jane could and should have said to this. The words thronged to her mouth—the correct, proper words that she'd been trained to say her entire life. That he was not plain, that he was not without grace, that she would be honored in his acquaintance, that she was sure his parents prized him.

She opened her mouth and, to her horror, what came out, in a still, even tone, was the absolute and unvarnished truth. "I am the plain one in my family," she said. "And I'm sure that all my relatives wish me gone."

She realized with a shock what she had said, and she looked up at him and met his astonished expression as she said, "Yesterday my youngest siblings died of the sweating sickness, Margery and Anthony, they were, and likely children, accomplished and bright. I should be mourning them, except . . ." She paused a moment and thought that having disgraced herself already before this acquaintance of less than an hour, she might as well continue and fully destroy his opinion of her. "Except that I think my parents mourn them as they would not mourn me, that they feel regret over them, because they were likely to do well in life. They would not had I been the one to die."

She did not know what she expected from him—revulsion, shock, or a sudden recoiling. What she got instead was a melting, a relaxing.

His face softened as if it were wax under the hot sun, and suddenly all the features looked more like they fit together. "I know exactly what you mean," he said. And cleared his throat. "I don't mean that you are—"

But she shook her head. "There should be no deception between us," she said, astonished at her own boldness. "I am plain, and you should not deceive me about it."

"No," he said and inclined his head. "I suppose not."

He was quiet a while, and she thought surely she'd finally shocked him, surely he would now make an excuse to go away from this very improper encounter.

Instead, he inclined his great head, where the overlarge ears protruded, too noticeable beneath the jeweled hat. "Mistress Seymour, I don't suppose you'd do me the very great honor of walking with me?"

Three

⚜

WERE they lovers? In truth Jane didn't know.

Oh, if her parents found that she'd been meeting William Dormer, unchaperoned in the depths of the forest, in the quiet of summer evenings or in the early dawn coolness of the day when they both were presumed to be listening to Mass with their respective families, Jane would have no doubt at all they'd accuse her of having a secret lover.

But it wasn't like that. In the two months they'd been meeting and talking, sometimes walking together when fields and paths looked deserted enough that it was not likely any farmers or servants would see them, they'd not even touched fingertips. What tenderness there was between them was like the tenderness between angels, all confined to the mind and not at all of the body.

The truth was while they were together, she could forget her plainness, and he could gratify his sense of social awkwardness by knowing she looked kindly upon him, was impressed by his title and grateful of his attention.

They shielded each other from the feeling that each one alone was singularly unsuited to their roles in life.

And William was fond of word games and of reading, and together they discoursed on theology and other matters of great mental import. It was said that the king was seeking a way of putting aside his long-suffering wife Catherine and sought to marry a much younger woman who might give him children.

Without ever having seen any of the participants, knowing no more of it than she had heard her parents discuss late at night while they sat together and quite forgot her presence, while she plied her needle near them, Jane felt a great sympathy with the queen whom they said had once been beautiful but whom time and many childbirths had left worn out and coarse and unattractive.

William discussed it from the viewpoint of the theological justification for it and said that after all, the Good Book said that if a man married his brother's wife they would be cursed and not have children.

It seemed to Jane that this overlooked the very real existence of Princess Mary, who was definitely a child of the king, even if not a son. And then, did not the Good Book also say that a man should take his dead brother's wife and raise up a progeny for his brother?

It was hardly the stuff of heady lovemaking, or the high-minded poetry of courting, but they could discuss all and do battle of wits between them and in the end part as good friends as when they'd started.

To Jane, it was enough to make her heart beat faster, to make her feet speed stealthily away from her seat in the back pew of the family chapel during the celebration of the early service. She ducked out of the chapel while everyone—her parents and the servants and other attendants who had Mass with the family—was rising for the gospels, so that her leaving might not be noticed.

Her desire to sit in the back pew so that no one would stare at her had long ago been gratified with a smile by her mother, less, Jane thought, out of respect for Jane's modesty than to avoid displaying Jane to the world.

Jane's plainness wouldn't be so hard on the whole family, Jane believed, if her mother in her youth had not been re- puted far and wide as a famous beauty. But Miss Margery Wentworth—as Jane's mother had been—had been talked of all over the shire, her beauty praised in song and poem. She could not understand, much less accept, how Jane had been born to her. And, on her more rational days, Jane understood her mother's disappointment.

But she was glad for William, who understood *her*. And who talked to her and asked her opinion.

He was practically the only person to do so.

So Jane escaped the chapel and made her way through now-accustomed halls to the side entrance of the home. Since everyone who mattered was within at chapel and the other servants and field workers already busy at their early morning tasks, she rarely crossed paths with anyone, and even when she did, no one dared question her.

She ran up the path in the forest to their appointed meeting place, much closer to the hall now as William feared that Jane would be attacked by footpads if she went too far.

Jane had taken some care over her attire of late. Oh, her clothes were the very same that she'd always gotten from her parents—worn dresses that her mother set aside or gowns that her sisters, out and about in the larger households of her mother's friends, thought too humble or plain for them.

But now when Jane modified them, cutting away a worn bit or pinning up the hem—for of all her family she was the smallest and slightest—she covered the worn part with a scrap of lace or did some embroidery to disguise where she had pulled up the hem. And she made sure her hair was properly combed, even if it took her a bit longer in front of the mirror and tempted the demon of vanity. And she never left home without her coif and headdress, and that the prettiest she could command.

Oh, she knew she was probably being foolish, as, no matter how washed, a russet wool sack would not become a velvet gown. But she felt as though she were at least showing William she was willing to try.

He had changed, too. She wasn't quite sure in what. His features were still not so much unpleasing as inharmonious and unremarkable. And his frame was still too thin for his height. But his shoulders looked more square, and he held himself with more dignity.

Meeting, they smiled at each other nervously, then veered off the main path and onto one of the side ones, which crossed the forest solidly between the trees and where they were less likely to run into any curious passersby.

Today he seemed to Jane more silent than normal. He'd not even made any comment on the weather, which was balmy early September, with the faintest tinge of crispness in the air, nor the quiet of the forest, which was great at this time of morning, broken only by birdsong and the occasional scurry from the undergrowth.

Even his great horse Samson, pacing sedately beside him, seemed to Jane more reserved and distant than normal.

"The summer is coming to an end," Jane said at last. "And harvest will be upon us soon."

It sounded, she thought, like some page from a great book of hours, but the truth was that they often resorted to such platitudes. And one such nonthreatening comment on weather or season was usually enough to allow William to overcome his shyness and start talking.

Instead he nodded, a slow, ponderous nod, as if she'd stated some great and momentous truth. And it seemed to Jane as if their footsteps on the mossy path were loud as the shriek of a nightingale upon a summer evening. Was he being sent somewhere, perhaps? Away from her? Or was there some other matter weighing on his mind? Or had he, perhaps, simply tired of her unstinting but plain company?

"Listen, Mistress Seymour . . . Jane . . ." he said at last. He had, for some time, been taking the liberty of her first name, as he should not and as she should not have allowed him. But without being lovers they had committed themselves to some sort of relationship where it seemed only fair that their given names should be used, without pretense, as she'd first told him.

She now looked at him, alarmed by his reverting to her family name and not quite certain what to expect.

"My parents are talking of . . . marrying me." He sighed, a deep, ponderous sigh that expanded his chest beneath its expensive doublet.

"Marrying you?" Jane asked without comprehending.

"They speak of betrothing me to one of the daughters of the Sidneys," he said, naming another of the great families in the region as if they'd been no more than beggars at the door. "Mary, they say her name is. A pretty, lively thing."

On those words, *pretty* and *lively,* his tongue delayed and demurred, as if wishing anything else upon the future companion of his days but those two characteristics. And, looking at William, Jane could see how a pretty and lively spouse would either terrify him or suffocate him, either scaring him into silence and mute conscience of his inadequacy or conquering him wholly and trailing him behind herself as it was said that great barbarian queens of old took their captives, tied to their chariot wheels and dragged behind.

"I don't suppose," she said, "that you could talk to your parents . . . Marrying your sons with no regard to their attachment is acknowledged by many to be wrong. I don't suppose you could tell them that you'd prefer . . ."

Here she hesitated because he'd never told her that he'd prefer to marry her. Nor, indeed, had there ever been any tender word between them to indicate he loved her or thought of her as the future companion or his fate. There had been nothing, in fact, between them, but these walks and talk of politics and religion and sometimes discussion of the old legends of the region.

He hesitated, too, his mouth opening and closing but no sound issuing, till Jane wondered if he was shocked at her daring or if he was looking for a way of letting her know that he'd never meant to marry her. But, instead, William shook his head, making the little hat he wore—red, this day, and with feathers—bob up and down unsteadily. "You don't know my parents," he said. "You don't know what they are like. I'd never get out three words together, much less . . ."

Jane's heart sped up, and something like a constriction formed in her throat. He'd never said that he didn't intend to marry her, never denied that his affections were attached. That meant that he wished in fact to marry Jane.

She wanted to laugh or cry or fling the light cloak she wore up in the air in rejoicing. Plain as she was, she had attached the son of a knight, and he wished to marry her.

Her mother would be shocked, and likewise her father. She could well imagine them looking at her, mouth agape, when she announced her betrothal.

She was so carried away with this thought that for some moments she did not think that she was not indeed betrothed, that the gentleman lacked his parents' consent and was not likely to obtain it, or not, at least, if she counted on William for the negotiations.

Not William with his shyness, his modesty, his fear of offending.

He was staring down at her in mute appeal, as if expecting that she would offer to talk to his parents for him. But even in as odd a courtship as theirs had been, such would, naturally, prove impossible.

As for her own parents, if they were to approach them first, Jane could well imagine that their incredulity, their low opinion of Jane's charms, would never allow them to make a case for their daughter's betrothal. It seemed a desperate cause.

But Jane, having labored long to engage the most eligible man she'd ever met, did not wish to lose him. And having found a friend who valued her as she was, for her talk, her thought, her earnestness—and who never made her feel plain or inadequate while she was with him—she did not wish to lose him and return to the lonely and hopeless days before she'd met him.

Something had to be done.

And then she remembered her mother telling her, early this morning, that she must get the linen sheets from the press and make the guest bed in the east guest bedroom for their cousin Sir Francis Bryan.

Sir Francis and Jane's brother, Tom, whom Sir Francis employed, were to come into town that very night.

Sir Francis was, of course, a very great personage at court, a friend of King Henry himself since their childhood days. And he was a good-humored man, old enough to be Jane's father and always full of song and talk and story.

Oh, true, his words were often bawdy and his stories often caused Jane's parents to cast her worried looks and imply that perhaps it was time that Jane retired to her bed. But in all his talk, all his good humor, Sir Francis had one excellent qualification to be Jane's advocate in this: it was that he alone in her parents' acquaintance seemed unable to see how plain Jane was.

Jane had often thought that Sir Francis liked all women so well that even the plainest of them still engaged his interest. Or perhaps it was that he heard of Jane from Tom, who still prized his sister as the companion of his childhood—he heard of her as lively and a good huntress, unafraid, and full of energy. And perhaps this served to mask the awkward reality of Jane's plain face and unlovely body.

What Jane knew for sure was that the old man was ever full of gentle jests and bawdy compliments to her person and always joked about her having a secret lover somewhere. He alone would not be surprised by William's existence, nor shocked that William wanted to marry Jane. Which meant he might very well undertake, in all earnestness, to pursue the negotiations between the parents. And he had standing enough at court to silence Jane's parents in the unlikely event they should raise objections, and to convince the proud Dormers that Jane had connections worth knowing.

"Be at my house," she told William, "this evening, after the supper hour. Come quietly into the garden. Leave your horse without the walls, and come softly. Wait for me outside the eastern entrance, where I shall come and get you."

William looked shocked indeed, a high blush tingeing his fleshy cheeks.

It occurred to Jane that it sounded as if she were arranging for an illicit assignation. She smiled at the thought as she added, "My cousin, Sir Francis Bryan, the king's friend, is visiting us. I will arrange for you to talk with him, as will I, and plead our case. There is some chance he will intercede for us and our attachment with each of our parents."

She ran home, to be at the chapel's entrance when the Mass ended, and to go prepare the guest bedroom for a guest who, of a sudden, seemed much more important to her than he'd ever been.

Four

SUPPER had dragged on, interminable. Sir Francis Bryan's jests and stories, which had always entertained Jane in the past, now seemed to have no color to them and no scent—just stories about an alien land that mattered not at all to Jane's everyday life.

When her parents looked at her with the meaning look that implied Sir Francis's stories had gone in risky directions and she should not hear them with her unstained ears, Jane had risen and gone to her room.

But instead of removing her outer clothes, keeping only her underdress and getting in her bed, she sat upon it, her hands on her lap, listening. Waiting.

From the dining room came sounds of men laughing. From her mother's quarters her mother's voice, and a soft reply, possibly of a maid. So her mother had left, and the men were now left utterly to themselves and free to talk of whatever subjects men discussed when they were alone. Jane hoped they would make quick work of it.

From the kitchen, sounds had died down, the meal and its cleanup probably done, the cooks getting ready to retire. From outside the house, if Jane listened very carefully, there came a sound of trees rustling in the wind and a desultory horse's neigh.

Was it one of the Seymour horses, restless in his stall in the stable? Or was it Samson? Had William come, and was his horse growing impatient outside the walls?

Jane did not know, and not knowing consumed her. She liked William. She would not go so far as to say she loved him. What knew she of love?

What she felt had nothing at all to do with those long-winded poems of the troubadours, their panegyrics and painful sighs. It was just that William had become, over the course of the last two months, her dearest friend and companion. The thought of living without him seemed to her like a dull and dreary life. But the idea of parting gave her only a calm sense of doom and no great despair, no animated sorrow; no overarching tragedy tinged her thoughts as it should have if she were in love.

Perhaps because she was not in love—or thought she wasn't—she saw William for what he was. A good man—or he would be one someday. But for now, he was a hesitant boy in a grown man's body.

He wanted her hand; he wanted their marriage. But how long would it take him to grow tired of waiting out there in the dark, with the night wind rising? How long till he decided he did not have the courage to face Sir Francis?

For in William, shyness overrode all other feelings.

With relief, at long last, Jane perceived footsteps past her door. Sir Francis's guest quarters were at the end of the family quarters and to the right. She heard Sir Francis slur something to her father, then her father's door open and close, steps down the hall, and finally Sir Francis's door opening and closing.

She rose immediately. Her hands had gotten damp with sweat, and she wiped them on the front of her skirt.

Her candle that she'd brought with her into the room still burned in its candle holder, though much lower than she would normally have burned it in one night. Jane's mother would have words on the wasting of good wax. But that was a worry for another day.

Jane took up her candle, opened her door as silently as she could, and closed it again with hardly a sound, then tiptoed down the hallway where the candle was insufficient to do more than make the shadows longer upon the ancient walls.

Knocking on Sir Francis's door was an art. It had to be loud enough for the man to hear, yet not so loud that it would startle those not yet sleeping in the house.

She knocked once; then again she knocked. When nothing but silence answered, she raised her hand to knock yet again.

From within came Sir Francis's "Aye," and Jane opened the door.

The man was in his shirt, having removed all his outer garments. The shirt, freed from the restraints of doublet and hose and stockings fell, loosely, to the middle of his thighs. Beneath those, an expanse of surprisingly hairy legs showed, and beneath that, against the stone floor, great feet with splayed toes and yellowed nails.

"Jane," Sir Francis said, looking a little alarmed. "Bless my soul."

His voice was a little too loud, and she put her finger to her lips.

The man looked at her with great big, wide-open eyes, and

it occurred to Jane that he might think she had designs on him. She felt a great need to laugh and had to control it. If she laughed like an abandoned woman, what would he not think? She looked away. But possibly before she did, the merriment had shown in her gaze. Sir Francis looked confused and terror-stricken, no doubt already contemplating how to explain to Sir John Seymour that Jane had come to his room of her own accord and that Sir Francis had not the slightest interest in attempting against her virtue.

She stepped into the room hastily and closed the door behind her, quietly. "You must not be alarmed," she said with tardy reassurance. "You must not be alarmed, Sir Francis. I come only to ask you a great favor, which I do not wish to have my parents hear of, just yet." She hesitated and then, because she could sense her words were opaque to him and might not reassure him quite well enough, she added. "It concerns a young gentleman."

Like that, the alarmed expression went from his face, replaced by a sly, cunning look and a smiling glance that seemed to say he'd seen all manner of folly, and hers was nothing new nor unexpected. "A young man is it, Jane? You've got a dove cooing around the flowering hedges, is it?"

Again his voice was too loud. She took her finger to her lips, but she did it smiling, for she had a boon to ask him and didn't wish to displease him.

"His name is William Dormer," Jane said as reasonably as she could. "He is the son of Sir Robert and Lady Jane Dormer. We've met . . . and become attached."

Sir Francis was smiling and nodding at her, showing no surprise at all that she should have captured a young man's heart. "Become attached, have you. And does he wish to marry you, Jane? Has he asked for your hand?"

"He's—" Jane's voice caught in her throat. "He's said he would like me to be the chosen partner of his life, yes."

"And would it please you?" Sir Francis asked.

"Very much," Jane said. "Very much."

Sir Francis beamed on her. "Our little Jane has become a woman and will be a pretty bride of seventeen."

Jane noticed he called her pretty without irony and once more thought that, liking all women, Sir Francis was unable to distinguish between them by degrees of beauty.

"And has he spoken to your parents?"

Jane shook her head. "We wish you to speak to my parents for us. And his parents also. We think that Sir Robert Dormer might raise objections to our betrothal, since they have grander plans for him. They're seeking to match William with a Sidney girl."

Sir Francis arched his eyebrows high above his merry eyes. "Indeed. Well, we are in new times, and provided the match is not too disparate in station, fortune, nor form, no family should gainsay young people's attachment." But there was something like doubt at the back of his amused gaze. "And will your young man speak with me, Jane, or not even with me?"

"He will speak with you," Jane said and smiled. "If you will listen to him. I have asked him to wait without this nearby entrance and I will fetch him for you now."

"Go on, then," Sir Francis said and, walking to the basin and ewer atop the clothes press in his room, he poured water from the ewer into the basin and washed his hands and face.

"Go on," he told Jane.

Jane went out again with her candle, careful to close Sir Francis's door so quietly that no one in the house could have heard it.

The hallway was silent, save for a snore issuing from her father's room. She hurried down the corridor on tiptoes, shielding her candle flame from the breeze created by the haste of her passage.

At the end of the hallway, she opened the door and found William there, waiting.

He wore his best doublet of fine blue velvet and a simple matching hat, with no jewels, no plumes, nor other decoration—perhaps because he thought it might catch the light as he entered the Seymour garden.

His eyes were wide with concern, and his whole face was set in a sort of stern eagerness. To Jane's eyes he'd never looked so handsome. She held her finger to her lips, but she needn't have bothered. William understood the need for secrecy as well as she.

He closed the door quietly behind them, and they tiptoed down the hallway to Sir Francis's room.

The worthy opened the door as they reached it, clearly having waited for them this long while and listened for the slightest sign of footsteps.

They came in, and Sir Francis surveyed William doubtfully. It seemed to Jane that the worthy noble had some misgivings about the enterprise.

At last Sir Francis smiled what he no doubt thought was a paternal smile. "You're young William Dormer, are you?" Sir Francis asked.

William bowed hastily.

"I know your father," Sir Francis said.

William nodded in silence.

"You are attached to our sweet Jane, here, are you?" Sir Francis asked. He'd not bothered to dry his face after washing it, and as he turned to look on William, the glint of water on his hair and beard caught the light like sweat, as if the interrogation were costing him a great effort.

William seemed taken aback for a moment and swallowed hard, making his Adam's apple bob up and down upon his too-thin neck. But when he spoke his voice found a fullness and expression Jane had not often heard from him.

"I think Jane is a rare jewel," he said, "which has been preserved just for me, and I've been glad to find her, and with her I would fein spend the rest of my days."

Sir Francis cackled, delighted, and, taking a step back, sat upon his bed. "Would you now? Well, we must talk. You must satisfy me of your intent and your sensible attachment to Jane, too." He turned to Jane. "You may leave us, my dear. Go to your bed now and dream sweet dreams of not sleeping alone." He cackled knowingly. "For soon we'll see you two in bed together. Now be gone. I'll get your young man out of here without anyone perceiving him."

And thus dismissed, Jane hastened down the hallway to her room, where she blew out her candle and then sat in her bed, her heart beating hard and fast, dreaming of formless union, imagining the expression on her parents' face, and all in all contemplating how her life was about to change.

If it all went well. If their parents gave consent.

Five

 Jane intercepted the maid on the way to Sir Francis's room. She took the pitcher of water from her hands and dismissed the girl.

She'd wakened early, fretting over Sir Francis's talk with William. She'd caught just that look of uncertainty in the old man's face that told her he either misdoubted William's character or his steadiness of purpose towards Jane.

Carrying the cool white ceramic pitcher, she knocked at the door.

"Enter," came from within in the gruff tone of the recently wakened, and Jane slid in, carrying the pitcher.

To her great relief, Sir Francis was fully dressed. He grinned at her, "Ah, girl. I knew it would be you. You'd be about and sniffing to hear something of your young man." He winked and poured water into the recently emptied basin, splashing it all around.

While he washed his face, and since he seemed no more disposed to enlighten her than if she'd been a deaf-mute unable to communicate her doubts and her distress, she said, "Well, Sir Francis? What did you think of William?"

The gentleman grabbed for his towel—a double-quilted linen piece set beside the basin atop the press and said, "Give me leave, girl. I'm ill awake yet."

Jane said nothing but looked steadily at him.

He let out with a great roar of laughter. "You girls and your love affairs," he said. "I have spoken with your young man, Jane, and if I may say so, you could have picked better. He's broad of jaw and small of eye, with large feet and awkward legs."

"Never mind his legs," Jane said. "I did not complain of him."

"Aye, but mayhap you should have. For in intelligence and grace he's nowhere near your equal, dear Jane, and you could do much better than him. Have you considered perhaps applying to become a lady-in-waiting at the court, where greater men, and better, could come and court you?"

It seemed to Jane the worst of the injustices and the most foolish of temptations for Sir Francis to dangle the court before her—before her, who could not even engage the interest of locals. Everyone knew that Queen Catherine, older and not so handsome as she used to be, yet liked her ladies in waiting to be handsome and liked them around her all in array, like beautiful flowers in a plain room that they might, perhaps, with their grace lend grace to her plainness.

"Never mind the court," she said. "What think you of William's suit? Will you help us?"

"Aye, girl," he said, and gave her a whimsical, startled look. "Are you so hot?" He seemed surprised at the idea that she could be, and for William yet. "Well, very well, I see I shouldn't toy with your eagerness. Love chooses not where it rests, does it not. Your William will do well enough, I daresay. Pay not attention to the ideas of this old reprobate who thinks that a woman of your blood, your grace, and your intelligence could do better. I've spoken with your father early this dawn."

"You have?" Jane asked and, all alarmed, had to reach for the clothespress and rest her hand on it to steady herself. What could her father have said? And how surprised had he been?

"Aye, and he's pleased enough and gave me his leave to pursue the suit with the Dormers."

"He did?"

"What, girl, you expected he would not? Sir Robert Dormer is a knight, and his wife is from a right noble family. What father in his right mind would refuse her daughter such a worthy conquest? You did well, Jane, at least for your parents' purpose."

"And was he surprised?"

Sir Francis raised his eyebrows at her. "Surprised? Why should he be? That you found yourself an admirer while you're living here in the middle of the forest? Ah, Jane, your father is a man of the world. He knows when the stag is in season the hunter will beat a path to it, and so will it be." He winked at her again. "And now to Mass, girl, and it's no use at all your asking me again before tonight, because I mean to talk to the Dormers this afternoon."

Jane went to Mass with an unquiet spirit and dared not shift from her pew to go meet William in the woods. Not today. It was not worth the risk.

Six

The sun was setting, tingeing the horizon beyond the trees and the sky above a pale shade of red. Jane had paced her room, unable to concentrate or settle at anything.

At the noon hour, or a little after, Sir Robert had left upon his horse, possessed of all assurances and good wishes of the Seymours.

For Jane the day had slipped into a daydream of anxious longing—longing for an answer, longing for certainty. In her mind she could find none.

Sometimes it seemed to her an assured thing—of course the Dormers would agree. How could they fail to on the inducement of such a great personage as Sir Francis, the king's own friend? And when he was interceding for Jane with all his might? How could they withstand his wit, his court knowledge? What could they do, but give in and say yes?

At other times she thought that her parents would not have anything disposed for her dowry, nothing set aside. They thought of sending her to the convent when they could get the money together. And not much money at that. And even so much was not to be done right away. What if they could not give enough of a dowry to tempt the Dormers?

She bustled here and there all day, doing she hardly knew what. If anyone had asked her afterwards, she would have been unable to name a single thing she'd accomplished that day. Her needlework lay started in three different places, and her music forgotten upon the virginal in the small room.

All day long her parents gave her startled and astonished looks, as if she'd turned overnight into a marvelous creature who might very well, at any moment, grow wings and fly away or perhaps gain a second, marvelous head beside her own.

As the end of the day neared, unable to bear their questioning looks and gentle handling any longer, she went to her room and there spent her time, waiting—now getting up and now sitting herself down, only to get up again. At long last, as the sky lost its light and the sun its vigor, she heard the sound of approaching hooves.

She took a moment to compose her hair and arrange her expression so that it betrayed nothing of her inner turmoil.

Looking in the mirror, at her very same face—plain Jane with the protruding eyes, the receding chin, the thin lips—she willed herself to show nothing. She would display neither sorrow nor triumph.

If Sir Francis had succeeded, she would greet her upcoming union with equanimous condescension. And if her union with William were refused, she would show no grief. Already her parents were looking at her with that anxious look parents always gave a child who was ill. If she showed disappointment at the result of a failed suit, she would only be confirming their opinion of her—that Jane was not worthy of being loved and that anyone who thought to unite his fate with her must not be serious enough to persuade anyone.

Too afraid of running into one of her parents, or Tom, who was visiting with Sir Francis and who was sure to mock her and make sport of her over her impending betrothal, Jane walked out of the door nearest her room and then outside, through the rose garden, towards the door of the great parlor, where Sir Francis would be meeting with her parents.

Before she ever reached the parlor, she heard Sir Francis's voice carrying, full and loud, through the night air. It had some great emotion behind it, but what that emotion might be, Jane could not say. She was not yet close enough to hear words. She ran forward to listen.

And then, right outside the door, she heard Sir Francis's voice again, "It's a wretched business."

The sentence stopped her. A wretched business? Then it couldn't possibly have gone well. She stopped just outside the great parlor. Inside, candles were lit, and she could see her mother standing by the fireplace and her father sitting in a great chair. Sir Francis paced the room, still attired as he'd been when riding his horse.

His fine doublet looked wrinkled and stained from the ride, and his face was knit in a great frown of disapproval. He'd removed one of his gloves and carried it in his hand, now holding it tight in his fingers, now slapping it across the palm of his other hand. "A wretched business," he repeated. "I tell you."

"But . . . I don't understand," Jane's mother said. "You mean to tell me the Dormers dismissed the match out of hand? They won't consider their own son's attachment?"

Jane felt a knot form in her throat. She stood amid the rose

garden. The mild end of summer kept quite a few roses flowering. Their fragrance, full and heady in the air, caught in Jane's
throat and brought bile burning to the back of her mouth.

Sir Francis made an inarticulate sound and slapped his
glove on his hand. "We are to understand," he said, "that the
Seymours have not enough of a pedigree for the Dormers."

"The scoundrels," John Seymour said, rising, his hand upon
his sword pommel, his face reddening with immediate anger.
"The scoundrels. How dare they? Not enough pedigree? Why
my family is as old as theirs and comes from the Normans,
too. And before the Normans came there were the Esturmis
here, whose blood runs full in my veins, because their last
daughter married my ancestor."

Sir Francis sighed. He stopped for a moment, looking at
John, as though evaluating his friend's temper and his ability to
endure insult. "Well, there is the matter of your son's bride—"

He looked at Lady Seymour, who pressed her lips tight in
disapproval.

"What mean you, my son's wife? My son Edward's wife, I
assume? What mean they by that?" Sir John asked. But he had
waited too long, and his voice lacked the note of indignation
it would have had, had he been wholly innocent.

Jane remembered hearing some gossip. Maids and cooks
and the farmers who overnighted had sometimes whispered
behind their hands that Sir John liked Catherine Filliol Seymour far too well.

She knew not the details. No one before had been bold
enough to throw the story in Sir John's teeth. Catherine was
her brother Edward's wife some years married, and Jane had
never seen a hint of such a thing. But then Jane hadn't looked.

Now she wondered how far abroad such a scandal could
have spread and what it meant.

"And this is all?" Jane's mother asked. "This is how Lord and Lady Dormer dismiss us, with a sneering comment about our lack of nobility and some hints about unproven scandals?"

"Well, truth be told, Lady Dormer did all the talking," Sir Francis said. "And how she talks, endlessly. She also said . . ." He looked around and at the room, then at the Seymours from beneath lowered eyelids, as if wondering what their reaction would be to such news. "Well, the truth is, Lady Dormer also said that Jane . . . well, that she hoped to secure a better daughter-in-law than Jane so that her son's daughters wouldn't be ill-favored."

If Sir Francis expected protest from the Seymours, he was disappointed. Lady Seymour and Sir John Seymour looked one on the other and sighed.

"Oh, believe me," Lady Seymour said at long last. "Beauty and plainness are not easily inherited, else we'd not be having this problem."

Sir Francis frowned. "I never understood why Jane is considered plain," he said. "She has lively eyes and as good a mind as any in creation, and I told Lady Dormer so and that I'd liefer have Jane in my family than a hundred such as Lady Dormer."

Jane could not listen anymore. She admired Sir Francis's efforts and the gallant way in which he'd tried to defend her, but she could endure no more.

In the end, it had come to this. After all of Jane's efforts. After her very true kinship and attachment with William, after their hours of talk in the gardens, after their silent betrothal, it would come to this. She would be rejected for being plain, and there would be no appeal.

She could not endure to sit there outside the door and to listen to her mother and father utter platitudes as if the Dormers' disdain were justified.

She turned away blindly, in the dark, and—in the dark—came up against a tall, dark shape, a larger bulk. Confused, she backed away, thinking she had bumped into a tree or some bush she'd failed to notice. Then she realized her hand was touching fine velvet and an edge of lawn, and that the obstacle in her path smelled familiar.

"Jane," William's voice said. "Jane, I beg you—"

She blinked the tears from her eyes to see him standing there, earnest, tall, with that expression like he was an unwitting passenger in his own body.

"Jane . . ." he said, and lifted a hand to caress her pale, too-smooth hair.

She pulled away from him; she wrenched herself from his warm, reaching arms. "Stop. Stop. What are you doing here?"

"I came to let you know I care not what my parents say. I care not what they think. Jane—we were meant to be, you and I. You are the one I want, and not some stranger."

Looking up into his gaze, for the first time, Jane read there a naked glance of desire such as she'd never surprised in any man's expression before. Or not aimed at her. He wanted her. Indeed, he wanted her. But what did that mean but that he wanted to make her body his? What did that mean but illegitimate children, and shame, and more of the same taint upon the Seymour family as Lady Dormer had already complained about?

"No," she stepped away from him, as he stepped forward. "No. You must see it is not right. I am a poor woman, and my only endowment is my virtue. If your parents will not let you marry me, then you have nothing to offer me. Nothing I could accept."

"But we could run," he said. "We could—"

"And how would we live, pray?" she asked. "Removed from

the approval and favor of the world, how would we live? Go you home and leave me to my grief."

And yet he kept coming towards her, and she kept stepping back to get away from him. But she knew the paths and secrets of this garden as he did not—without thinking, and in the dark she still knew them. She stepped back and back and back, and rounded a corner, till the path she was on had a root of an ancient oak stretched right across it a few steps in.

She reached the root and then turned and ran. William ran also and fell across the path.

Jane heard the sound of his fall and felt the slight tremor of the path under the impact of his weight. But she stopped not. She delayed not.

The entrance loomed before her. She opened the door and entered. She avoided colliding with two servants. She gained her room with a sense of relief and locked her door behind her.

She sat down on her bed and cried.

It wasn't that she thought William wished her ill. It wasn't that she thought he would knowingly force himself on her. It wasn't any of that.

It was that she believed William's body was no longer controlled by his mind and that, in the disarrangement of his emotions, he'd do things he'd never do else, if fully himself. And it was that she realized there was nothing remaining for her there.

William would marry his Mary Sidney, and she wished him joy of her, and the fact that she could, so calmly, wish him joy showed her she'd never truly loved him. Her affection for him had been that affection of two lonely creatures bruited about in the world, without purpose, who cling to each other and hope, in the other, to find consolation for what nature failed to give them. Had they married they'd have been deluding themselves and each other.

She had wanted no more from him than escape—escape from her plainness, from her parents' disdain, from Wolf Hall and its enclosing, surrounding forest.

And now she was consigned to live here forever.

Seven

EARLY morning, Sir Francis came to find Jane where she sat at the virginal in her mother's small room, playing desultorily a string of jarring notes that wounded the cool morning air like falling hail.

"Mistress Jane," he said, and waited in the doorway. She could see him reflected on the raised front of the virginal—a fine piece brought by her mother at her wedding and worked with glass and stones all about into a scene of country delight with shepherds and their huts and everything disposed to beauty as never happened in the real country.

She could see Sir Francis standing there—a blurry impression of the tall, broad man. He'd removed his hat and held it in his hand, deferring to her as though she'd been some great personage. Or a dead or sickly person.

Jane continued playing. Her fingers tickled the keys on and

on aimlessly till the consciousness of him there made her fingers slow down and eventually stop.

"Jane, do not distress yourself," Sir Francis said. "You are a young girl, comely and serene, and other men will come. And as for that Lady Dormer, I don't give a fig for her opinions. Just because people are born to the nobility doesn't make them noble. You know that, Jane. And she's no better than a common bawd. Indeed, I've known bawds . . ." He seemed to recall himself and with whom he spoke, and he coughed hastily to cover his mistake.

Jane had stopped playing. She could not command the presence of mind to move her fingers while being consoled. It was such a rare occurrence for anyone to even notice her distress in this household that someone seeking to console her struck her dumb and devoid of all her power to respond or reply.

Sir Francis cleared his throat again. He came into the room slowly, as if her feelings were some small bug or cowering animal that he might tread on, unawares.

The way the small room was disposed, the virginal was up against the wall, and its polished walnut coffin was the only thing somber in the furnishings. This was Jane's mother's room, and as such it had been fashioned for the gentle, happy girl her mother had been upon the time of her marriage.

Its tapestry hangings showed roses and ivy worked in pale tones and very skillfully. The bench standing by the broad window that let in the early morning light was covered in matching tapestry, as was Jane's stool and the great armchair on the other side of the virginal—which normally served for Jane's father when he sat in that room to discuss any matter with his wife.

Sir Francis now dropped onto it heavily, as if concerns or thoughts wearied him beyond his ability to stand. He sat there a moment in silence.

Jane contemplated her own white hands, her delicate, thin fingers on the keyboard. If she moved a finger, it would make a noise, and making a noise might break the tension in the room. But Jane had no intention of moving at all.

"Aye, Jane," the old man said, his voice heavy and somber. "It is a wretched business."

The repetition of what he said before, adding nothing new to her thought did not oblige her to answer. She did not. Instead, she contemplated the dark keys against the ivory, the scene carved behind the keyboard on the open lid of the virginal, and thought how beautiful it would be if the countryside were really like that, every shepherd a swain, every bush ever flowering, every lawn rolling and green.

"Jane, look at me, now," Sir Francis said.

And at his commanding tone, she didn't know what else to do but look at him. He looked, much as he always did, a ruddy fellow in his middle age, with blond hair excellently cut in the best manner of the court and a luxurious beard well-trimmed.

On this day he wore his blue doublet, and a snowy white lawn collar peeked above it. His face looked creased, as if from lack of sleep, and his eyes somewhat bloodshot as if he'd drunk too much in search of slumber that had not come. "Jane, I feel wretchedly about it, because I promised you to intercede, and I feel you and young Dormer put your trust in me to bring the matter to a good conclusion."

Jane lowered her head. "It is not your fault if—"

"Oh, I know it's not my fault, but still I feel as if you trusted me, and I failed you."

Jane looked up again, and she tried to give her face the most earnest expression. The truth was that she was not sure exactly what she was feeling, save she knew it was not grief over lost love. She had known since the day before that she did not love William. She had no scruples in marrying for less than love. But she thought that what truly pained her was seeing herself confirmed as worthless in her parents' eyes, and her whole life extending before her as nothing but living here, at Wolf Hall, the unmarried daughter of the Seymours. Or going to a convent. Which would be worse.

"I do not in any wise blame you, Sir Francis."

The man sighed as if she were withholding her pardon or being, all in all, obstinate. After a while, he cleared his throat. "But you know," he said, as if she had opposed him with some heavy argument, "sometimes the good Lord disposes things in His wise that make us all the better and enrich our lives and ourselves beyond our seeking. If you will but mind me, you remember I said young William would do but that I thought he was no fit mate for you and well beneath that level you could attain on your own or with help . . ."

Jane contemplated the fabric of her gown—a purplish thing that she had fashioned over from one of her mother's old ones, and where she had disguised thin spots with a fantastical embroidery of phoenixes and flowers. She must look a fright in this gown, the color leaching her already pale skin of all tint.

What but foolishness and belief in William's infatuation could have caused her to pick such an unbecoming color or to spend so much time embellishing this piece?

"I think I can solve all of this problem and show you that the Lord can be merciful beyond your praying, if you will simply trust in me," Sir Francis said. He heaved a great big sigh. "How would you like to be maid of honor to our lady the queen Catherine of Aragon?"

Jane raised her wondering gaze to his face, surprised at such an outrageous promise.

The man seemed to take her look as an indication of lack of

enthusiasm and hastened to say, "You know that our kind lady makes sure that all her ladies-in-waiting have good dowries and lack for nothing, do you not? You will be sure to have a marriage in no time, and one that will leave William and the Dormers in no doubt that you were the one condescending to them."

"Oh, no, Sir Francis," she said. "I did not doubt it would be a good and honorable position, but, as such, surely many young women of birth, spirit, and good looks will seek it, and I—"

"Leave be, Jane. Leave be," Sir Francis said. A huge hand patted at her arm with perhaps more familiarity than was warranted. "I will do it all and arrange all, and I will send your brothers to fetch you from home in due course. A few months, no more."

She still looked at him, thinking this was an odd promise.

But when he smiled at her, a great, avuncular smile, and said, "Will you be pleased with that, Jane? Pleased to come to court with your brothers, and be more in the stream of life? And mayhap get a good marriage withal?" She didn't want to displease him.

She bobbed her head down quickly. "Aye, Sir Francis," she said. "It would please me very much."

She hoped the inclination of her head hid the doubtful expression on her face.

Sir Francis seemed satisfied enough. By the corner of her eye, she saw him grin. He patted her arm again, familiarly. "You're a good girl, Jane," he said.

And with that he was gone, out of the room, and calling for Tom and Jane's father and inquiring of some hunt they had planned for today.

And Jane stayed behind at the virginal. She pressed a few keys tentatively. She was glad Sir Francis had left the room before he saw she didn't put much faith in his promises.

But how could she? Was not Jane well aware that the women picked for the royal court were all beautiful? The queen, no longer beautiful herself, liked to have decorative young women around her. And then there was a certain apparel and jewelry required and worn at all the occasions. She didn't think her parents would gladly furnish her with such, not when her chances of her gaining matrimony thereby were so scant.

Her playing gained in vigor as she grew accustomed to the idea that her days would be spent here, in Wolf Hall, maidenhood to death. And nothing would relieve her boredom or tension but this playing . . .

The notes, discordant, jarring, rose from her fingers to permeate the house, as she looked out the window at the sky that was becoming overcast.

A few drops of water fell and splashed against the window. Autumn was coming fast.

Eight

PHOENIX ON THE WING

JANE rose from the unaccustomed bed in the inn where Sir Francis had boarded her for the night.

Outside her window, all night long, she'd heard sounds of people and of carts, great rumblings of conversations and wheels, such as she had never heard in her own home.

It had disturbed her sleep, seeping into her dreams and wakening her to worries of how likely or not likely it was that she should realize her desire of becoming a maid of honor to the queen.

Sometimes, lying in the little narrow room, staring at the stained ceiling, she imagined that she was being foolish. After all, she was a daughter of the Seymours, and two of her brothers, Edward and Tom, were already serving at court, there carrying on functions in great closeness to the king. Why should she not be accepted?

At other times, it seemed to her that all was lost. Because

surely the queen would look at Jane and say this was not a face she wished to confront every morning when she woke. And at those times, Jane marveled at her audacity in having applied for the post, much less in expecting to carry it.

Thus spending the night torn between hope and despair, she woke to find that her features were not at their best. Her eyes were bruised, a bruising that showed beneath the very pale, thin skin.

A maid from the inn came to help her dress, taking the place of the lady's maid she needed—though she'd never had one at home—for the very elaborate dress her mother had set aside for her this day. To Jane, there was the added novelty of this being the first time she could remember, since she was very young, when she got wholly new clothing, no part of which had ever belonged to anyone else.

She had a white chemise of finest lawn, black velvet petticoat, and black velvet mantle, as she'd been instructed to wear by the queen or at least whoever amid the queen's entourage took on such duty. She put it on with trepidation, finding it accentuated her paleness.

Once the maid was done adjusting the headdress, also made of black velvet, on Jane's small head, it seemed to Jane as if her pale, oval face all but disappeared in the midst of the gloom.

Which, she thought, with a worried look at her bruised eyes, might not be a bad thing at all.

Tom came in, boisterous, starting, as he always did, as if he were in the middle of a sentence before reaching the door. "Not bad, Jane, you look not bad at all. Sir Francis will be here any moment and will escort you to see the queen."

"The queen?" Jane asked in surprise, feeling a dark red climb her cheeks in an effusion of heat. "The queen herself?"

Tom laughed loudly. He had grown into a handsome man

with a round face, a beard, and a full mustache. But there remained about him much of the boisterous little boy who'd been Jane's immediately younger brother, companion of childhood hunts and friend in childhood scrapes. Although to be honest, most of the trouble Jane ever got in as a child had been instigated by Tom, himself.

"You do realize if you get this position you shall see the queen every day, do you not, Jane?"

Jane nodded and sighed, still not sure whether she hoped to get the position or hoped not to get it. On the one hand, the prospect of slipping back into Wolf Hall, increasingly more deserted as her siblings left and her parents stayed alone behind, was not pleasing.

On the other hand, the court opened up before her as a frightening prospect, the waters of new acquaintance, the squalls of possible rivalries and of calling attention to herself, all conspiring to make her feel as if turning back now would be the safer course.

"Upon what are you thinking, Jane?" Sir Francis asked.

He'd come in without her noticing.

"Nothing, sir. Just worried."

"Oh, worry not." He walked around her, inspecting her, as a buyer would inspect a horse at the cattle market. "You look very well indeed. The carriage is waiting, and I shall take you to the palace, though it's a short way."

He escorted her down the stairs to the carriage, with her brother Tom following close behind. In the carriage, Sir Francis sat with Tom beside him and leaned across to talk to Jane, while Tom looked out the window, seemingly ignoring all of his master's words.

"Look here, Jane, what you've got to know is this: court is all in an uproar. The king wants to divorce the queen."

"I heard, milord. For lack of male issue."

Sir Francis shot her a sudden sharp look that gave her to know that was not all. "There is another," he said. "A lady who has caught his fancy."

"But surely—" Jane said, knowing well enough from all the tales of her childhood and everyone who gloried in being descended from the bastard of this king or other, that kings rarely viewed their marriage vows as confining them as well as their wives.

"There have been others—" she added in embarrassment, the names Bessie Blount and Mary Boleyn dancing about her head, overheard in some talk by her father and Sir Francis. But she wasn't even sure those were the right names and much less sure of what the women were like who bore them.

"Ah, yes, there have been others," Sir Francis said and smiled. "I see our young Jane is not as innocent or rural as we thought. There have been many others, this is true, and why not, since our king is a virile man, locked up with an older wife, well past her prime? But Jane, this one is different, and you would do well to hear about it."

He paused, and Jane looked earnestly at him, indicating that if he was disposed to tell the story, she was quite willing to listen.

"The lady's name is Anne Boleyn, and she's the daughter of a family that's been much at court, and she's connected to the Howards, too, that great ducal family. Her father sent her to the court of France when she was but a little girl, and there she learned . . ." He shook his head. "Well, there it is, she came back educated and with a certain style that is not often seen in these parts. She and her sister came back, and first the sister caught our king's fancy. Then Anne."

He paused again and looked at her slyly, as though expecting to see her embarrassed. Jane strived to give him only a straight-forward look of interest and attention.

"If Mistress Anne had given in to him," Sir Francis said, "as her sister did . . . then would all have been over, for he would have had his . . . pleasure, and it would be done. But she would not. She will not. She will not have aught than marriage. And so our king is seeking to divorce Queen Catherine."

"But I heard it was because of his conscience tormenting him. Over Queen Catherine's having been his brother's bride once."

Sir Francis laughed. "King Henry has always been good at letting his conscience be controlled only by his heart," he said. Then he looked at her in some alarm, as though he feared that she would repeat what he'd said. As though she, new at court, had any such contacts.

He frowned. "True, perhaps his conscience does torment him. I think he views the death of all his male babies as a punishment from God, and set about to find a reason for it. But the truth is, if he divorces the queen, he'll marry Anne Boleyn. Cardinal Wolsey might flatter himself that the king is only getting a divorce to marry some French princess or other, but I think even the good cardinal has seen the truth at last, and that's why he saddled us with a papal legate that—"

He glanced outside the carriage as if to see where they were. They had been traveling through crowded streets, where colorfully dressed women and men dove out of the way of the carriage and flattened themselves against walls to let it pass. Jane had been giving the scene outside the carriage window at least half her mind, curious and interested in what was passing.

She was fascinated by the loud sounds of metal and wood issuing from workshops, amazed by the various songs being sung by merchants all around, and drawn to the color and movement outside. A good horsewoman and connoisseur of horseflesh, she wished she could get out of the carriage and visit the horse market they passed.

"But no matter," Sir Francis said. "We'll be there soon. What you must know is this: that for all the purposes of your life at court, there are two queens, Queen Catherine, at least for now the rightful queen and married to King Henry, and Queen Anne, who, though she not be queen is said to command the monarch's heart in such a wise that everything she does and everything she sees is of interest to him. Don't fall athwart of either of them, and you'll be fine, Jane."

"You mean to tell me that the maid of honor who—" Jane swallowed hard. "That she's still living in the queen's household? But why? It must be an impossible situation."

"It is a situation as the king wants it, to have both his women close at hand. And nothing we can do about it." He nodded to Jane. "Just trim your sails to fit the wind, and you will be well, Jane."

And with that they pulled into some enclosed yard. Jane was not aware of having reached the palace, because she was not aware of the place where they had stopped being any different than a hundred other small plazas around town.

Only there were no merchants around, though there were plenty of men engaged in piling hay and brushing horses and other tasks of the stable yard.

Sir Francis helped Jane out. Flanked by Sir Francis and Tom, she went through a bewildering succession of chambers, antechambers, and corridors, all of them much grander than anything she had ever imagined. Great paintings and tapestries hung from walls painted in the brightest colors. The ceiling above was wood, carved in panels representing heraldic animals and initials and she knew not what. And the windows were leaded and had, upon them, in stained glass panels, the arms of both king and queen.

She was hurried to a small room, where Sir Francis spoke earnestly to a young gentleman who disappeared through two doors at the far end. He came out and said, "Her Majesty says she will receive you now."

Her Majesty. Jane was about to be face-to-face with the queen, the daughter of royalty, the noble princess of Spain and wife of King Henry.

Trembling, not quite sure how, she advanced. They entered a yet smaller room, where a small, fat woman sat in a large chair, sewing something out of white linen. She looked up at them as they entered.

Tom and Sir Francis bowed, but Jane prostrated herself on the floor and whispered, "Your Majesty," in a tone where the real terror was supplied by her being so near the greatest in the land.

"Get up, girl," a voice with a Spanish accent said. "Get up now. That is not needed. Get up."

Jane found that Tom and Sir Francis both seized hold of her arms and started helping her rise.

Standing, Jane found herself face-to-face with a small, over-weight woman. She had faded hair—not so much white as discolored. It had once been a tawny gold, and it was now half white and half a pale yellow, as though it had lost not so much pigment as courage. And the woman's broad face was wrinkled and also faded, as if she'd stayed too long out of the sun, and darkness had bleached her color away. But her eyes were blue, lively and kind, and they turned towards Jane with interest and appreciation.

Standing very still, in the queen's scrutiny, it seemed to Jane that the queen could see into her, and past her, through her countenance into her soul. Jane shifted, unsure she would pass muster.

"My lord Bryan says you are Edward Seymour's sister," the queen said. "And Thomas Seymour's, too?"

Jane nodded.

"And that you're a good girl and pleasing and very clever with your needle. He has shown me your needlework, very fine and well done."

Confused, Jane heard herself mumble something about how well her mother had taught her needlework. She was thinking that the queen looked tired and ill. And kind. As though kindness were a light shining within her tired body.

"And that you are good at your devotions and a nice, modest girl," Queen Catherine said.

"I try to be," Jane said softly. "I try to be modest, Your Majesty."

"Good," the queen said. "Good. For we've had immodesty aplenty."

And with those words and very little more instruction on her duties and appearance, Jane was accepted as the queen's maid of honor and given her own narrow little room at court.

There Sir Francis and Tom left her, with a box of her things and an assurance that she would see them very often indeed in the normal course of court affairs.

Nine

❖

HE looked closely at her, his eyes very near. Around them, conversations ebbed and flowed.

They were in the queen's chambers, where the king had descended with all his gentlemen for dining and an evening of entertainment.

Jane fancied they had been drawn there more by Anne Boleyn's dark beauty, her intemperate laughter, than by the queen's gracious countenance and hospitality, which had afforded them dinner, dancing, and music, and which now extended to games and pleasurable conversation.

The king had retired with his gentlemen to the far window, and they stood there and talked. His face was grave, his expression dark. Perhaps he was discussing the divorce. Or perhaps some other matter of great import.

Other people were playing at various card games or engaged in their own conversations.

Jane sat in a corner by the fire and was giving as much attention to her work as her tired eyes allowed.

Beside her, the fire roared fully, for it was frosty cold November outside, the wind whistling around the walls and penetrating through the stone to chill the occupants.

The two queens, the real one and the one everyone treated as a queen, were involved in some complicated game of cards that Jane, new to some of them, only dimly understood.

"Why are you not playing at cards, Jane?" Wyatt asked. "It's a merry assembly. Why are you at your needlework?"

Jane looked up. The tables were filled with the more fashionable and senior ladies-in-waiting, many of them from great titled houses. It seemed a most unlikely pastime for her to join in. Instead she said, "They're playing a game I don't understand. You know that I was never much good at card games."

"Oh, but the game is simplicity itself, you see." Wyatt pointed to the table at which the queen sat. "Where Her Majesty and Mistress Boleyn are playing, for instance, all you have to do to win is draw a king."

At that moment Boleyn laughed. She had a laughter like silver bells: cold and jangling, cutting through all the other noise in the room like breaking glass.

"A king she means to have," Wyatt said. He looked at the fire, his expression roiled with disturbance. Jane had heard stories that Thomas Wyatt had gone to Italy to escape his love for Anne Boleyn and that he'd followed Dante's footsteps.

But it had not rescued him from his inferno. He looked back at Anne Boleyn, his eyes hungry and intent.

Anne Boleyn was smiling, her expressive face bathed in joy. She advanced her hand—the one upon which she always kept her fingers folded in a strange manner, which some said was to hide a sixth finger.

"You see, I know I will win," she said. She threw back her head, and the light of the candles dazzled on her eyes and teeth. "For I am always very lucky at games."

The words seemed to echo in the small chamber, and Queen Catherine appeared to have been rendered speechless by them, but when she spoke, her low, vibrant voice eclipsed that of her rival. "Perhaps, Mistress Anne, perhaps, but you must know that those who are lucky at cards are unlucky at love."

Silence fell on this statement, and it seemed to Jane that the king looked over at the two women from his perch by the window where he was disputing something or other with two of his gentlemen, and frowned at the two women who shared his life and his palaces and who each claimed some share of his affections.

"I fancy," Wyatt said, "even *he* feels the smarting of her whip. She is a magnificent witch."

Jane said nothing. She wasn't sure what her feelings for Thomas Wyatt were. Ever since coming to town, six months ago, she'd found herself drawn to him, to his company.

She did not know why she should be drawn to him unless it were love.

He was not, after all—unlike William Dormer—a creature for whom she could feel any measure of empathy as to a fellow sufferer buffeted by fortune he could not control.

And yet . . .

Jane looked at him, only to find his gaze riveted—as she knew it would be—upon Anne Boleyn's curtain of black, silken hair, her sharp, entrancing profile, her shining eyes.

Without asking but simply by keeping her eyes and ears open, she had found that Thomas Wyatt was divorced. He'd put aside his wife for infidelity.

And then Anne Boleyn had put him aside for the king.

Perhaps brave Wyatt, world traveler, gifted poet, man of the world, had the same type of weakness as William.

But the thing Wyatt couldn't control was his desire for dangerous women.

Jane looked up at the dark, handsome face and wondered why that should be.

She inclined her head towards her altar cloth and sewed some more, delicate stitches outlining some flowers in a darker thread.

She must put Thomas Wyatt from her mind. He might be honest and truly wish to love Jane, but both of them knew he never would.

Another burst of laughter from Anne Boleyn, this one interrupted by the queen's angry voice, "Give over, Mistress Boleyn, for you see that not enough cards are left to you, and you have no chance of winning this game."

"Of what does she speak?" Jane asked Wyatt.

Wyatt shrugged. "Oh, there's a system of points to the game, and only the king can overcome some number of points from the adversary. I assume the queen is ahead." He spoke in an undertone, as though it were treason to support the queen in aught.

But Anne was yelling over the queen's words, "But no, I shall yet win. Why should I give over while I'm winning?"

The two women rose in their agitation, both hands reaching for the pile of cards in the center of the oak table at which they played. Mistress Boleyn was pale as death, and the queen was flushed, both of them visibly angry.

The king, himself, disturbed at his conversation, stood and came near the table where the women were both talking at the same time, upholding each her end, and clearly giving no quarter to the other.

"Ladies," he said. "Ladies. This much argument? And over a mere game? Can we not play quietly and be sociable?"

At this Anne Boleyn laughed, as she was apt to do when she was nervous or embarrassed or not sure what else to do. She laughed, but her fingers drummed on the table, as if marking a nervous counterpoint to her laughter.

The queen looked at her rival, her lips compressed, but the rest of her face in such stillness that no one could guess at what went on in her mind.

But when Anne's laughter died down, she said in her clear and cutting voice, "Ah, Your Majesty, you see, I fear Mistress Anne is playing for the king."

It was just a sentence, but of course, like everything said in this room, it was fraught with silences and full of meaning that mere words should not have. The whole room fell silent, as though none were sure what to say.

And in that silence, Jane looked up, perturbed, searching her mind for something she might say that might diffuse the tension and the anger.

At the same time the king looked away from the table and the two women involved in their dispute.

Their gazes met, and in his gaze—in the gaze of the most powerful man she knew, a very pillar of the universe—Jane read weariness and impotent anger. She'd spent all her time at court thinking of the unfairness of the situation to Queen Catherine and wondering if Mistress Anne's bouts of laughter hid some insecurity, some deep wound, wondering if the other woman also suffered in the uncertainty of this love suspended.

At this moment, for the first time, she realized that the king, too, suffered. He was, Jane thought—reading in the features of that round face the lines of every male she'd ever known—probably very simple, as she'd found most males were simple. He would want his table and his bed, both set according to his wishes. And at the end of the day he would like nothing so much as to have his own way.

But Henry had his way denied again and again, by fate or God or whoever disposed that all his male children by Catherine should be stillbirths and that the only child who should survive would be Mary. Mary was satisfactory enough—pious, obedient, and intelligent.

But she was a girl, and that one defect rendered her useless for her father's purpose, unable to hold the dynastically insecure throne of England, and subject to whatever whims whomever she might marry might bring with him.

In this, Henry had not had his way. Had Catherine given him a boy, he might still desire Anne Boleyn, but he would surely not be amenable to her play for marriage and the throne.

As it was, all he wished and all he wanted was Anne in his bed as his legitimate wife, giving him sons. But Catherine, his ever-obedient wife in everything but this, would not give way. She did not wish to go quietly into a convent, for which Jane couldn't quite blame her. Jane herself, who'd never tasted the joys of the marriage bed, had no taste for the cloister.

So the two women, locked in dispute, were making life very difficult indeed for the most powerful man in England.

All this passed into Jane's understanding in that moment when their gazes met. All this, plus the understanding that the king was very tired and likely to pass from tiredness into anger at any moment.

Beside her, Thomas Wyatt heaved a great, chest-expanding sigh. "Aye," he said in an undertone. "She plays for the king."

And Jane, marking the sadness of his countenance, wished she could give comfort where Anne Boleyn caused such great ache.

But it would never do. Thomas Wyatt might *wish* to love Jane Seymour, but he did not. Like the king. He was heart and soul in the thrall of the bewitchingly cruel Anne Boleyn.

Ten

JANE followed her mistress and a half-dozen other ladies-in-waiting over the tapestried bridge that connected Bridewell Palace, where the court tarried, to the Parliament Chamber of Blackfriars, where the papal inquisition into the king's marriage was located.

She had not yet made up her mind what to believe over the validity or lack thereof of the royal marriage. It was all a muddle as she trusted her mistress who swore that she'd come to King Henry a true maiden, but on the other hand she was bound to believe her king, her temporal lord, who said that Catherine of Aragon had lived with his brother Arthur as a wife with a husband well in advance of marrying him.

But it seemed to her this was not the point or the fact of the trial. And Jane thought that perhaps she was missing something, or perhaps she was not intelligent enough to understand it.

It seemed to her, however, that her mistress's crime hinged

less on whether or not she had been a virgin at her wedding and more on the fact that she had failed to produce a living son, an heir for the throne of England, and that she had now entered the age when such a son was impossible.

A marriage between princes was less a matter of love or right or law than a matter of ensuring the survival of nations. And Catherine could not give England an heir, and on that note she was being swept away.

Not that Jane thought this was right or just, but she accepted it as she accepted her own plain face staring out of her mirror every morning. At an early age she had learned that justice was not a normal thing in this world, nor should she expect it.

She thought on this and that the queen, Catherine, daughter of two monarchs who had united a peninsula and built an empire, was singularly unequipped to accept immutable fate or the fact that some necessities and facts defied justice.

So she followed her mistress in silence, as Catherine stormed across the bridge, her mouth pursed tight in disapproval, her eyes narrowed with self-righteous anger.

It was a beautiful day, the twenty-first of June, balmy and warm but not yet too hot for the rich clothing all wore—even Jane who had received from her parents an allowance of fabric to attire herself according to her new duties, and from Sir Francis himself a modest complement of pearls and such other jewels to enrich it. And Jane wondered if Sir Thomas Wyatt would be in the room. She knew there was no chance at all he would notice her or her new finery.

When Jane entered the great room where the judgment was to take place, she felt herself to be woefully underdressed.

The room itself, all black wood, fretted and carved and ornamented, was a room rich beyond the dreams of any provincial girl. Adding to that splendor were no less than two cardinals in the scarlet silk of their rank. Campeggio and Wolsey vied with each other for magnificence and riches, and each of them had several attendants—minor clerics and officious note takers—occupying a large portion of the chamber.

In the room were two large areas, each covered with a golden canopy. In the highest of these the king was already sitting, surrounded by his gentlemen of the chamber, among them a somber Edward Seymour. The king and all his attendants dressed at their richest, with such a display of feathers and colored jewels as dazzled by the light flowing in through the stained glass windows.

The lower canopied area was reserved for the queen and her ladies, and, as they flowed into it, and the queen took her seat, the higher-born and more resplendent ladies took the forefront, while Jane and other relative nobodies were pushed to stand at the back.

She looked towards the canopy beneath which the king and his gentlemen sat or stood.

And there she discerned a tall, lanky figure all in black.

It seemed to her perhaps that he looked towards her, but at that distance, she could hardly be sure.

Despite a numbing tiredness in her legs, which set in after a little while, Jane would not have missed this for anything because the proceedings were intricate, confusing but magnificent, and because Wyatt was here, across the room.

First the king rose to speak and said that he had his scruples about the marriage but that nothing would please him more than to have the marriage proven right and sound, and for him to take Queen Catherine back to his side.

Jane thought this echoed hollow. Who among the learned gentlemen and clerks listening to the deposition would believe it? Who would take it whole and unalloyed?

After all, did not all of them, like Jane, know the need the kingdom had of an heir and how unlikely Queen Catherine was to provide one at her advanced age and after several miscarriages? And did they not all know about Anne Boleyn? And how the king looked on her with unsatiable lust?

Still, the king maintained that all his bishops backed him in his doubts and that his doubts were the force behind his request for a divorce.

At this point there was a disruption in the proceedings as the elderly Bishop Fisher objected and said he did not agree. At which point the king dismissed him, saying he was but one man.

Then the queen rose. She spoke clearly and magnificently, only slightly hampered by the Spanish accent, which she'd never managed to lose. "Milord," she said, addressing herself wholly to the king. "I appeal to you and to your honor, to that sense of fear for our great and terrible everlasting Lord, the creator of worlds, who gave you power over these isles and holds your crown upon your brow, that you will recant of this unjust persecution. For you know as well as I that I came to you a maiden and untainted and that my first marriage was not such ever in the eyes of men or God Himself. In that spirit I appeal to you to cease offending against my honor and the great love of God who gave you such power over all your subjects and to return to my chamber and our conjugal bed and that happiness that was ours for twenty years."

When she finished speaking, Queen Catherine had tears in her eyes, and her pudgy hands knit themselves together, as though striving with each other in the greatest despair.

The king got up and explained how "the great love I bear the princess, Catherine of Aragon," was what had prevented him for so long from acting on his doubts and that "my dearest royal wish is to have the marriage declared valid." And yet he refused to have the case remandered to Rome for fear the emperor, Catherine's nephew, might force the pope to rule against him.

The two of these invalidated each other, since, how would the emperor rule but for his aunt? Yet the king swept on and smiled, sure of—seemingly—carrying the argument simply on the principle that he wished it so.

It seemed to be nothing more for it but for the queen to sit down and submit herself to a minute, public examination of her first marriage and of whether or not it had in true fact been a marriage.

Cardinal Wolsey spoke to the effect, saying that they must now hear witnesses about the queen's first marriage and what her late groom had said.

Against all expectation, the queen stood. Her ladies, in commotion and confusion, stood with her, and Jane found herself at the tail end of a movement crossing the room against the pressure of spectators who, sensing something new and unexpected, pressed closer and closer to see.

At the end of the train of ladies, Jane got more than her share of pushes and shoves, and for a moment it seemed likely she would be overwhelmed by the surrounding multitude and be quite unable to stay near her mistress or her companions.

She felt elbows at her side, a very rude hand grabbing at her petticoat, and it seemed to her she heard five or six different languages echo excitedly from the mouths of bearded, extravagantly attired men who pressed in from all sides.

By the time she reached the other side of the room, after the other ladies, the queen had climbed up to the canopied area that sheltered the king and fallen to her knees at his feet. And Jane could see Thomas Wyatt, with a bemused smile, looking over the heads of the other ladies at her, a questioning look in his eye, as if trying to see what was afoot and if Jane knew anything.

The king, confused, looking red in the face, reached down to raise the queen. But she knelt again in supplication before him. And again, he raised her up.

All the time she was talking, but in no language that Jane knew. It was expressive French followed by impassioned Spanish, with perhaps a mixture of Latin.

Her deep, rich voice flowed, full of emotion.

The king raised her up and said something, but she prostrated herself again and spoke, ever more loudly and this time in English. "Sir," she said. "I beseech you for all the love that has been between us, let me have justice and right, take of me some pity and compassion, for I am a poor woman and a stranger born out of your dominion. I have here no friend and much less indifferent counsel. I flee to you, as to the head of justice within this realm.

"I take God and all the world to witness that I have been to you a true, humble, and obedient wife, ever comfortable to your will and pleasure, being always well pleased and contented with all the things wherein you had any delight or dalliance. I loved those whom you loved, only for your sake, whether I had cause or no, and whether or not they were my friends or enemies."

She paused for breath. The king looked moved, but it was impossible to tell whether he was moved to pity or anger.

And Jane held her breath as the queen continued, "I am prepared to be put away if any just cause of law is found against me. Either of dishonesty or any other impediment. By me you have had many children, although it has pleased God to call them from this world. And when you had me first, I take God to be my judge, I was a true maid, without touch of man. Whether this be true or no, I put it to your conscience."

The king looked like a little boy hauled up before his masters and standing without excuse or explanation for some truancy. He held his hands down at his sides, where he had let them drop in readiness to help the queen up once more, when she'd started her plea in English.

His face was very red, and he pushed his lips in and out as some people do when deep in thought. But he looked most of all embarrassed, which went ill with his resplendent, embroidered attire and his purple cloak of royalty.

Queen Catherine rose up, swept King Henry a low curtsy and, leaning on the arm of a gentleman usher, moved slowly out of the court. Her four principal attendant ladies started to follow.

The official court crier called after the queen. The ladies in waiting stopped, as did those two others following them—Jane and another girl named Mary D'Arcs, recently arrived from the country.

The nervous usher said, "Madam, ye be called again."

Catherine shook her head. "It matters not. This is no unprejudiced court for me. I will not tarry."

She swept out, and her maids with her. Jane plunged through the massed crowd, sure she'd last seen something like an amused grin on Wyatt's face.

Outside the court, a press of women waited: ordinary women from the city of London, most probably merchants' wives and the daughters of common artificers and dressed after their kind.

As the queen emerged there were calls of support, and a great many women told "good Queen Catherine" to be "steady of purpose" and she would carry the day.

But Jane wondered if she would. Her mind in confusion, her senses oppressed from the grandeur and pomp of the day and from Wyatt's strange reactions, Jane wondered very much if any circumstance could cause Queen Catherine to win this battle.

Oh, she had justice on her side, and right, too. Jane, a religious woman herself, knew her kind. She doubted not that the queen—who only that morning had enjoined them all to pray for the king to return to his senses and her affections—was telling the truth when she swore by God and God's law that she'd been a maiden.

And if she'd been a maiden when she'd married the king, there was no justice in putting her away.

But justice was not all, and Jane knew, as the queen—her elder—didn't seem to know, that women's role in the world was fundamentally unjust. Her wit counted for nothing, nor her understanding. Only beauty counted and, for queens, bearing a prince who lived to maturity.

Jane inclined her head, following the queen on what she felt was a doomed war against fate that could not be combated. In her mind, having attained prominence as a queen's lady, was the vague idea that when the queen was finally put away and sent to some convent, so would Jane be put away and sent to the convent with her. And then she would no more see Thomas Wyatt's grief-filled gaze nor listen to his irony-sparkled voice.

As they cleared the press of common women, they started towards the palace. And there, before they reached it, was a group of ladies.

Most of them were ladies-in-waiting of the queen, but they paid their mistress scant attention. They congregated around Anne Boleyn, laughing and talking, looking onto Mistress Boleyn as flowers turn to a new rising sun.

As Queen Catherine and her ladies passed, Anne Boleyn

looked at them and, throwing back her beautiful head, arching her graceful neck back, she laughed.

Her laugh was just a little loud and went on a trifle too long.

Eleven

❧

ON a July morning in 1531 Jane rose from her bed early and walked out, searching a spot of coolness in the halls of Windsor Castle.

She hoped with some fervor that there would be hunting on for today, and she thought there would.

For all that had changed in the last two years, the court still seemed to have two queens, and the routine of the days and their duties had become well established.

The king left every morning to go riding and hunting with Mistress Boleyn. Those of the ladies of honor who enjoyed the sport were free to join in, and Jane, a good huntress, almost always did.

She enjoyed the freedom of the fields, and the mad chase, and she usually stayed on the chase to the end, long after the king and Mistress Boleyn had disappeared to enjoy each other's company in some shaded glen away from prying eyes. For that always happened.

At night, however, the queen was the queen, and the king was ever courteous to her in public and spent time in her chambers, often having supper with her. And despite his denials in public, Jane knew, as every other lady knew, that he sometimes visited her in her chamber at night.

Despite the blistering scenes of jealousy that Anne Boleyn would inflict on the king whenever this happened.

It was these visits that caused Jane to believe that Anne Boleyn, for all her idyls with the king, had not yielded to him the ultimate favor. Because the king had the fever of wanting, not of satiety, that fever that must and would be slaked on every available object, even his despised wife.

Which, of course, increased Mistress Anne's jealousy.

Many things had changed in the kingdom at large. Cardinal Wolsey had fallen from his position of power, and the king seemed to be edging dangerously close to a break with the pope and the Catholic religion. He claimed for himself the right to choose bishops and cardinals who agreed with him. In his temper tantrums, he claimed for himself the right to decide his own divorce.

But in the ultimate instance, the king was not strong enough to break with his wife, not strong enough to force his will on his mistress. And so Anne remained untouched, and Catherine remained his legal wife, and the tension in the court remained, thick and unbearable.

And Thomas Wyatt might be out early morning. Jane hadn't seen the dark, brooding courtier around court. She missed him greatly.

So she rose early and started to wend her way here and

there in search of breezes and cool air, and just in case she might end up somewhere near Thomas Wyatt.

She walked down a hallway, down a staircase, then along a long room and up a staircase again, pausing at open windows that admitted the cool morning air and, all in all, not quite knowing where her feet took her.

On a whim she decided to climb up a flight of stairs at random, intending to gain an upper gallery and look from it onto the roofs of the city in the quiet morning.

Looking down at her own feet on the stone stairways, she almost missed the man going the other way. She saw his feet first and, looking up, trembled to recognize the king, who'd been running down at full tilt and who now stopped in front of her, frowning a vague frown of confusion at finding his way blocked.

He was attired in his full hunting attire and carried his hat in his hand. None of his gentlemen were with him.

"Milord," Jane said, and dropped on her knees hastily.

The king reached down with that gallantry for which he was known and, grabbing her by the arms, pulled her firmly to her feet again. "No, Mistress Seymour," he said and smiled at her. Close by, his smile was a little overwhelming. He smiled as he did everything—full force and full of intent. It was a bit like being too close to the sun. "No, Mistress Seymour. You are too sensible for that. No need to prostrate yourself. Only stand aside, for the hunt is about to depart. They are already waiting for me below."

Jane stood aside to let him pass, and then, almost without thinking, started following him down. Because if there was hunting, she always went along.

"The hunt?" she said, as she stepped down, hurriedly, after

him. There were duties she performed for her mistress, but, she being one of the least visible of the ladies-in-waiting, her duties were hardly anything of any import. She read for the queen if no one else were available, she played indifferently upon the virginal, and she did an awful lot of needlework. Nothing that couldn't wait for another day if there was a hunt afoot.

The king could have been offended at being interrogated by a mere lady of the queen. By all that was right he should have been offended, and Jane realized this as soon as the question was out of her mouth, and she hesitated, her foot partway down to the step.

But he only turned back and said, over his shoulder. "Aye, we're hunting at Woodstock today. Anne has chosen it, and she insists we are to leave early."

"And may I come?" Jane asked.

The king stopped. He turned around. There was, to his expression a sadness and a tension that Jane did not fully understand. He looked at her a long time, his russet eyebrows low over his eyes.

Again she thought he was about to censure her for her daring or blame her for being too forward.

But instead, when he spoke it was in a heavy tone, and what he said was civil and curt. "I would very much prefer, Mistress Jane, if you did not come. This one time."

It seemed very strange, but Jane, trained from childhood to obey and full of respect and awe for her king, dropped a curtsy before she thought of it.

And then she was left on the stairs, frowning, while the king hurried down the stairs. Why would the king not want her to join the hunt? It was a strange thing.

After all, perhaps he wished to have private time with

Mistress Boleyn. But did he not have such time at every hunt? What difference did Jane's presence along make?

Perhaps Anne Boleyn had taken some great dislike to Jane?

This seemed to Jane so ridiculous that she almost laughed aloud. In the normal manner of such things, Mistress Boleyn had, now and then, made a joke at Jane's expense. Jane had been sitting in some corner, sewing or playing her dutiful songs upon the virginal, and Anne would notice her and, with two quick words, make her an object of ridicule.

Then Madge Shelton, Anne's cousin, and the bevy of gentlemen Anne kept around her, including Wyatt and Anne's brother George, would all join in and laugh at Jane, who had learned to bear it all as if she didn't understand she was being mocked.

She fancied Wyatt only did it to avoid having the same mockery and laughter turned upon him.

She was not a fool, and she knew where she stood in the court and that her status did not bear making herself unpleasant to the king's favorite.

Besides, Anne and her crowd made fun of everyone. Sometimes, when they thought no one was about—and since they didn't regard Jane as anyone worth remarking—she'd heard them mock the king himself.

But in the end, Jane would wager that Anne had no more than a vague idea of who Jane was and that, if pressed with the name and the description, she would say something about needlework or about Jane's lack of skill at the virginal.

No, the king might know Jane's name, but Anne Boleyn wouldn't. And why should she? She was not very good, at any time, at making friends. Anne was one of those people who made slaves or enemies. And Jane was not willing to be either.

So what mystery was here that the king seemed to dread—or fear—the idea of Jane's joining the hunt?

Jane heard the neighing of horses and the echo of Anne's laughter coming from below, on the other side of the wall. She climbed up the flight of stairs to a little recessed alcove, from which a window looked down upon a courtyard.

There, Jane stood on tiptoe to see out the window.

What she saw in the courtyard below was a merry company arrayed for the hunting: Anne and her brother George, and Wyatt and Norris and Madge Shelton.

The king mounted his horse, and Anne said something to him, cast too low for Jane to understand from where she stood.

The king's face clouded like a winter day, and he spoke once, decisively and so loudly that Jane understood him as clearly as if he'd been right by her. "The queen will have to console herself," he said. "I do not want any of her good-byes. She might put her trust in the emperor, but she'll find that the almighty God is yet more powerful." He cast a withering glance at the palace. "Let us be off. I can't wait to be shod of this place."

Anne Boleyn laughed loudly, and in the sound of that laughter, Jane distinguished triumph and joy.

It was then that she understood the king was leaving. He was deserting Queen Catherine without even the courtesy of a good-bye after twenty years of marriage.

And Thomas Wyatt was leaving. Used to considering the courtier the only man she could ever love—even if she was sure she rated no higher in his notice than some of the court furniture—Jane felt as if he were deserting her, and not merely following his king and the woman the king and Wyatt both loved, on their flight from the rightful queen and the accustomed court.

As she heard the hooves beat down in the courtyard,

headed for the gate and the freedom of the beautiful summer morning, Jane started running on her own.

She did not know why she was running, nor what her heart thought the urgency might be, but her feet sped upon the stairs.

She must reach the queen, she must. She must tell her that the king was leaving.

In her mind were confused images of the queen mounting and giving pursuit. No. That would never happen. Not Catherine, who had borne all with stubborn patience.

But she must do something. She would do something. And Jane must tell her. She could not allow the king to leave like that, without at least presenting his regrets to the woman who'd loved him for over twenty years, to the mother of his children.

And Jane must go and catch up to Wyatt—whom she couldn't possibly love, but nonetheless did.

She ran madly up the stairs, faster and faster, till she entered the queen's quarters where all was still quiet and there was just a soft hush of a lady-in-waiting preparing water for her mistress's morning wash.

The lady, Maria de Salinas, now widowed Lady Willoughby, the queen's oldest friend, her lady-in-waiting from Spain, moved to bar Jane's way as she made for the queen's bedchamber.

"I must . . ." Jane said, and paused to gather her breath. "I must tell our lady of what has befallen."

Her haste, and, she was sure, the discomposure of her features, the disarray of her attire after her race up a flight of stairs and down the corridor alarmed the other woman. She took her hand from Jane's shoulder, where she had laid it to stop Jane's race. "What has befallen? Is it the king?"

Jane nodded, still trying to gather breath.

"What of the king? What?" Maria de Salinas asked.

Jane shook her head. "He has left. Just now. To go to Wood-stock."

The woman looked uncomprehending, and Jane sighed in exasperation. "He has left with Mistress Boleyn."

"To go hunting?" Maria said. "He does it every day."

But Jane shook her head. "Not to go hunting. I think . . . I heard . . . It seems to me that he is leaving."

As de Salinas looked at her, in horrified disbelief, Jane made her way around her.

Only on entering the royal chamber proper did she think that she was committing a great trespass, that she wasn't sure the king was leaving, and that the fate of messengers bearing bad news was not always enviable.

But she thought of Thomas Wyatt going with that company and away from the rest of them.

She remembered her nursemaid's stories about men taken away by supernatural creatures to dangerous magical realms. In her mind Thomas Wyatt might as well have been carried off in such a way. Jane fancied he wasn't quite safe.

But the queen was standing by the window, already awake, and as Jane bobbed a confused curtsy, Catherine turned her tired face towards Jane.

The queen's eyes were red, her cheeks pale. "I know, Mistress Jane," she said. "I know. We must pray a lot."

Jane blinked, confused at this much composure. It was for this, then, that queens were trained. To see their kingdoms burn before their eyes. Or to see their husbands seduced away. All without giving way to the wailing a more common woman would allow.

But Jane was no queen.

"Pray for his return?" she asked, thinking that they'd done that long enough with no visible effect, till one would think the Almighty was deaf or that His will was dead set against Catherine.

But Queen Catherine shook her head, her kindly face, worn by so many griefs, the loss of so many children, looking even older and more worn. "No, Mistress Jane, we must pray for her. Anne Boleyn thinks it's all a game, you see. And she doesn't know with what she's playing."

Twelve

THE chapel was somber, lit only by tapers.

Jane stood, exhausted. All day long and into the night, they'd been praying and singing, singing and praying.

The others prayed for the king, but in her mind she prayed for Thomas Wyatt.

Over the months he'd been away from her, she'd come to understand the harrowing torture of his position.

Wyatt loved Anne Boleyn and therefore must follow her, as much in the thrall of her as a beast in thrall of its master. And yet, the best he could hope for from Anne Boleyn was that his love wouldn't remark him. For if she did, and the king noticed it, Thomas Wyatt's life wouldn't be worth a fig.

It had been this way for six months now, and it seemed to Jane that she might as well have joined a convent as joined the court of Queen Catherine, the deposed queen of England.

Oh, Catherine was still the queen, at least as far as the common people were concerned. They still linked her name to the king's every Sunday at Mass throughout the land and asked for people's prayers for her health and happiness.

But her husband had left with his mistress, and in truth Catherine's life was circumscribed here at Ampthill Castle, where she'd been asked to remove with her household—all two hundred people, including her ladies-in-waiting.

Ampthill Castle was very impressive, with five stone towers and a gatehouse said to have been built by Henry IV's brother-in-law. But situated in Bedfordshire, it was too far from the normal progress or residence of the court for Queen Catherine to have any involvement at all with it in the daily course of business.

Also, its gardens had been allowed to fall into neglect, and though the place was accounted fine for good health and clean air, it was surrounded by a veritable wilderness of unkempt trees and untended grounds.

Jane didn't mind this so much, as she found it reminded her of home and Savernake Forest. For all her attempts to get out of it, she now found she missed the shaded glades, the green shadows of the forest, and that solitude which was possible to procure in its recesses.

But she missed Thomas Wyatt's witty tongue also.

Here at Ampthill the queen's ladies were all too much together and too much apart from all the world. Oh, the place was spacious enough for two hundred people. Vast indeed. Unlike at court where often the ladies had to room together, Jane had her own room, which suited her fine, giving her a place to hide and claim a headache when the somber atmosphere depressed her.

But this court of women, either reflecting their sovereign's grief or desolate at finding that their own prospects of finding a husband were diminished with their removal from the court, all clung together in despondency.

More often than not, the crying queen and her principal lady-in-waiting, Maria de Salinas, spent their day here in the chapel, and here in the chapel they commanded that the other ladies should be, praying and crying: now for the king's health, then for him to recover his senses; now for the concubine's salvation, then for her to see her own interest lay not in this course. And then sometimes they prayed for England, that it be spared God's wrath for what its monarch was doing.

Over and over the prayers and the Latin, the sermons, and the blessings went, until Jane felt as if she were not only living in a convent, but surely a convent which celebrated only the darker holiday—the day of all saints, or a protracted Lenten expiation. The smell of wax, the waft of the censers, all of it drove Jane into a trance of despondency.

It seemed to Jane as though she had died and were condemned to forever spend her days in prayer for the sin of wanting to leave her mother and her father, the sin of vanity in her own mental prowess, the sin of wishing for an elevation neither her looks nor her birth warranted.

And then, one day, while she knelt in the pew, repeating prayers she no longer felt and to which she could no longer give any rational thought, a lady touched her shoulder and whispered in her ear that Thomas Seymour had come and waited for Jane in Jane's own chamber.

Jane felt guilty as she left the somber atmosphere of the chapel and hurried outside and through hallways that suddenly appeared filled with light and air, towards her room. It was like escaping purgatory for sweet paradise.

Her room was at the end of the house that looked out over

the wild gardens. It was light and airy, being furnished only with a narrow curtained bed—whose curtains Jane rarely closed—and a clothing trunk where she kept the enlarged attire she now rarely got to display, and it gave the impression of vast proportions.

Atop the trunk were three books that she had brought with her—a book of devotions, one on the obligations of a young lady towards her family and class, and a very beautiful book of spiritual poems which the queen had given to Jane in thanks, the queen had said, for the young lady's calm and gentling ways.

But the window of her room let in only a greenish light, being obscured by green branches that filtered the sun reaching it. It seemed to Jane that this light and this shuttering were designed to give her repose and bring her happy memories of her walks through Savernake Forest.

The truth was that were it not for her parents' palpable disappointment and disapproval of her, Jane would have been happy enough to spend the rest of her life hunting and walking the forest paths or gardening in the little rose garden outside Wolf Hall.

This time when she came into her room, it seemed all transformed. The only difference was, truth be told, the presence of her brother Tom, who stood in the middle of the room with the look of one arrested in the midst of pacing.

His face was red, his clothing was a brilliant, clashing blue, his hair was styled according to the latest fashion, and all of him bristled with impatience and vitality. He seemed to push everything else in the room into the background and make it all seem quite faded and feminine by comparison.

"Jane," he said. "Here you are at last."

Though she'd hurried from the chapel as soon as called, he

contrived to make her feel as though she'd kept him waiting for days, months, perhaps centuries.

He resumed his pacing, walking away from her. "You must pack your bags and come with me this instant," he said.

She stared at him, openmouthed, her words deserting her. She was aware that she must look quite foolish, but she had no idea what he meant. "Come with you?" she asked at last. "Where?"

"To the court, of course."

"But . . . the queen's court is here," Jane said.

Tom looked impatient. He stopped in front of the window, its greeny-leafy shade behind him, and crossed his arms, looking like the forest god of some lost civilization. "Oh, Jane, don't be a fool," he said.

And when she failed to answer, quite at a loss as to how she could be a fool, he looked at her with withering disdain. "You really do not understand it, do you? You wish to spend the rest of your life here, with all these women, praying and singing and imploring God for what's never going to happen?"

The weariness of the last months came over Jane, and she sighed heavily. "I don't see much point in all of it," she said. "I don't think God is disposed to hear it, or else He's trying us in a most frightful way."

Tom snorted, a rude noise he would never have indulged in his mother's presence. "Frightful indeed. Jane, the queen's sway over court and king is gone, and another reigns in her stead. You came to court not out of any great friendship for Queen Catherine, but because Sir Francis thought it would improve your chances to make a good match. Well, you're not likely to make a good match shut up here." He tapped his foot. "So pack your things and come away."

But Jane had been watching Tom since earliest childhood.

She knew his sudden enthusiasms, his lightning-rapid decisions. She also knew that her brother, while sharp and what
was commonly thought witty, was not an intelligent man.

When it came to thinking through the consequences of his
decisions and anticipating what would result from this or that,
he could, in fact, be rather stupid. He always viewed things as
he wanted them to be rather than as they truly were, which
was a dangerous characteristic in anyone seeking to make his
way in any court in the world.

"Tom, the other lady has no court. And besides, she never
liked me."

"Did she dislike you then?" Tom asked, staring at her, as if
trying to figure out how Jane could be important enough for
anyone to dislike her.

Jane shrugged. "I don't think she knew I existed."

"Then worry not about it. Except for a few people she
markedly dislikes, the Marquess of Pembroke has said she will
welcome all of the former queen's ladies into her establishment."

"The marquess?" Jane said. "Her establishment?" She could
hardly make out of what her brother was talking. What could
the Marquess, of Pembroke or otherwise, have to do with her
life and with the king's affairs?

Tom looked impatient enough that Jane thought for a moment that he would just stride away from her and disappear.
He'd been known to do that when they were both little and
she disappointed him by not grasping some game or intrigue
of his. Sometimes he would disappear into the forest for days,
until she—and their parents also—was frantic with worry that
he would get attacked by footpads or some beast.

But now he merely sighed. "Jane, Jane, Jane, I despair of
you," he said. "In this mausoleum, I suppose it's no wonder that

news does not reach you, particularly news that pertains to a certain person who, within these walls, must be regarded as Satan himself.

"Some months ago, the king has created Anne Boleyn the Marquess of Pembroke, with lands and dependencies of her own, and last month they've gone to Calais and been received by King Francis there, as though the marquess were a queen. Now they're back, and rumor has it that a wedding and coronation won't be far off. Now you see why you have to come with me back to the real court?"

Oh, Jane wanted to go back to the court. Not for advantage, not for the possibility of marriage. Early on at court she had decided her chances of marriage were not greatly improved by her being exposed to even more men who thought she was plain and uninteresting.

And she thought that the court of Anne Boleyn would be a different place from Queen Catherine's court and that they would likely all be the object of those crude jests that Anne's group of friends was so likely to make.

But it was the court. And Sir Thomas Wyatt would be there with his wit and poetry, and though he'd never truly look on her with favor, she could perhaps ease some of his suffering with her calm talk. And perhaps she could keep him from making himself too obvious, keep him from bringing on himself the kingly wrath.

And there would be hunts. The king would lead them. And there would be those moments of inexpressible honor when the king looked at her and she thought that he could guess her thought—that he knew her and understood her as she knew and understood him.

This was such a rare event in her life that even though she, of course, in no way expected to ever be closer to the king than that, yet that experience of knowing herself understood was enough.

All of this and her attraction to life and liveliness as opposed to the dead air, the dead feeling of this place, called her back to court.

But there were other considerations that pulled her heart and mind in a different direction. She looked towards the book on top of her clothing trunk. How could she abandon the queen who had been so good to her? How could she presume to leave her behind?

Oh, Jane wasn't foolish enough to flatter herself that the queen knew her much better than Anne Boleyn did. She suspected the queen would hardly miss the sound of another voice in the choir of lamentations around her.

But the queen had been deserted by her husband. If now her ladies, too, started leaving, one after the other, how would that look?

She would feel indeed abandoned and the most dejected woman in the whole world.

"Tom, I cannot," Jane said, and—in saying it—knew she was consigning herself to a life of darkness and prayers. Perhaps there was something to fate. Perhaps she had been destined to the convent from birth and perhaps that was why the Lord had ensured her plainness. Perhaps she should never have fought it.

Tom looked impatient. "Jane, you have no choice. I am not asking you if you wish to come. I am telling you that our parents, and Sir Francis, who has reason to have some authority over you, all have ordered that you come, and promptly, too, back to the court where your presence might be of some advantage to yourself and them."

She hesitated. Tom glowered. "Now, Jane. I have the carriage waiting, and I'll take you back to court now."

"I must say good-bye to my mistress," Jane said. In her affliction her hands gathered her skirts and clutched them to her, as if by holding them she could save herself.

Torn between the enticing duty that she was forced to perform and what she felt to be her obligation but dreaded with all her heart, she felt guilty and scared and bullied. "You must allow me, for she has been very good to me."

Tom grunted his permission. "I'll have your trunk taken down now," he added. "If all your belongings are in it. Come to the carriage in the main yard when you are done with your foolish errand. It is Sir Francis's carriage."

Jane nodded, not sure what she was nodding to—that her belongings were in the trunk, or that her errand was foolish. Both were true enough, she'd warrant.

She ran out of the room and back on her way to the chapel, not sure how to interrupt her mistress at her prayers.

Relieved, she saw the queen and the others come out of the chapel.

Jane curtsied in front of the queen, a deep curtsy, and for a moment words would not come to explain what was happening.

When words came, they tumbled out of her in confusion, "Madam, my brother has come to fetch me. He says I am to go with him."

The queen looked neither surprised nor offended. She nodded and said, "Doubtless a lot of families will have their daughters go to the concubine's court. Royal favor is worth more than my meager approval, and I cannot blame them."

Jane felt her face flame with embarrassment, and she bowed low and said, "Your Majesty, I would not for the world leave you in your dark hour. But my brother brings the orders of my parents and my protector and they say—"

Queen Catherine looked intently at Jane. The queen had

never been pretty since Jane had met her, but these years in exile had given her face a refinement of feature, as though suffering were a forge, and it was beating a new shape out of the unfortunate woman.

She still did not look pretty. It might be that she never had but had merely possessed that surfeit of prettiness granted by youth and high rank. Now, as Jane looked at her, it seemed to Jane that she was looking on one of those portraits of saints at the moment of their martyrdom, when their gross essence was purged and turned into something glorified.

"You are a good girl, Jane," she said softly, almost in benediction. "And you need not feel guilty towards me for obeying your mother and father."

She raised her hand to forestall Jane's protest. "No, you listen. You should not feel guilty, first because it is your parents' order, and that makes it your earthly duty. The Lord commands you to honor thy mother and thy father, and so you shall. And second, because I would not disdain having someone I know I can trust at court, to give me information and tell me all that happens." She smiled again, that soft, gentle smile that seemed to only have started gracing her of late. "So, go, Jane, go with my blessing."

And so Jane, still feeling guilty for enjoying her deliverance, left behind her exile and headed back into the world of court and of life.

Thirteen

I T was February, and Jane was in Anne's room, the queen's room in all but name.

Anne Boleyn was still abed, and Jane had come in to fill her basin with fresh water. Anne was ever more likely to treat her ladies-in-waiting as true maids than her predecessor had been.

Perhaps aware of being herself baseborn, she felt she must elevate herself further before them, or else they would not respect her.

Her court both confirmed Jane's worst fears and dispelled them. If anything, Mistress Anne was more rigorous a mistress in matters of dress and behavior than Queen Catherine had been. On the other hand, this did not apply to Anne herself.

Everyone knew the king shared her bed. Oh, half the court said that she'd already married the king in secret. But if that were the case, it would be a most irregular thing, would it not? When the king was still by all rights married to Queen Catherine? And if there had been no marriage, then Anne Boleyn had now fully given way to the king's wooing and deserved no better honor and no better treatment than Bessie Blount or Mary Boleyn.

And yet her power was as strong as ever, and all had to give way and bow to her and treat her as more than royal blood or risk the king's wrath.

Now that the queen was gone from court, Jane had herself often witnessed the king's sudden wrath at those who displeased Anne.

And yet he still looked tired. He still looked as though he had at least two brawling women on his neck.

Jane could make no sense of it. All she knew was that right now Anne Boleyn was still abed, or at least, judging from the noise and the occasional bouncing or ruffling of the curtains, she seemed to be dressing within the enclosure of the bed curtains.

Jane poured the washing water into the basin, set the linen towel by it, and started to back away. She did not like to be near when Anne Boleyn woke, as she was as likely as not to be in a foul temper and discharge it on whomever chanced to be near, without cause or regard for circumstances.

She could hear, from muffled voices, that Anne had at least one other lady in there with her—perhaps Madge Shelton— who was helping her dress.

Outside the curtains and in quite improper fashion there were a bevy of men waiting. The usual men who followed Anne Boleyn around and trailed from her every word as if she were a goddess and they those smitten by her arrows.

There was Norris, who seemed to be quite close to the king;

Anne's brother George, whom the king had made Lord Rocheford; and Wyatt—Wyatt whom Jane flattered herself of late to think her pet, though he'd hardly noticed her—the poet, Anne's former suitor.

Now, while Wyatt was talking to George Boleyn, Anne's head popped from between her bed curtains, dark and mischievous, black eyes twinkling like those of a wood nymph bent on tempting unwary travelers.

"Wyatt," she said. "I am hungry all the time. I have a powerful craving for apples such as never before. Do you know why that is?"

Wyatt went pale. Jane didn't quite understand his reason for paling, but he started stammering something that made not much sense, words, disconnected and hesitant.

Her heart clenched in her chest at his suffering.

And then, Anne laughed and said. "The king says he knows. The king says I'm pregnant."

Pregnant? By Wyatt? Jane dropped the ewer she was carrying away, and shards of ceramic flew all over the floor.

In confusion, Jane bent to pick them up, thinking she could not have heard what she thought she had just heard.

But no, Anne Boleyn had said that she'd talked of the pregnancy to the king. So, for certain the baby would be the king's and not Thomas Wyatt's.

Because, surely, Anne Boleyn, wanton though she might be, was no fool. She must know, in her heart she must know, that the reason the king wanted to marry her was to produce an heir, and that if she conceived this child before they were legally and visibly married, he would be a bastard and no better than Henry Fitzroy.

Her hands picked up the shards, frantically, while her mind

worked through all this. And she realized everyone, Anne Boleyn included, were staring at her.

"You are very clumsy, Jane," Anne said, sharply.

Jane stammered, "I didn't mean . . . I was only surprised that . . ."

Anne laughed, her loud, piercing laughter. "Mistress Jane," she said, in her high, declaiming voice, sounding like an actor upon the stage. "Mistress Jane disapproves of me, you see, Wyatt. Mistress Jane, the fine flower of modesty and the model of every English maiden thinks I am an abandoned libertine for allowing the king his way of me, and for bragging of the product. And why should I not brag?"

Anne Boleyn's wanton, dancing gaze looked all around, at all of them. "Why should I not brag, since my issue will one day rule over you all and, when the king my sovereign and master is gone, he can cut off all your heads, if it so pleases him?"

She grinned at them like an elf, no more conscious of sin or trespass than an elf. With her hands on the shards of the ewer, Jane wondered if she, herself, could ever be that confident and abandoned. She also wondered what Anne meant by saying that her child would be king.

But Anne laughed, loud, incontinently, that strange laughter of hers. "Oh, it matters not, because I've told the king he must be wrong. He is wrong, I am certain. I cannot be with child."

And with that and another peal of laughter, the dark, elfin head disappeared within the curtains of her bed once more, leaving Jane to pick up the shards very fast, holding them in a fold of her skirt.

Thomas Wyatt was still pale, looking shaken. How it must wound him to know that the king had enjoyed the delights of that body which bewitched him but which must remain, forever, out of his reach.

As Jane darted out of the door, confused and abashed, she thought it took a little long for conversations to resume behind her. As if the gentlemen of the chamber were no more reassured of the propriety of all this than she was.

Fourteen

THE divorce had been declared.

Since there seemed now that there had been a secret marriage all along, and since the marriage with Catherine Aragon had not been so much rescinded as annulled, Bishop Cramner declaring that it had never been a true marriage as such, the king and his new queen could not get married again, publicly.

That would be the same as saying that the first marriage hadn't been valid and that the issue now thickening Anne Boleyn's figure must, therefore, be illegitimate. So, instead, to give people a glimpse of their new queen, the king was planning a grand coronation for May, and it was said he meant to do wonders for this his new lady who had already proven so fecund.

Doubtless the preparations for such a ceremony occupied the king and kept him from visiting his queen or spending as much time in his chambers as he was wont to. And so life had been very quiet, at least for Jane.

It turned out that Queen Anne liked tapestry and embroidery as much as the old queen had, and therefore Jane got to sit in her quiet corner and do her work, while in the queen's chamber witty conversation and dance went on.

Even while Thomas Wyatt was by. Since his beloved had become queen, the poet had become very quiet and dull.

But Jane had not seen the king, and she wondered if he were happy. Yes, doubtless he was, for how could he not be when he'd attained his heart's desire and had a child on the way at last?

Jane contented herself with the thought that she would probably never share those moments of quiet understanding with the king. Her thoughts on it were mixed. For if he only understood her when he was unhappy, did she wish him to be unhappy that he might understand her?

She was in the garden on this March morning. The weather, still cool in the main, had let up for one glorious day of mild temperatures, and Jane had taken herself to the palace garden for a look at the herbs, the borders, the roses, thinking of their health against the coming spring.

Though the itinerant lifestyle of the court, in general, left her very little time and interest in tending the gardens as she had at Savernake—because chances were she would not be around to enjoy the result when winter turned to spring again—yet she missed her work with the dirt and the green shoots.

She was steadying some of the roses and wondering how to get rid of the white larvae she found on some leaves, and thinking of what she had lost, and laughing to herself.

She could not flatter herself that she had lost the king's friendship after all. She very much doubted the king knew much more about her than her name and that she usually looked calm and unruffled. Of course, that was perhaps enough when all around him had been in turmoil.

But now that the days ahead promised to be halcyon, with the long-hoped-for son and his beloved lady, he would not remember Jane even for that much.

She caught herself sighing and smiled at her presumption.

She heard a small sound behind her, and she jumped.

The king stood behind her, fully attired, his hat in his hand, blinking up at the sun in the sky as though it were a marvelous and never-seen thing.

"Good morrow, Mistress Seymour," he said. "And a glorious morning it is, is it not?"

She curtsied. "Your Majesty. Indeed. It is as balmy as we could hope, as sunny. And as . . . well, as blessed, we would say?"

He looked at her, his great eyes rolling with something like skepticism or doubt. "Blessed, Mistress Seymour?"

She felt heat on her cheeks, which, as ever, must mean she had a raging blush that she could neither hide nor disguise. "Oh, certainly. For Your Highness has now a new—or should I say—a legitimate marriage," she amended, recalling herself. "And this legitimate marriage will soon have fruit."

The king's face wrinkled, as though in deep thought. "Aye," he said. But it was a heavy sound.

He looked at Jane's hands, which were unfolding a leaf that looked somewhat blighted. "You are a gardener, Mistress Seymour?"

She blushed again, a wave of heat and doubtless color in her cheeks. "In my parents' house," she said. "When I lived with them, I was a gardener," she said. "Or at least I helped tend some tender plants, and I was exceedingly fond of cucumbers. Which, indeed, everyone was when I grew them."

The king gave her a puzzled smile, and she realized his question had been rhetorical or, at any rate, he'd never expected from her such a complete answer as he'd got.

He looked away from her and over the wall of the garden from beyond which the sound of a city wakening—the sounds of shouts and cartwheels, the rumblings of songs and calls of vendors—were starting to be heard. "Well, Mistress Seymour, supposing you have a tree which overspreads every parcel of your garden and causes all the rest to stop flourishing. Would you not resent that tree?"

Confused, Jane swallowed. "Certainly. It would best it were trimmed."

"Well, then, but if the tree gives delicious and sweet fruit, what then?"

Jane didn't know what to answer. She had some vague idea the king was talking about Anne Boleyn. But why would the king, less than a year married to the lady, think of her as a tree that overspread his garden and blighted all his other plantings?

He smiled at her silence and said, "Exactly. If the fruit were rare enough one might well endure a lot for the sake of it, would one not. And I hope the fruit is rare enough. Good morrow to you, Mistress Seymour, at your gardening."

And with that, the king was gone. He had looked just as anxious and tired as ever.

Jane picked up a handful of fine, loamy dirt and let it run out between her fingers. She wondered, if the fruit should prove not as he expected, how long Anne Boleyn, the tree, would retain her power.

But then she told herself she was being foolish, for surely Anne would produce a prince. All the astrologers said she would, and besides, what king had deserved such outcome more than Henry?

A man walked out of the shadows. He wore all black, and his grief-marked features were those of Thomas Wyatt.

He looked as full of regret as ever for the love that could not be his. But his lips twisted in a little, sardonic smile.

Approaching Jane, he spoke without preamble as he usually did to her, as though their entire acquaintance had been one long, unhurried conversation.

"I think already His Majesty is starting to find that the wanting is better than the having," he said, looking towards where the king had disappeared. "For she's wild to hold, though she seem tame."

Fifteen

QUEEN Anne, for now Jane must think of her that way, was appareled in white crimson brocade and cloth of gold. Around her neck was a necklace of pearls larger than chickpeas and a large jewel made of diamonds of great value. A robe of royal purple velvet surmounted it all.

The day before, she made a parade of her attire before her tame gentlemen admirers and received many well-deserved compliments. Jane still flinched from the love-wounded look she'd glimpsed on Thomas Wyatt's face.

Jane, one of her ladies, largely unseen and—she believed—brought to London with the new queen simply because if some dress or stay should break, Jane could be trusted not only to fix it but to do a quick embroidery or ornament upon it that would look as if the effect were meant, anyway.

The day was suffocatingly hot, enclosed and uncomfortable

like the exhalation of an oven. Jane's own clothing, crimson and powdered with ermines instead of encrusted all in jewels, and lacking the royal purple robe, felt hot and clinging to her, and she wondered how the queen must feel six months' pregnant and great with child.

Yet Anne looked happy. Or at least, she did not look unhappy. She sat on a litter, with the canopy over her head, borne by noble barons, at the head of a large procession of nobles.

The way from the Tower to Westminster for the coronation was littered with displays mounted by the guilds and the various organizations of the city. Children declaimed and poets wrote long panegyrics to Anne Boleyn, in which they compared her now to an angel come from heaven, now to Saint Anne, grandmother of Jesus Christ, and now her emblematic crowned falcon to the dove of the Pentecost, which approached fast on Whitsunday.

To Jane the whole pageant was so fascinating that despite the heat and her discomfort—mounted on a horse as she was, following behind the queen's litter at the slowest of possible paces—she felt like a child witnessing marvels.

She had scarce seen the city of London, though she'd lived in it for years. Her progress to it had always been from one place to the other in a carriage, and then she had been let out only in the well-known confines of the court, which was like a city unto itself, and where she was known and her own environment well-delimited.

Jane watched, fascinated, all the people who'd come out—laboring people, who worked every day of their lives at professions she could hardly imagine and that for this occasion had put aside their labors and come to the street to celebrate. She marked several women plainer than she and several with children at their skirts, and she thought that perhaps not all was lost. Perhaps she could convince someone that she had true worth.

But then she looked at Anne Boleyn's long curtain of black, silky hair, as the queen was carried in her litter just ahead of Jane. And she remembered Wyatt repeating so many times that he would love Jane if he could. But in Jane's world, heart and mind must be wholly eclipsed by a fascinating body, as men of power could have what they wished, and what they wished was a comely face and bewitching figure. Dreaming otherwise was mere make-believe, a foolishness she should have outgrown with her childhood.

Slowly, as the procession continued, and yet another assembly of children recited their poems to the queen's virtue or greatness or generosity, Jane started noticing something odd.

Before, whenever she'd progressed through the city of London with Queen Catherine, most often unscheduled and within the confines of a great, trundling carriage, every common man and woman out there had shouted to the coach as it passed, "Long live good Queen Catherine."

Now, at this grand, scheduled ceremony, the people of London had all come out to see, but they looked sullen and distant, their hats on their heads, their arms alongside their bodies.

There were no shouts at all, save the occasional "The king's whore," which all of them pretended not to hear, though Jane was sure once or twice she had seen Anne look in the direction of the shout.

Slowly, hour by hour of the interminable progression, it dawned on Jane that this marriage, so much to the king's heart, was disapproved of by the people. It became apparent that the multitude, the crowds of London that labored and played in the great metropolis, thought what their king was doing was wrong.

And though they had no more say on the king's marriage

than did the sheep in the meadow, yet, in their massed multitude they seemed to Jane to represent an irresistible force. Like loosened water, like a river at the flood. And she wondered if after all perhaps they wouldn't move the kingdom with their force.

Jane's mother used to say that soft water will pierce the thick stone, and so it would in time. How long could a king live so far separated from his people's will and thought?

"They will love her enough and throw flowers at her feet and offer prayers for her once the prince is born," Thomas Wyatt told her that evening, when the great ceremony of the coronation had taken place and the two of them were standing in a gallery at Westminster Hall, far enough from anyone else that Jane had dared speak her feelings.

Jane must have looked her doubt at him, because Thomas looked exasperated. "Look, Jane," he said. "Be not a fool. The lady Anne is not a comfortable wife. But as she is, she is our sovereign, and we must get used to it. Perhaps then the pain will dull enough we may consider . . ."

He looked towards her, his eyes full of intent and meaning. She was, she felt, meant to think of their life together, once he'd grown accustomed to the loss of what he truly wanted.

And she could think of that life, too. Of being left behind in his castle, to sew and mend, to play the virginal and tend to the children while Thomas looked elsewhere for a mistress who would despise and ill-treat him. And if he found one willing to be cruel enough, Jane might look to be falsely accused of adultery and put away. As had, perhaps, happened to his first wife.

She looked at Thomas Wyatt's handsome and melancholy face, and she said, "You know, milord, you speak great foolishness."

He looked startled, as if she'd pulled the glove off from her fingers and swatted him full across the face. "And why is that, milady?" he asked. "Would you not have me if I offered?"

Jane smiled at him but did not answer.

"Am I to think that I am too lowly for you?" Thomas Wyatt asked. "And where would your ambitions rest, milady spite? The king himself?"

Jane was startled. Here for the first time she saw a true spark of interest in her, expressed of course in wounded reproach, as it was the only way Thomas Wyatt seemed to be able to communicate love at all. She hastened to appease him before his intemperate voice attracted attention to them.

"Oh, milord," she said. "I would never aim my bow so high. But neither do I wish to hunt on another's preserve or be pleased with her leavings."

He frowned at her but did not say any more. Perhaps the pretense of wanting him but not being sanguine enough to claim him had appeased him.

And Jane had realized that for some time and at the back of her own mind, she'd thought of Thomas Wyatt as someone who needed suffering.

A Christ enamored of His own cross, eternally climbing the calvary. A martyr rushing to the lion with glad cries. And enjoying the journey.

There would never be any happiness for the handsome, dashing poet, Thomas Wyatt. And none for Jane as long as she had hopes of him.

Sixteen

SEPTEMBER seventh dawned dark, and the queen had gone into labor. Intemperate in her pain as in all else, Anne Boleyn had screamed and screamed, till all the halls of the palace echoed of her torment and rang of her pain, like giant bells forged to toll suffering.

Jane had not been thought important enough to attend at the birth, and for that she was glad, for even in her room, or in the more distant recesses of the garden, she could hear Anne scream and implore—of God, of the king, of the mercy of whoever was listening—that she might be relieved of this great pass.

To be fair, Jane could not say she liked the queen. She'd come to Anne's court in obedience to her parents and her brother. But a prince was to the good of the whole country, even if it saddled them with Anne as a queen forever. And besides, Jane didn't like to see anyone suffer.

So she prayed under the shade of an apple tree in the garden, where she'd sought refuge. She looked up the grey sky above, and she prayed earnestly that God would grant England a prince and the queen swift delivery.

So absorbed was she in her prayer that when the screams stopped she was not at first aware of it.

The feeling was, rather, as though there had been a pressure upon her that was suddenly lifted and, from that lifting of pressure, she was able to breathe more deeply.

Only afterwards did she realize that the screams had stopped and what it might mean. Or at least what she hoped it might mean. She did not want to think that Anne Boleyn might be dead. And it wasn't only because then Jane must go back home, but also because she imagined the disappointment in the king's eyes if he lost his hoped-for son and his wife, too.

She hurried towards the room where the queen had given birth, but as she got close she found that she was struggling more and more against people coming in the other direction. And that those people looked in no wise happy.

Her heart beating fast, her breath catching in her throat, she hurried forward. Had Anne Boleyn died? If she had, Jane would feel guilty for never having liked the queen. She would also worry for the kingdom and its sovereign.

Rushing forward, she came upon Thomas Wyatt walking the other way, shaking his head.

Amid the great crowd, Jane made for him, and he ambled towards her, till they met.

"What of our prince, Sir Wyatt?" Jane asked.

He shook his head, looking more somber than usual. "There is no prince."

Jane clutched her hands to her chest. "Dead?" she asked. All the present feelings of guilt for not liking or approving of the queen haunted her, as if her dislike could in any way call down tragedy.

Unexpectedly, Wyatt grinned. "Not dead, Mistress Jane, worse. The child is female." His grin exuded bitterness. "We have a princess. Again."

Jane wondered how the king would accept a princess. But not wanting to discuss it with Wyatt here, in the midst of a crowded corridor, she curtsied to him and walked off towards the royal room.

She could feel his gaze on her as she left.

Jane approached the royal room but didn't enter, only hovered at the door. People were still in the room, highborn people and some of Anne's circle, among them the Lord Rochford, her brother. They all looked as if they were at a funeral rather than at a birth.

But looking in at the door, Jane saw that the queen sat up on the bed, wan and tired looking, her hair matted with sweat, but quite visibly alive. She, too, however, looked as if she'd lost if not her life then everything which gave that life value.

Did she fear the king and the king's wrath? Having tempted him as much with the delights of her body as with the chance that she could give him a male heir, how would Anne Boleyn be treated now that she had failed to fulfill the most important part of the contract that had made her queen?

Just then the king, who'd had his back turned to Jane, turned around, and she saw in his arms a babe—healthy looking, with a ruddy complexion and a tuft of reddish hair.

"Well, never mind," he said, looking back at Anne Boleyn, without having even noticed Jane at all. "Never mind. For she is hale and hearty, and she will have brothers. We'll call her Elizabeth. After my mother."

A girl. After all the turmoil in the kingdom, after unseating the rightful queen, Anne Boleyn had done no more than Queen Catherine had done. She had given the king issue. But not male.

And in that moment, as though a shadow fell upon her, Jane thought that Queen Anne would do no more than Queen Catherine. That after this one girl all the children would be stillbirths or soon dead. God in His mercy would not permit the concubine to outperform the wife.

Jane had best ingratiate herself to someone at court. Some minor gentleman, perhaps a widower. Thomas Wyatt was not to be, and Jane must find it in her heart to give her attention to someone else, and quickly. Someone she could endure to be married to.

Perhaps one of the king's grooms, she thought, and smiled to herself, or a stableboy. At least life with him would be interesting, if not in any way pleasant. And she would shock her parents enough.

But she let go of the passing amusing fancy. She must think seriously and plan her future if there was any hope of not having to return to Savernake and live as the maiden daughter forever.

The queen's months of ascendance and Jane's months at court might well be numbered.

Seventeen

❧

THE queen was raging. What in the unmarried Anne had been an occasional, almost fetching temper tantrum had become in Queen Anne a raging frenzy.

The problem was that again she'd delivered. But she'd delivered before her time, the child dead, though developed enough to see it as male issue. And this time the king was holding her responsible.

They were in the queen's apartments, and they should have been at supper. But King Henry had sat there, quiet and still, looking sad. The queen had just got up from her childbirth bed and was, for the first time, in company.

Anne looked gaunt. That curious, frail thinness that had made her look like she was not quite a creature of this world but of another, a woodland elf or a creature of magic, had changed.

She was now so thin her bones showed through the features like a presage of death—the too-square chin, the too-prominent eye sockets within which her dark eyes seemed to have sunk and dulled, like jewels that had lost their luster.

It was an intimate dinner with just the king, the queen, and two of her maids, Madge Shelton, picked, Jane believed, because she'd already been debauched by the king and could not present him with fresh temptation, and Jane Seymour, chosen because Anne Boleyn couldn't imagine Jane tempting anyone.

Despite herself, Jane wondered where Thomas Wyatt was, but pushed the thought down.

After half an hour of being served and eating in silence—the queen picking at her food, the king with his usual hearty appetite—Anne spoke, her voice with an edge of sharp shrewishness. "You do not speak," she said.

The king caught Jane's eye. Incongruously for a man much older than her and so corpulent that he could easily be two of the frail Anne, he looked to Jane like a truant boy—a handsome child who has been at his father's wine and does not want to admit it. And to whom all wrong is usually forgiven.

Or a child whose toy was broken and who did not understand that he had any part in this. He looked at Queen Anne with his lower lip somewhat advanced, in an expression of peevish disappointment.

"You promised me that if I married you, you'd give me a boy," he said. "And it's all been for nothing. I have another princess. Well, I had a princess before."

The right course, or so it seemed to Jane, was to be gentle with the little boy the king resembled, the child within the grown, powerful man, whose lower lip was clearly just away from a trembling sulk. It was to tell him that there would be boys and reassure him it would all still turn out as he wished.

But Queen Anne did not seem to see the scared little boy in her husband. Instead, she raised her eyebrows, and she set her lips in one thin line, which made them thinner and less appetizing than Jane's own lips. "Aye," she said. "You had a princess. Mary will be the death of me, or I of her. And so will the Dowager Princess of Wales, Catherine."

King Henry looked exactly like Tom Seymour when the household priest, Father James—in Jane's long-ago childhood—tried to get the spoiled and truant boy of the Seymour family to do a difficult sum or to learn his Latin verbs. Tom had a way of looking away from Father James and off into the distance till it seemed that though his body was there, his spirit was miles away. Whenever he made this face, he would later claim never to have heard the request or the reproach.

The king did it now, looking over Anne's shoulder and over Jane's head, as if a tapestry on the wall absorbed all his thought.

Any woman, anyone who'd ever been around children, would know that look. But since the man playing the child was the king of England, Queen Anne should have known this was not the time to speak.

Clearly she did not. She rose from her seat, her glass in her hand, an expensive crystal glass filled with expensive wine. "You ignore me," she said. "You want me to give you a prince, but you will do nothing to rid me of the witches that make that impossible."

She threw the glass across the room, where it shattered against the wall. Red wine dripped, staining the molding.

In another time, Jane would have flinched from this. But she had grown accustomed to the spectacle. Queen Anne screamed, she threatened, and she often threw objects. Jane's only response was to go to where the glasses were kept in the next room and bring another one, which she set in front of the queen. Madge poured wine again into the glass.

All this scene might have been pure routine. Save for the queen.

She remained standing, her face haggard, her countenance all out of jointure. "You will not hear me. You'll do nothing for me. You do not care for me anymore."

The king ate his supper quietly.

And Jane thought what fools beauty made of women, causing them to think that their power over men was ironclad and would last forever, and that in the balance they would always hold their suitors in the same thrall as they'd first held them.

Queen Anne didn't seem to realize how much her beauty had faded during the many years that she'd waited for the king to marry her. Nor did she seem to realize—she, who had exerted over the king a fascination few women had ever exerted over a man—that part of her power over him was to keep him longing for her. She didn't seem to understand it was thirst and desire that had made him give her the Crown and that satiety must have the effect of loosening the bonds of her fascination.

How could someone achieve so much by such a simple trick and not be aware of it?

"Think you I've not heard? That you dally? That there is some lady at court who attracts your eyes and your attention?" the queen asked, her voice increasingly shrill.

The king stared at her now, as if from far away.

"Oh, you do not love me. Both your false first wife and your daughter, they plot against me. I can feel it, their spells like needles on my skin." As she spoke, she swept her lovely, elongated hands up and down on her arms. "They are witches,

I tell you, and they have bewitched me and you and our bed. Every child I have by you will be dead until those two are resting in their graves."

Her face now crumpled into grief. "Oh, how can you sit there and do nothing? How can you sit there and not have them killed? What would it cost you to execute them? You were never truly married to her, do you not understand that? And the other one, what is she but the vilest bastard in the world? And she refuses to admit it. She refuses to admit our daughter has rights to the throne before she does." The words had been spoken in a crescendo of fury and intensity, till the last was a scream. "How can you not punish such disobedience?"

She leaned forward on the table, her hands flat on the white linen cloth, her face as close to the king's as it could get, so that her last sound of indignation must have been piercingly loud in his ears.

The king, who, up till that last moment was eating calmly, now dropped his knife and, folding his napkin, said, "Madam, you go too far."

Anne did not move, her face still close to his, even as he raised his face and looked at her steadily, with an expression of such disapproval that Jane thought if it had been directed at her, she should have quaked.

"The women you speak of are the daughter and sister of great sovereigns and the daughter of a great prince—myself. I have no reason to believe they are other than good, religious, and obeying. In fact, the Dowager Princess of Wales has always come close to sanctity. You will moderate your speech when talking about them, and in all things you will refer to them with the respect of one who speaks of her betters. Do I make myself rightly understood?"

There was a silence. The queen did not move.

The king reached forward, and his hand wrapped around her wrist. "Do I make myself rightly understood, madam?"

Anne didn't answer. Perhaps she couldn't. What issued forth between her lips was a shriek of rage, a scream of impotent fury.

Suddenly she was animated, possessed with fury, like a cat or a hawk or a wild creature caught in an embrace by an unwary man. She wrenched her wrist away from his grasp. She screamed at him, without words and, when he reached again to hold her wrist, she slapped and clawed at him in incoherent fury.

Then she stood suddenly and took off running for her inner apartment.

The king made no move to follow her. He lifted the cup from the table and took a long, slow draught of the ruby wine. Then he walked slowly to the door and left.

Madge Shelton had gone after the queen. She walked past the two or three antechambers left quite wide open, and Jane could hear her pleading at the inner door. "Your Majesty, please, open the door."

But Jane surveyed the table, with the wine, the stained napkins, and the uneaten food. The servants would clear the table later. And after the scene she'd just witnessed, Jane was scarcely in the mood to sit quietly by the fire and embroider.

Instead, she, too, went out, the way the king had gone.

In this palace the queen's apartments gave out onto a sort of covered walk, a promenade where Anne and her ladies would gather of a fair day and from which it was possible to watch jousting in the courtyard below.

Now it was nighttime, and the gallery was deserted and the courtyard, too. The king, Jane thought, must have gone to calm his own nerves with his gentlemen at his own quarters. In fact, these days he brought his gentlemen to most of his dinners with the queen. Why he'd left them behind this time, Jane could only hazard. She guessed he did not wish to have them witness scenes such as had just taken place.

As for Jane herself, she welcomed the cooler air outside, and she walked back and forth. Though it was dark, there was a bright full moon, and by its light the courtyard appeared a place of dreams.

Somewhere, far away, she could hear a woman laugh, and somewhere from a chamber to her left came the sound of the virginal expertly played and the sound of a man declaiming poetry.

Jane walked ten steps away from the door to the queen's lodging, in either direction, daring not to go too far because these days the queen's disposition was so mutable and her rages so sudden that Jane did not dare not be nearby should Anne call her.

She thought what a strange creature this Anne Boleyn was, so ambitious and full of purpose and yet so seemingly unable to do anything with her position once she arrived at it.

If Jane had half of her beauty, or if Jane were ever to get half her chance at a good marriage, she would not let it go to waste.

The women of the court said that Anne Boleyn had bewitched the king and that as such charms, all witches' glamour failed after three years and that this was why she was so insecure, knowing that her power over the king was waning and that soon she would be bereft of it, and should a son not materialize, she would be lost.

But Jane believed not in witches. Or she did not believe that Anne Boleyn was one. She'd been present for enough of the present queen's courtship with the king, and she remembered the looks he gave her, like the looks of a boy faced with a locked pie cupboard.

Jane thought it was only inevitable that once the cupboard sprang open, the boy would eat himself to surfeit.

At that moment one of the pillars that held up the roof of this gallery stirred. And Jane, her mind full of witchcraft and the supernatural, jumped back and stifled a scream.

The pillar laughed and turned, revealing himself as none other than the king.

"Milord," Jane said. "Your Majesty. I beg your pardon. I was only taking the air and . . ."

The king looked at her, his face tired and drawn under the moonlight, his eyes narrowing as if with worry. "What Queen Anne said, in there, Mistress Seymour? Think you it's true?"

"Your Majesty?" Jane said, knowing full well what the queen had said, but knowing also it was not advisable for her lady-in-waiting to repeat it. Words forgiven a queen and a wife would come oddly from her servant, almost a stranger to the king for all the times they had met around the palace.

He made a click of impatience with his tongue against his palate. "Do not pretend you did not hear it, you who are, more than other women, devoid of feminine wiles. Do not pretend you couldn't hear that. Indeed, the way my lady wife screams, only the dead and the deaf could avoid hearing it."

He looked up at the moon, and it bathed his face and bleached it, making him appear at once younger and not quite alive. The pale light washed away all the wrinkles from his face, restoring youth to it, but it also made him look like a statue, a king sculpted in marble, something incredibly majestic and ancient.

Jane had the thought that she would like to touch his hair, that she very much wished to advance her hand and caress his beard. She was not fool enough to attempt it.

"She said that Catherine and Mary are witches," the king

said. "That they wish her . . . and me ill and that they have cast spells that would deprive me of a son." He looked down at her. "You were Catherine's lady-in-waiting, too. Do you think Queen Anne is right?"

"Milord," Jane said. "Far be it from me . . . I am but Queen Anne's lady-in-waiting. . . . I would not presume . . ."

She was thinking that the king and the queen's affair was such that one day they were mortal enemies or near enough and the next they would be bound in the closest love that had ever bound man and woman. If Jane said something about the queen that the king disliked, would not the king remember it later, when his love for the lady returned in full force?

Stronger heads than Jane had rolled off their shoulders on less provocation.

Standing here with him under the moonlight, and him looking young and almost gallant, it was easy to forget that he was a king, the most powerful man in these isles.

But that he was, and Jane would not and could not presume to ignore it.

The king looked at her, all steady and serious. "I did not ask you to give me your opinion of Queen Anne, Mistress Seymour. I asked you to tell me if you think Catherine, my—the Dowager Princess of Wales—is in any wise guilty of witchcraft or of plotting against me. And if it's possible that she has turned my natural daughter, Mary, against me and taught her the same craft."

Jane shook her head. Before he had fully stopped speaking, she was shaking her head. "Your Majesty, the . . . the Dowager Princess is the kindest, most gentle lady that ever breathed and fearful of the Lord our God and loving of the gospels. While I stayed with her, she prayed, over and over, for Your Grace's health. She would not . . . She could not . . . Indeed."

Jane floundered. To her eternal confusion, she felt the king reach for her hand, his soft, warm hand enveloping hers. He lifted her hand to his lips and kissed it, an earnest kiss of seeming chaste devotion. "Thank you, Mistress Seymour, you have comforted me marvelous much. Perhaps I can now find sleep in my bed."

And with that he bowed to her, the slightest of bows, and he walked away through the night, whistling the tune he had written for Queen Anne.

Jane felt she had indeed relieved his spirits, though she was not quite sure how she had done it. Nor was she sure why for a brief moment there on the promenade, she'd thought of the king as a man, and a man she wished to embrace and console.

Eighteen

PHOENIX IN THE FIRE

SPRING in Wiltshire seemed quite different to Jane as she traveled towards her family home with the royal progress. Castles and manors she was used to considering grand and even magnificent from childhood now seemed narrow and humble. Forests and preserves seemed more full of animals and birds and more deserted of people than she remembered. And in between there were stretches of rolling land, the fields turned and raw in the sunlight, not yet cloaked with the green that would cover them as the crops grew with the swelling of summer.

Jane sometimes rode on a horse, sometimes on a litter, following the progress with the other ladies-in-waiting.

Queen Anne also now rode and now was carried. The king and queen were going though a period of good understanding. She was pregnant again, and her temper had subdued somewhat. And he, ever hopeful of the elusive prince, treated her as a precious jewel or a fragile flower, minding what she ate and how she ate it and what she wore and how she traveled.

It was at his insistence that fiery Anne Boleyn rode far less time than she spent reclining in her litter, amid cushions and blankets, her still-svelte figure swathed and treated as something of immense value that might at any minute shatter.

Thomas Wyatt was subdued, too, perhaps because the king rode beside the queen and allowed little opportunity for his courtiers to get close to her, much less talk to her. And Wyatt, therefore, often made bid to talk fair to Jane through the long journey.

"Ah, Jane," he would say. "If you could live with me knowing my heart is with another, I could learn to like of you."

But Jane made him some light response or none at all. There was nothing for it. Since she had realized that Thomas Wyatt would never be happy unless he was suffering, she'd realized she had nothing for him or he for her. There was nothing she could do to improve his happiness.

She also suspected that Wyatt had perceived her interest in him early on and, since the coronation, had been aware of its waning. And though he didn't love her or have any interest in her, it wounded him that he should have lost her unrequited regard.

Now, she felt, he was merely seeking to revive her attention, to get her to look to him again and spend her days in either fear or expectation of a look from him. In a way it was as though he regarded her feelings as a piece of jewelry and his rightful prerogative. He wanted to wear her attention to him upon his sleeve and display it to the admiring—or mocking—world.

But Jane, though she remained plain and perhaps unable to

attract any other gentleman's eyes, had learned that there were gentlemen whose attentions were not worth attracting.

It was as though, through being at court, even if she'd been ignored there, she'd learned a measure of self-possession and self-value. She would not give it up to be walked upon by Thomas Wyatt's haughty disdain nor trampled beneath his boots like dust.

So Jane rode into Wiltshire and approached Wolf Hall with no love prospects, noting only how small everything appeared and how insignificant.

In Wolf Hall, she was received by her parents with both kindness and a sort of odd puzzlement because here she was, returned with the court, and yet here she was, still unmarried after years of exposure to a society where most women found husbands.

She got her childhood room back, while the king, the queen, and the rest of the court were disposed in many newly built rooms, many newly furnished apartments.

In a way it was like being at court. In another it was like the suffocating days of her childhood—returning to her room and her solitude, her needlework and her virginal.

"Master Wyatt seems to prefer you, Jane," her mother said, seeing Jane at her virginal on the third morning of her stay there. "He says that if he could love you, he would be very pleased indeed."

"If he could love me, mother, but he cannot."

Lady Seymour looked at Jane with an expression somewhere between vexation and impatience. "Jane, love . . ." She looked outside the small window, where the rose garden showed but dimly, shrouded in fog. "Love is not . . ."

Jane shook her head. She imagined her mother was going

to explain to Jane that love was not necessary for a happy marriage, that most marriages were contracted without love. To
Jane who had been quite ready to marry William Dormer on
no stronger attachment than her feeling kinship with him.

"No mother, love is not all, love is not even important. And
I'm well aware that as a plain woman I should not and will
probably not get love from anyone." She let her hands fall, together, upon the keyboard of the virginal, producing discordant harmonies.

"Jane!" Lady Seymour said in shock.

"Mother, you've made me aware early enough that I was
not a beauty. It is true, and I do not blame you for making me
aware of the truth."

"Jane," her mother said, now in consternation.

"No, Mother, please hear me out. I would gladly marry Sir
Thomas Wyatt if he truly wanted me or if I could in any way
make him a happy and comfortable home. But I cannot. You
must see that Master Wyatt, whom I know quite well, can only
be happy with a woman who despises him. You've taught me
too well, mother. I could never behave that way to my husband."

She saw her mother's shocked look, and she could not
stand it. She could not stand to sit there and dispute with her
mother.

Besides, she had this great fear that her mother—who
looked tired and ill-used by the intervening years—would tell
Jane of some trespass of her father's. She feared that Lady
Margery would confess to some wrenching unhappiness. Perhaps to that rumored affair between Jane's father and Jane's
sister-in-law. And whatever she confessed would be too much
and, far from convincing Jane that it would be right and meet
to marry simply because the gentleman wanted her, would
convince her of the foolishness of such a step.

Jane didn't feel she could endure such confidences and, looking at her mother's earnest and sad expression, she was very much sure it would come at any second.

She got up in confusion, curtsied hastily, and ran out.

Outside, the freedom of the forest called her, and she hastened towards her accustomed path. A great desire to see if her refuge amid the hedge was still there, and if it were still the same, overtook her. She walked along the path, quickly. The smells of the fields in spring, the smells of turned earth and flowering hedges, entered her consciousness and seemed to erase the last few years at court and take her back to the fields of her childhood and to riding free with Tom and Edward, without a care in the world. Back before she was nine, back before she knew she was plain, back when she was so young that she did not understand her duty in the world was to marry someone and thus create fresh alliance and honor for her family.

She ran along the path, seeking her way back to that young Jane and her carefree childhood. Somewhere on one of the fields, which descended in a slow slope from the path and was thus visible from behind the edge, a farmer had made a great bonfire of branches—and probably rubbish. The acrid smell of burning stung Jane's nose, and the grey plume of it climbed like a banner towards the sky.

Thus running, she came to her secret hideout. Some fear at the back of her mind, that an overzealous farmer or industrious servant might have cut it clear away, vanished when she glimpsed the thickening in the hedge and the small space she'd used, before, to enter that area.

It was a little more overgrown, but not so much that she could not enter by forcing her body in between two flowering bushes. And then again, perhaps the inside was wholly overgrown.

She wondered if William ever made his way away from his reportedly happy home to this secret hideout, to enjoy the memories and the silence. Of if Jane had been wholly swept away from his mind by his far comelier and more pleasing wife, the former Mary Sidney.

With that thought in mind, Jane pushed into the hedge and, halfway through, heard a man's sharp intake of breath. William was in there. She must back away now. How embarrassing, how impossible for both of them if she were to find him here. Not only because it must revive both of their fond memories of their youthful foolishness—to no good effect—but also because William would think her reason in coming here was to revive those memories, and that she pined for him still.

But her efforts at retreating were thwarted by a branch from the hedge, which had got caught in the ample, slashed-through sleeve of her gown—a finery she was not used to wearing in the countryside—and held her immobile.

With a sound of frustration, she turned to free herself. But her struggle, or the sound, had called the attention of the man within her erstwhile refuge. He now came towards her in great strides.

"Mistress Seymour," he said. "Pray let me help."

It was the king. She tried to curtsy or kneel, all impaired by the bush holding onto her sleeve. One of the king's large hands, for all its thickness and massive proportions, gripped her sleeve delicately. The other bent back the bough till it snapped.

His voice was full of humor as he said, "There you are, Mistress Seymour. You are quite free."

In confusion, Jane dropped to her knees on the soft ground, but the king raised her and said, "None of that, for you see, we are not in company. I was taking a stroll amid fields and forest and came upon this delightful hideaway. Did you just discover it, also?" he asked.

And then, as though remembering, "But no, you grew up here. Was it perhaps—"

"A favorite place of mine as a child, Your Grace," she said, lowering her gaze to the moss-covered ground.

He looked on her with something of a quizzical smile. "A place you resorted to often enough, if I can guess, your coming from such a large family." There was a wishful note to his voice as he said the last words.

"Yes. It often got quite noisy in our house," she said. The situation was impossible. She stood half-in, half-out of her hideout, and the king within it seemed to fill the entire space. Oh, not with his physical being, though he was a portly man, but with his presence and majesty. To go in any further, she must violate his space, get closer to His Majesty.

The hideout was just as she remembered—shadowy and green, full of the murmur of water and the whispers of birds.

"A noisy house can be a happy place," the king said. "I myself remember fondly my days at court with my sisters and brother." He sighed deeply. "Everything passes, Mistress Seymour. Such is the way of the world. And those of whom you thought you were so fond that you would die if you should spend a day without them, go from you forever, never to be recaptured."

There was nothing Jane could answer to that, so she bobbed a curtsy by way of agreement.

He smiled on her. "But sure your memories cannot be as melancholy. I'm sure you had many a happy game, many a glad chase through these paths, and perhaps used to meet with some swain in this very hideout."

Jane blushed deeply. "Indeed, Your Grace, I never—"

He looked at her seriously. "No, perhaps you never," he said.

And Jane felt suddenly stung. She knew well enough she was plain, but must men notice her merely to remark on her lack of looks?

She drew her shoulders up and took breath in deeply, "Not that there was never a gentleman that wished to marry me, but that I—"

The king looked surprised. "I never thought you lacked for suitors, Mistress Seymour. Often I've noticed men look at you at court." He laughed suddenly. "Which I suppose means I was looking myself."

The shock took Jane like a slap. That he would speak to her like this. She'd often witnessed such flirting, notably with Madge Shelton, whom everyone said had shared the king's bed often enough. As well as many other gentlemen's beds, if one were to believe court gossip.

And the king would treat Jane as one such? Jane who had always believed herself protected by her plainness? She drew herself up, very straight. "Your Majesty. You are a married man."

His eyebrows rose on his great forehead, and his mouth formed a round O of surprise, and Jane thought he had not meant anything improper, that he was just flirting with her, one of those endless bouts of flirting that went on at court and which meant exactly nothing.

Why, Norris, Wyatt, and many of the others continuously professed to love Anne so well that they could never marry another woman, or even look at another woman—all while they seduced and debauched a great round of ladies-in-waiting. Jane was not stupid, and though she might be left out of the general misbehavior, yet she was aware of it and could name names.

She had long ago realized that such declarations of undying love and unending devotion, of fidelity and worship, were no more than a game and no more real than were poems that called a woman fair though she be dark or said the stars of the heavens sparked within her eyes—something that, had it been real, would have been frightening and doubtless painful.

Looking at the king's surprised face, realizing she'd treated courtly jest as reality, Jane felt a wave of heat climb her pale cheeks, and she inclined her head, curtsied, and pulled at the fingers of her left-hand glove, all in a panic. "Your Grace, I beg your pardon. I did not mean to presume that you meant—"

But the king shook his head at her, and she thought for sure he would now punish her, perhaps tell her to remain at Wolf Hall while they all left.

"Mistress Seymour," he said at long last. "You must pardon me. I have lived too long in company that minds neither its words nor its manners, and I've forgotten the proper respect due to a gentlewoman."

"Indeed, Your Grace," Jane said, still quite bent on apologizing, sure that the king was angry at her. "I meant not what—"

"Jane, Jane," the king said, shocking her with using her proper name.

He reached out, and his great hand grabbed at Jane's shoulders, his fingers appearing immense and all out of proportion in relation to her own thin, small build. "Do not apologize for doing what is proper, Jane. You must never do that. You are right. I am a married man, and your reproaching me for my familiarity to you is all that's proper." As if it had only occurred to him that he was, if anything, being more familiar now, he took his hand away, but not without patting her shoulder lightly, as though he might have ruffled the fabric or her skin and must put it right before leaving. "I've lived too long in the middle of wantons and debauches, and it is no wonder my sensibilities are dulled. Your answer was all that is proper."

He smiled at her, and it was a dazzling smile that transformed his whole countenance and changed his face from that of a man in his middle years to that of a boy, radiant over a toy or a surprise. It was a sudden effect she had seen when—in ages past—the king had smiled at the woman who was then Mistress Boleyn.

At the same time, it was as if his presence and power, that personality that seemed to radiate from him and have its own existence, extended towards her, infringing on her space with a physical weight. His smile, radiant and dazzling, seemed to touch her and press against her and cut her breath short as she inhaled.

He didn't seem aware of it, as he stepped closer to her. "In fact, in my days here, in your parents' excellently disposed home, I've been thinking that Wolf Hall—this manor, this forest, these fields, the farmers, and your servants—are all exactly as England ought to be, and the core and beauty of my country."

He gestured animatedly with his great hands as he went on, "My loyal subjects, hardworking, clean living, live in places such as this."

Jane had a flash of thought for the villagers in nearby villages who'd be very surprised to hear their abodes compared to Wolf Hall in any way. But then, she supposed her family was as far beneath the king as the peasants were beneath Jane's family and perhaps Jane's level was as far down as the king could perceive from his great height.

She dropped a quick curtsy and looked at the ground to hide the smile that had come upon her face at the thought of her family being typical subjects of His Majesty. "Your Majesty is too kind," she said.

"Perhaps not kind enough," the king said. "Perhaps I have too long bestowed favors on the wrong people."

He stopped suddenly, and his smile vanished as quickly as though it had never been. A great sigh filled his chest. "But perhaps," he said, speaking as if to himself or to some distant divinity that wouldn't listen to him, "perhaps the child will be a boy?"

Jane blinked, realizing that the king's thoughts had now bent once more around the queen's condition and that he seemed once more to be considering, in his own metaphor from so long ago, the rarity and worthiness of the fruit compared to the tree that overspread and killed all other plants.

Jane chose to say nothing. The queen's condition or the state of the royal marriage were not topics to be impunely touched upon. Or at least not by a mere gentlewoman.

The king looked up at the sky above the little enclosed space among the hedges. The sun had risen considerably further than it had when Jane had hurried here. She wondered where the time had gone.

After surveying the sky for a moment, as if trying to calculate the time of day, the king turned towards Jane. His voice was as formal as it had ever been in addressing her. "Mistress Seymour, I seem to remember that you hunt?"

She took a deep breath, glad that the conversation had moved away from more dangerous talk. "I do enjoy the chase now and then."

"And have on occasion caught more meat for the court than the gentlemen have," the king said, and laughed at her surprised face. "Think you I've failed to mark the Diana in our midst, who plies her bow better than some of my gentlemen? I' faith, Mistress Seymour, it does not seem fair that a lady, good at her needlework, should also be so good at the hunt."

Jane felt her face heat once more. "If Your Majesty judges it to be improper—"

"Oh, not improper at all," the king said and smiled, not his dazzling smile this time, but a great, benevolent grin somewhat paternal or gently affectionate. "You see, Mistress Seymour, all of us educated men know well enough that Diana the great huntress was a chaste virgin. So what could be more proper?"

Confused by his gallantry, puzzled by his compliment, Jane looked down and could not speak. She knew, too, to her great shame, that her face must be suffused of that dark pink color that always attended her embarrassment.

The king laughed, a great guffaw, and grabbed her hand in his engulfing one.

Before Jane knew what to do or, indeed, thought she could do anything, he took her hand to his lips. She felt the brief touch of his moist, warm lips upon the back of her hand.

"I'll not disturb you further, Mistress Seymour," the king said. "Tomorrow, my gentlemen and I enjoy a deer hunt your father was kind enough to have organized for us. If you'd like to join us, I'm sure your father can have no objection."

Jane's breath caught in her throat. Ever since coming back to Wolf Hall, she'd felt as if her life had fallen into a routine she could not avoid—the sewing and the music and sometimes walks along the path. But here was a departure.

Her father, though in general not disapproving of Jane's taste for the hunt, and while allowing and often encouraging her on smaller hunts with her brothers, would never have thought of letting her join a great hunt with invited guests, much less a royal hunt.

"If it would displease you—" the king started.

But Jane shook her head. "Oh, no. It would please me very much."

"Good, good," the king said and bowed to her with a courtier's gallantry. "Then I bid you good-bye, for I will see you tomorrow very early for the hunt."

And he left Jane alone in the moss-covered space between hedges, listening to the brook and smelling the acrid smell of smoke and the sweeter smells of overturned earth and flowering roses.

Her life had changed at last, or at the very least she would be afforded a break from her routine.

She laughed in sudden delight; then, hearing herself, she remembered Anne Boleyn's great, intemperate laughter and stopped abruptly.

Nineteen

❧

JANE met with the king and his company in the courtyard of her own father's house early in the morning and was surprised—shocked—to see she was the only lady in the company.

Her father and her brother seemed surprised, too. Though, doubtless, her father must have been apprised of her joining them, as the king would have told him he wished Jane to be of the company. In fact, Jane's own mount was ready, the mare she used to ride when at Wolf Hall.

But all the same, her father and brother looked at her with such wondering looks that she thought they must have misunderstood the king's words, or perhaps felt that she was being too daring in joining a wholly male entertainment.

This last thought put a blush on her cheeks, as she hurried towards the horses.

"Holla, Mistress Seymour, how does Diana this fine

morning?" the king asked. He was already mounted and had trotted towards her. He now stopped next to her mare and grinned at her.

Jane curtsied and blushed and knew not at all what issued forth from her mouth, save for knowing it would make no sense, whatever it was. She was further confused by seeing that three grooms had rushed forward, each one vying to attend her in mounting.

She climbed on her horse, half dazed, in time to hear Lord Rochford, ask, "Diana, milord?"

The king chuckled. "It is but a jest between Mistress Seymour and myself. Do we hunt, gentlemen? Or do we stand about talking?"

The horn sounded, and they started towards the part of the forest where beaters would have been busy for some hours already, scaring the game towards them.

Jane found the joy she remembered and the happiness of riding through the early morning fields. The morning was fine, with just that hint of cold that often presages a scalding day.

The fields lay wreathed in early morning fog, and the horses were full of spirit and ready to ride however long it took. The party separated, as it would.

Some of the party fell back or fell out, tired of the long-drawn pursuit or of the time on horseback. Others went down what they deemed more promising paths, where they fancied the game would come to them.

Jane stayed with the main part, keeping pace with the king's fast riding for a while, until she came to a path crossing where she thought she heard the noise of game headed down the other path.

She took off from the party, so intent on following her

quarry that she neither noticed that she was at the lead of this chase, nor that only one person was following right behind her.

The path ended in a clearing, and here she could see more clearly than she had from the path, the movement of the brush as a deer came towards her. From the look of it and the way the brush parted for the creature, it would be a large animal.

Jane took her bow from her back and nocked an arrow. Though she was small, she had, from long training, the upper body strength necessary to pull a bow almost as large as that of any male hunter.

Still, if this were a very large buck, she knew she might not be able to pierce its skin and also that, when wounded, deer often charged.

Looking over her shoulder to make sure of being covered by several male hunters, she saw only one, her brother, Tom Seymour, who regarded Jane with raised eyebrows and a puzzled smile on his face.

A rustle from her prey called Jane's attention, and she turned just in time to see the deer emerge from the underbrush. It was no buck, but a doe—a large doe, her sides swollen with enormous pregnancy.

Jane took in breath suddenly, regarding the animal's moist nose and soft eyes and thinking of such a pregnancy and of the strain it must cost the animal to run in front of the beaters through the undergrowth of Savernake Forest.

The doe looked scared and harassed and so tired that she might have dropped on her front legs at any minute.

Jane lowered her bow slowly. She had never been a squeamish maiden, and she normally enjoyed the killing part of the hunt as much as she enjoyed the pursuit. There was something to a buck—large and defiant to the end, at bay and tossing mutts on his antlers—that made her heart race and, when she sped an arrow towards its heart, made her feel she'd met a worthy foe.

But she would not take a doe in foal. Nor did she have any interest in killing an animal that looked already defeated.

From behind her, she heard the twang of a bowstring pulled and looked back in shock to see Tom let an arrow fly from his bow. A sound not quite a bleat and almost a scream from the doe told Jane that the arrow had met its mark.

Jane turned back, indignant, "Tom, she was in foal."

"Don't be a fool Jane. Your heart is too soft." He climbed down from his horse and blew his trumpet to call his attendants to him.

They came rushing in and set about preparing the carcass for transport. The doe lay, bloodied, amid the underbrush through which she'd run, her large, moist eyes turned towards Jane in an expression that Jane fancied was accusatory.

Jane realized she was breathing hard, either from reaction to the doe's death or from her brother's unexpectedly cruel act.

After inspecting his kill, her brother left it to the care of his grooms and approached Jane. He stood by her horse, his leather-gloved hand on the horse's neck. "Your heart is too soft, Jane. A creature so turned from its nature that it will still be great with foal while its kind is nursing bucks in the underbrush would have died anyway. Better that we should have the eating of it than that it should die in the forest and be eaten by wild wolves."

Jane swallowed. She was shaking, and she still felt as though the doe had met an unjust end. Even though she knew her feeling was quite irrational, she felt as though the animal had run to her for protection, and Jane had failed her.

She removed her arrow and put it back in her quiver, and she put up the bow, all without looking at her brother directly. She felt angry at him for his unwarranted cruelty.

Tom, meanwhile, looked over his shoulder towards his attendants who were far enough away and occupied in their preparing of the carcass.

As if having satisfied himself that no one was paying attention to them, he spoke in a low voice, "And you're too soft-hearted in other ways, too. Take care Jane, you run great peril."

Jane had no idea at all what Tom meant and was sure her face showed only total astonishment.

Tom looked angry. "Jane, you great fool. Can you not see that the king looks at you a great deal and has gone through some trouble to have you be of his hunting party?"

"Oh, it was no trouble," Jane said, then realizing this was not what she meant at all, she said, "It's only that he found me on a walk through the forest and he asked if I liked to hunt and . . . my having said yes, he asked me to join in this hunt. You see, brother. Perfectly innocent."

"Perfectly innocent," Thomas said, mimicking her accents. "When did you become a fool, Jane? You used to perceive intents and ideas as well as any woman, perhaps better. Why think you that you're the only lady invited to a hunting party of gentlemen?"

The vague discomfort that Jane had felt at first, when coming down and noticing that she was the only female in the expedition, now revisited her, putting heat on her cheeks and making her lower her eyes.

"I suppose His Grace could not invite his wife. The queen is being careful of the child she carries. And I suppose that none of the other ladies wanted to join."

"Jane, you suppose far wrong. The king, to my knowledge, sought only your company."

"But why?" Jane asked.

Tom gave her a surprised look, as if wondering of his sister's wits. "For the reason gentlemen seek a lady's company, Jane. You cannot be that innocent."

"Oh, Tom, I'm not such a fool as you think. But you must see that I have no great endowment of beauty that would attract the king. There are women at court who are far fairer than I and that . . ."

"I don't know," Tom said. "Except that I've thought you are the exact opposite of the queen, both in coloration and temper, and perhaps the king seeks that?"

"I don't—" Jane started and swallowed. "He has made no advances and shown no particular marks of his favor." Even as she said this, she wondered if she was lying, thinking of their talk in the clearing and of his kissing her hand and making remarks on how chaste Diana had been.

Tom tilted his head, as though considering this. "Perhaps not," he said. "Perhaps he has not. But you must see where you are, Jane, and understand your position . . ."

"I know to guard my honor," Jane said. And blushed. "Once already, when he paid a compliment that I'm sure he did not consider, I reminded him he is a married man."

"You reminded him of what?" Tom asked and looked surprised, till he perceived that some of his attendants had looked towards them because of his raising his voice. And then he wiped all expression from his face and leaned yet closer to Jane and spoke in a low voice, full of intent and menace. "You know, Jane, sometimes I despair of you." He gestured towards the doe and then towards Jane as if such a gesture encompassed everything that was wrong with his sister. "You have such a soft heart that you seem to neglect to be good to yourself. Jane, in another time this might not be so, but the king is pursuing you, and if you play your cards right, you could be the queen."

It was Jane's turn to look shocked. "The queen is my age, or a little older," she said. "There's little chance she'll die, leaving the king widowed."

Tom waved the objections away. "The queen is an uneasy woman to live with and so full of venom and so self-willed that she'll step her foot wrong sooner than later and be put away as Catherine was."

"Tom," Jane said, her patience failing her. "The queen is with child."

At this, her brother fell pensive. "That is true, and that might be a problem. At least if the child lives. And if it is a son. Another girl or another stillbirth will only further exasperate the king against her and clear the path for you that much sooner."

Jane felt as if her brother were insane. Surely what he was saying was the sheerest madness. She had never had any mark of affection from the king that denoted a wish to marry her. Nor, indeed, a wish to debauch her. The only times the king had been too familiar, it had been that kind of familiarity that is sometimes offered to children and other people considered of no consequence.

"I will not listen to this," she said, and, pulling on the reins, made to turn her horse and get away from a brother who had clearly gone raving mad, and towards the rest of the hunt, where Tom would not dare repeat these inanities.

But Tom grabbed at Jane's arm. "Jane, listen to me. Think me insane if you will, only listen to me. I do not care if you think the king loves you . . . or doesn't. I care only that you listen to me. There is one way you could ruin this enterprise before it begins. If the queen has a son, there might be some advantage in becoming royal mistress, though not as much as there once was, since the present queen is not inclined to let the king reward his past amours—"

"The king's mistress, Tom?" Jane asked, insulted, revolted, and struggling for words and expressions to speak her disgust to her brother. "How can you say that? I would never consent to being the king's mistress, no matter what advantage you think it might bring."

To her surprise, he grinned a broad, delighted grin. "That's the spirit. Nor should you. Not unless the queen provides a living son. For in the meantime there is a very good chance that you might be able to become queen. Provided you don't give in to the king, and you don't allow yourself to be seduced."

Jane was outraged. So outraged that she couldn't find words for her disgust. She wrenched her arm away from her brother's grasp and succeeded, at last, in turning her horse around.

Her brother's laughter followed her, as she rushed out of the clearing.

She made it to the principal group of the hunt—where the king had just killed a majestic buck—in time to express her congratulations over his prowess.

And thus, in a merry mood, they made back to the manor, while Jane tried to forget her brother's very foolish words.

Twenty

"WILL there be a response, ma'am?" the page asked and took a step back to wait.

Jane, sitting on a chair by the window in her room, her embroidery by her side, held in her trembling hands the package she had just received and looked up at the young boy—one of the king's youngest and most pleasing servants.

The king had sent her something? What could it mean?

She swallowed hard, but even then she was sure her voice would come out trembling, as it did when she said, "No response. No . . ." She shook her head.

The page bowed low, his blond hair falling over his eyes, then into place again, as he straightened. "Good day, then, madam."

And Jane was left holding a letter and a small, neatly wrapped parcel.

She broke the seal on the letter and read hastily, "To Diana, in memory of our friendship in the woods." It was signed "Your servant and King, Henry," and Jane blushed to think what anyone might imagine if they read such a note addressed to her.

Of course, their encounter in the hedge had been completely innocent, and so the king's letter, seen in view of that, must seem to Jane's eyes as just as innocent. But not many people would understand it thus.

Her hands trembling, she broke the string that tied the other parcel and pulled out . . .

She gasped. In her trembling hand—ungloved, since she had removed her gloves the better to ply her embroidery needle upon a petticoat she was sewing as part of Queen Anne's large intended donation to the poor—she held a small tablet, of the sort a lady might wear at her necklace or her girdle. The tablet was gold and hemmed all around with sparkling diamonds. In the center of it, enameled with exquisite exactness and painted in such a way that it looked like the very man to life was a miniature of King Henry.

Jane stared at it a long time, turning the precious tablet over and over in her hand.

Too late, she remembered her brother's admonitions against giving in to the king. Surely it looked improper to accept the king's gifts, and, of course, as with the letter, she could well imagine how it would look if anyone were to see it.

In fact, Jane had accepted it only because she had been taken so completely by surprise, in the middle hours of the day and while she was quietly with her thoughts, working at her needlework.

Besides, since they had come from Wolf Hall, she'd rarely seen the king, much less had any reason to imagine that he was thinking of her.

The queen's pregnancy progressed, and all her ladies were kept busy with charity sewing, as though to petition God for the favor of a son in return for the queen's great kindness to the poor.

The evenings at court had been quiet indeed, save for occasional visits to the queen's quarters by the gentlemen of the chamber and the king. But even in those, perhaps fearing harm to his unborn child, the king had banned dancing and concentrated only on those softer entertainments of music and poetry, which would not be unduly exciting or fatiguing for the queen.

In fact, the king had been so careful of his wife as to answer all her censure in a gentle voice and calmly, and to treat her opinions as always being right. And in his visits to the queen's chamber, he'd danced attendance to the queen and never paid the slightest attention to Jane. Not even a stray look.

Jane had not resented this. Whatever Tom might say, she had no hopes of the king. She had no hopes of anyone, once her foolish hopes of Thomas Wyatt had been given over.

Which was why this gift from the king had taken Jane so much by surprise that she couldn't quite refuse it in time.

She turned it in her fingers, feeling the cool smoothness of the gold back, the diamonds beneath her fingers, and looking at the miniature of the king in between.

Should she give it back now? It would, doubtless, be the proper and decent thing to do. She should wrap it tightly in a package and call a page and have it delivered to the king.

But she was far too sensible to think this course was possible, much less desirable.

First, if she were to send something to the king now, no matter what her intention, pages, servants, and courtiers would rumor it about as a gift from her to the king. And no matter how unlikely it was that the king should ever take any interest of that kind in Jane, the story would be struck abroad that she was trying to court him.

This alone, even if unlikely that such foolish "courtship" would have any result, would be enough to spark Queen Anne's jealousy and to have Queen Anne send Jane from the court. It had happened before because Queen Anne had fancied that one of her ladies looked too long at the king, or that one had, perhaps, praised him too eloquently over a win at cards or a witty saying. And Jane had no intention of being sent home.

Add to that the look that she had long seen in the king in his unguarded moments when talking to either of the wives whom Jane had served as lady-in-waiting.

When the king was himself and unencumbered by protocol of state or his own wish to present a certain image—in the unguarded moment when his thoughts and actions were most his own—in the midst of a fight with Anne Boleyn, or while playing at cards with his first wife Catherine, Jane had seen a look come over the king's eyes that was very much the look of a self-willed, spoiled child.

That self-willed, spoiled child had probably meant no more, in sending the miniature to Jane, than what he'd put on his note—the memory of a pleasant encounter in a quiet forest place, amid the hedges.

He'd meant it as something less than friendship and far less than love—the gift of a child to a secret playmate, easily bestowed and quickly forgotten. The tablet with its diamonds about it might be, for Jane, a great and costly gift, but surely it meant nothing or less than nothing to the king who possessed, after all, all the wealth of the kingdom.

If Jane sent this gift back, it would tell the king that she had viewed his gift as far more than what he'd meant it to be. On such a personality as King Henry's, this might spark amusement, but it might also spark anger.

In fact, the thought that she was turning his gift away, that she didn't want his gift nor his kindness, would almost surely spark anger in the little boy that lived inside the king's soul, the little boy who wished to be loved and cared for and always the center of everyone's attention.

She stared at the gold tablet, till it seemed to her it might have melted and disappeared just from her scrutiny. But the tablet remained solid, and there was nothing for it.

Jane could not return it. And she must wear it. For surely the king would expect her to wear it and show the pride she had in what he would consider his simple gift.

Sighing, Jane clipped it to her girdle in such a way that it would fall half-obscured by her skirt. If she was very lucky, no one would notice it.

Then again, there was a good chance no one would notice it in any case, Jane thought, because, since Thomas Wyatt had desisted of making Jane show any feeling towards him again, no one had paid any attention to Jane at all.

Most evenings in the queen's chambers she was suffered to sit silently beside the fire sewing and, doubtless, tonight would not be any different.

She put her hand down and fingered the tablet diffidently. She was making too much of this. Chances were no one would notice it. Not even the king. Chances were the king wouldn't notice if she didn't wear it, either—but it was a risk she didn't wish to run.

No, she'd wear her tablet for a few more months, probably unnoticed, and when the queen had delivered herself of a prince, and the king had forgotten all about Jane, even as a friend chance-met in the woods, it would be safe to unclip it from her girdle and perhaps to give it to Edward or Tom, as a gift.

Surely with them it could not be construed to mean anything but a mark of royal favor and, as such, they'd prize it.

Jane returned to her work with a lighter heart, embroidering a simple sprig of flowers along the hem of the petticoat.

Queen Anne had said that there was to be no heavy embroidery and no elaborate work on these, since they were for the poor.

And Jane smiled at the queen's thought that these petticoats should have any embroidery at all. But she judged that Anne's life, passed at the French and English courts, had not given her much knowledge of peasants, much less poor ones.

Twenty-one

EVENING came, and Jane could not recall ever having viewed evening at court with such trepidation, at least not since her first night there.

But she need not have worried. After a late supper, the queen and her maids sat down to the normal entertainments of the evening. The king did not appear, but his gentlemen were there—or at least Thomas Wyatt and Lord Rochford had joined the crowd, as well as Norris, recently betrothed to the light Madge Shelton.

As they arranged themselves for card games, Thomas Wyatt and Jane were the only ones left out—Jane by the fire, sewing upon her work by this light now that daylight was gone. That was the only change between the work she'd done in her room and the work she did now. And Wyatt stood by the window, looking out and giving every impression of sulking, with his expressive, dissatisfied mouth set in an expression of great discontent.

"Come," Anne Boleyn said to Wyatt. "Come join my table, Thomas. I have need of your wit."

Wyatt turned from the window and regarded the acknowledged beloved of his heart with an expression that bordered on anger. "What you have need of, madam, is of another unfortunate who is guaranteed to lose all his money to you."

Anne laughed, loudly and much longer than the feeble joke warranted.

It seemed to Jane that the queen's laughter had become more frequent of late, and less dependent on what might be passing around her. Perhaps it was an effect of the disordered emotions of pregnancy.

George Boleyn regarded his sister with a faint, quizzical look, but then smiled and turned to Thomas Wyatt. "Come, man, come. You must supply your purse to support her habit. What's the use of all of you, her purported knights in shining armor, when you leave the family to bear the brunt of her gaming depredations?"

Wyatt glowered at the mention of his being Anne's knight. He hooked his thumbs deeply on either side of the dark belt, which scarcely made a break in the unrelieved black he wore and which seemed to accentuate the gauntness and height of his body.

"Mistress Jane does not play either," he said. "And she hasn't played in much longer. Why call you not on her?"

Anne Boleyn looked towards Jane, a quick, dismissive glance. Then the queen looked back at Thomas Wyatt. "Mistress Jane does not play. She has no use for the cards, despises the amusement, and has religious or moral objections to ladies who play cards. Is that not so, Jane?" Anne asked, and laughed, even though Jane had made no answer at all.

The truth was that Jane did play cards and had often played them with her erstwhile mistress, Catherine, who—after praying and supplication—was fond of nothing so much as a good game of cards.

In the worthy lady's company, particularly over the months of exile from king and court, Jane had become adept at most games of cards, be they moved by cunning or by chance.

But she saw no reason to enlighten Queen Anne who, at any rate, sought only to make sport and laughed before Jane could make any reply and without guessing what the reply might be.

Instead, Jane bent her attention to her work, forgetting the queen and her set. She guessed there were a couple of other remarks addressed to her, but her answer not actually being needed and the whole thing being a scheme concocted by Queen Anne for her own amusement, Jane ignored these remarks as well as everything else, and continued working.

She'd almost finished working the sprigs all the way around the edge of the petticoat.

From somewhere, at one of the gaming tables, she heard mention of the king and, without thinking, dropped her hand to where the tablet with His Majesty's likeness dangled, between the deep folds of her skirt.

She wondered if the king would come by later—as he sometimes did—to see how his wife had passed the day and if there were no disturbances in the pregnancy. After two children, which the physicians assured had been boys and which had been born early and dead, the king took no risks at all and often enquired of his wife's—or his heir's—health.

Jane's fingers toyed with the tablet. She wondered if the king came, whether he would ask her if she was wearing it. She doubted it very much, since he had not looked at her, much less addressed her, since they'd come back to court.

In fact, all his thoughts were bent to his wife, and it was to his wife that his attention went, trying to keep her happy and protected against the blessed day when she would deliver a prince. *As it should be,* Jane thought, playing with the tablet within the folds of her skirt and dismissing a faint prick of jealousy.

What call had she to be jealous? Was she letting Thomas Seymour's foolishness affect her? Did she think, truly, that the king had any designs on plain Jane, either as wife or mistress?

"You toy very much with something that's hanging from your girdle," Sir Thomas Wyatt said. He had slid across the room to her side while she was not attending, and now stood beside her, looking down at her with that sad, brooding look of his. He also appeared, though she could not imagine why, faintly disapproving, as though she had betrayed him in some way.

"It is that it's a little dark for sewing," Jane answered, looking towards the fire and ignoring his implied question.

The poet cackled, something that sounded not joyous at all. He walked from one side of the room to the other in front of the fireplace, causing a few heads to turn from the gaming tables to observe him.

"Sir Thomas," Anne Boleyn said. "You may sit down, sir. We scarce have need of the wind of your passage."

Her table laughed, and Sir Thomas Wyatt stopped and turned his back on Jane to look at them. Without being able to see his face at all, Jane would wager he was glowering.

He huffed expressively, a sound somewhere between sighing

and annoyance but perhaps closer to annoyance. "Mistress Jane has got a gift from our Lord King Henry yesterday," he said in a tone loud enough to be heard by the entire room. And, with a spiteful glare at Jane, "Or so a little bird told me."

"A gift?" Anne Boleyn looked up from the table.

The queen was ever so ready with her jealousy, so prepared to suspect any woman, young or old, of planning what Anne herself had done in supplanting the queen, that Jane cowered a little, expecting an explosion. And she said nothing to confirm or deny what Thomas Wyatt had said.

But Anne Boleyn only laughed loudly. "What can he mean by it?" she asked. "Come, Mistress Jane, what did he give you?"

Jane swallowed. She shook her head, then lowered it to her work. "It is nothing, Your Grace."

Anne Boleyn inclined her head a little, her expression puzzled and teasing. "Nothing at least seems rational enough. Thomas, are you sure you're not mistaken, now?"

Thomas Wyatt cast a withering look over his shoulder at Jane, his mouth set in definite disapproval. "There can be no mistake on it, Your Majesty. For it was the king's young page himself that told me, he was sent by the king to Mistress Jane, on an errand, to deliver a little packet and a letter. And that the lady sent him away with no response."

Again the queen laughed, and her perfect, curved eyebrows climbed her smooth forehead. "No response, indeed? Come, Jane, are royal gifts or missives so common that you send the messenger away with no response? The things I don't know about my own ladies. Apparently Mistress Jane Seymour is so used to being pursued by all men that a gift from the king himself brings forth no surprise and no reply. How quaint. I must talk to my ladies more, if such things go on, and without my ever perceiving them."

She played a hand of cards and, for a moment, Jane thought it would all be forgotten and the subject dropped. Thomas Wyatt continued to stand facing the queen's gaming table, his back to the fire. But he did not say anything, and Jane hoped the man's spite had worked itself out.

How could she ever have thought him gallant or as a man she could love? She now saw him as a small, spiteful man who only wanted that which he could not have. Jane had been a fool to ever think of him as more than that.

But her cards played and the money from the round collected, Anne Boleyn looked up once more. "Really, I am all astonishment that His Majesty sends you gifts. To you, of all people, Jane. I still wonder what he means by it." She gave Jane a bright, cheerful smile, for which Jane could gladly have killed her, and asked in a sweet tone, which compounded the offense, "Do you think he means to make you his mistress?"

Jane felt heat climb her cheeks. "Madam, I doubt very much he means any such thing."

The queen laughed. "And well you might. And so would I. But what else can he mean?" She perused the deck in her hands, then threw a card down upon the table. "Perhaps, Mistress Jane, if you tell us what he sent to you we might divine his purpose. What say you?"

Jane said nothing and took another stitch.

"Yes, show us the gift, and we'll play at imagining what can be in the king's mind," Thomas Wyatt said. "We know we will not succeed for we, mere mortals, must ever fall short of the royal thinking. But it will be like a riddle. An exceptionally difficult one."

Jane found the whole room looking at her, expressions ranging from Anne Boleyn's very amused one, through a whole range of diversion and amazement, to Thomas Wyatt's malicious glower.

She had to answer. There was nothing for it. Taking a stitch, she said, "I said it was nothing."

"You mean to tell us that the king sent you a parcel of nothing or a present of air?" Thomas Wyatt asked. "Poems have been made to such occurrences, but I have trouble believing it happened in real life."

"It was," Jane told the faces bent towards her. "Merely something in remembrance of a talk we had at Wolf Hall. A nothing that means nothing but that he was grateful for my parents' hospitality. Or appreciative of it."

A lot of people looked away at this, as if the answer had satisfied them. But Anne Boleyn continued to stare intently at Jane, her head slightly sideways and a smile playing upon her lips. "I have it," she said. "the king clearly sent Mistress Jane some herbal preparation of his own mixing for the benefit of her eyes, since she spends so much time over the needle and the embroidery thread."

Laughter echoed throughout the room. Anne didn't laugh, for once, but continued looking at Jane with the pleased expression of someone who made a joke at which others cannot help but laugh.

Of course, the thought of the king's mixing herbal remedies, much less favoring the queen's ladies with them, was funny, since this was the work of women, and the king was, if anything, too masculine a man to consider any such remedies, much less to make them.

Jane felt nettled that Anne Boleyn was making silly jokes at her expense. But Anne was the queen and likely soon to be the mother of the heir, and Jane could do nothing but endure it. She pretended great absorption in her needlework.

"Come, Mistress Jane," the queen said, after a small interval of silence. "You've delayed long enough. You know in my condition it is very dangerous to keep me in suspense. You never know what effect it might have on my child. Some old wives' tales say he will be born with weak eyes if my curiosity isn't satisfied. Do you want to tell the king that you are responsible for his heir's shortsightedness?"

Anne was smiling, but Jane feared that she might very well tell the king, the next time she saw him, that Jane Seymour had risked making their child blind rather than satisfy the queen's curiosity.

Jane could not risk it. She tried once more, in a humble tone, "But it is nothing that should excite Your Grace's curiosity."

"Indeed," Queen Anne said. "And yet it is excited."

She got up from her gaming table and walked to where Jane sat beside the fire. It was impossible to tell how far gone the queen might be in her pregnancy, since these days the lady started taking extraordinarily good care of herself and had told everyone she was with child the moment she missed her menses.

There was, right now, but a slight thickening of her waist beneath her exquisitely tailored dress. If the pregnancy progressed much further, Jane's needle would be called into work to add front panels to the queen's gowns.

Jane suppressed her thought about the pregnancy perhaps not lasting and substituted instead an earnest desire that it might last and bring a prince to the kingdom. Not only because the whole kingdom was in need of a prince but also because a prince would secure Queen Anne in the throne and put an end to all the foolishness that Jane's brother, Tom, might imagine for her.

She could well imagine Tom trying to get Jane to play the

part of seductress to a king who viewed her, if anything, as a daughter or an amusing child and nothing more.

"Mistress Jane," Anne said, extending her very pale, well-groomed hand towards Jane. It was the deformed hand, and on the side of her finger, Jane could see a little show of nail that was the vestiges of a sixth finger. "Show me my husband's present to you."

Jane knew there was no avoiding it. Trembling, fully prepared for the queen to make a scene or take the miniature away and refuse to give it back, Jane unhooked the little tablet from her girdle and handed it into Queen Anne's expectant hand.

She saw the queen's eyes open wide; she heard the queen draw breath in surprise. Jane put her needle in her fabric and prepared to pick up her fabric and run when the royal temper tantrum started, because Anne Boleyn was not averse to boxing her ladies' ears.

Queen Anne looked at the miniature in silence, a long time, when she held it aloft by the little clip from which it was meant to hang. "My kind husband sent Mistress Jane Seymour a miniature of himself worked upon a gold tablet and bordered all around with diamonds."

The faces in the room remained blank, as if not knowing how to react.

But Queen Anne's voice was light and amused as she continued. "We must admire his generosity for certainly—" She looked at Jane. "Being addressed to the likes of Mistress Jane, it must be disinterested."

Jane would like to think that the queen was referring to her honor, but knew she was referring to Jane's lack of beauty. She felt her cheeks heat and tears sting behind her eyes.

The queen's hand put the miniature down, carefully, on top

of the fabric that Jane had gathered between her hands, in anticipation of a storm.

"Keep it, Mistress Seymour, and make good use of it. A trinket such as that can fetch a good amount and likely is enough dowry to buy you a good husband." Under her breath, but still audible to the whole room, she added, "It is likely the only reason anyone would marry you."

Peals of laughter followed from all quarters. The queen and Thomas Wyatt joined in.

Jane felt tears behind her eyes and her heart racing with anger and distress. She had never showed that their mocking bothered her. She did not wish to show it now, but she could barely keep the tears back.

She gathered the fabric, with the miniature, against her chest and ran from the room.

Her departure, of course, brought fresh peals of laughter, which rang in Jane's ears as she leaned against the wall outside the door to the queen's quarters and, under the curious glance of the guards, felt her tears give way and course freely down her cheeks to fall on the white linen of the petticoat.

She clutched the fabric with all her strength. A great anger was surging beneath her humiliation and offense.

Queen Anne, so quick to be jealous of anyone, had only laughed when her husband gave Jane a costly gift. The laughter hurt Jane worse than any fury.

She thought that if the queen had been scared of the threat Jane posed, Jane might feel more kindly inclined towards Anne Boleyn than ever before. It would be the same as her acknowledging that Jane was a woman, too, and as a woman, might be desired by a man.

But, instead, the queen had laughed.

And Jane thought that, unlikely though it was, if it ever

should prove that the king truly thought of Jane as Thomas Seymour thought he did—that the king wanted Jane for his dalliance or even for his wife—Jane would play the game to the end.

Anne Boleyn's laughter was a glove of challenge flung in Jane's face. If Jane found she had the means, she would pick it up and strike to kill.

Twenty-two

✦

QUEEN Catherine's death burst upon Jane as a complete surprise.

Later, she would think that doubtless the king had dispatches about the illness of the woman he called the Dowager Princess of Wales. She would be aware that people at court had heard about it.

But, perhaps because Jane was so thrust out of the mainstream of the court, she never heard of it and was left to learn the news when she was summoned to a full court gathering and arrived to find both Anne Boleyn, King Henry, and the little Princess Elizabeth, now two years old, attired in gaudy yellow clothes of joy.

King Henry had put a little feather in his hat and came towards Jane, carrying Princess Elizabeth in his arms and smiling. "Have you heard, Mistress Seymour?" he asked.

Confused, Jane shook her head. She hadn't heard anything.

The princess Elizabeth smiled at her. She was a pretty child, a Tudor beyond doubt, but with her mother's eyes.

"The Dowager Princess of Wales is dead," King Henry said and, to what Jane was sure must be her blank expression, he added, "She slipped away yesterday afternoon, and the messenger has just come to tell me of it."

Jane's mouth dropped open. Words and images rushed through her, without ever reaching her lips. Any of those words reaching her lips might have been fatal.

But she thought of Queen Catherine as she had then been, playing an animated game of cards with her ladies. She thought of Queen Catherine handing her a book of prayers and telling her how much she prized Jane for her calm and gentleness.

Jane had been much better treated at Queen Catherine's hands, and a part of her felt a great kinship with the lady whose face had become ugly, whose body unappealing in the course of bearing many princes who had not lived long.

Looking up at the king, with his smiling face, Jane could only think that this man had shared a bed with the woman for twenty years, slept beside her many a night and, presumably, got up with her in the morning. And now she lay cold in her grave, and he was celebrating. The idea was repugnant and wounding, and Jane felt her tears come to her eyes and looked down to hide them.

She did not wish the king to see them and imagine she was reproaching him for his happiness. She knew better of His Majesty's quick temper and absolute belief in his own right to do whatever he wished to do.

But when he saw her bend her head, his own face crumpled, the conspicuous happiness vanishing from it. "Mistress Jane," he said, softly, addressing her by her first name, "I'd forgotten how gentle your heart is." He was quiet a moment. "Of course, you served the Dowager Princess of Wales, did you not?"

Jane nodded. "I did, Your Grace."

"Ah," he said. "Catherine was a kind mistress and very generous. In fact, she was very nearly a saint," he said.

Jane lifted her gaze with some surprise, to find his own gaze full of puzzled worry.

"Her only fault," the king said, "was that she would not admit our marriage was against the laws of God and that my natural daughter, Mary, must be illegitimate." He sighed. "But for that, she would have been a saint."

Jane looked past him at Anne Boleyn who, dressed all in bright yellow silk—which looked very odd with her sallow complexion—was receiving the congratulations of a group of courtiers. And of a sudden she knew, with certainty, that the idea of celebrating had been all hers and that the king was merely accommodating his pregnant wife.

Just as Jane thought this, she heard Anne Boleyn speak, while she drew the folds of her gown tight against her growing belly. "Today is a great day indeed, for now that the witch is dead, no one can help but recognize my son as the proper heir to the throne. And my son will be alive, now that she is dead. If only her daughter were dead, too, with her, I would be assured of it."

Queen Anne looked quickly towards the king, and the king pretended not to see her. Instead, he looked at Jane and said earnestly, "You see how it is, Mistress Jane. A lot of people say that Queen Anne is nothing but my concubine and that our daughter, Princess Elizabeth"—he gave the little girl a slight lift with the arm that supported her, causing her to giggle—"is nothing but a bastard. These doubts were bound to continue as long as the Dowager Princess of Wales, Catherine of Aragon, lived. Now they can be laid to rest, and all unpleasantness will soon be forgotten."

His voice descended in range as it rose in earnestness, and he said, "I beg you to believe I do not celebrate because the Dowager Princess is dead. Indeed, I loved Catherine of Aragon intemperately, which contributed to my taking so long to rectify the dreadful wrong our marriage represented. But for all my love for her, you must see she represented a bone of contention in my country, upon which factions must chew like rival mastiffs. She is gone, and the kingdom will be united again. That is what I celebrate."

Jane nodded, wishing to believe it so. She had come to consider King Henry with the sort of gentle regard reserved not for those one considers possible suitors but towards older, powerful people who bestow their kindness on someone young and powerless like Jane.

For all his faults, he'd always been kind to her. For all his faults, he joined Sir Francis Bryan in that very narrow group of men who did not seem aware of Jane's plainness.

She nodded to him and curtsied and made some cooing sounds in response to the cooing sounds Princess Elizabeth was making, till, at last, King Henry was called from her side by his wife's imperious voice.

Even if Queen Anne didn't want to risk dancing—not wanting to endanger herself, in her condition—she wanted music, and she wished others to dance.

Musicians were quickly assembled, among them Mark Smeaton, the king's favorite lute player, and the ladies-in-waiting were called forth to dance with the king's gentlemen.

Jane went obligingly and danced a turn with everyone, while the king—though he loved dancing almost above all things—sat beside the queen, holding their daughter and watching the sport. Princess Elizabeth was clapping her tiny, chubby hands in great appreciation.

After a number of dances, Jane found herself partnered with her brother Tom, who held her hand as he turned and turned in accustomed steps.

The dance floor was not the most convenient of places for private conversation. Couples changed partners very often, as the demands of the dance dictated, and a lady and gentleman might be separated for minutes altogether.

But Thomas Seymour's eagerness to speak to his sister defeated all this.

"Jane, Jane," he whispered when their hands touched and they were dancing side by side. "This is such a fine thing for you."

And on such a note, he passed her to another, the dandy Norris dressed in resplendent blue velvet slashed through to show golden yellow silk beneath. Norris was a light and graceful partner. Jane was a dutiful and well-schooled one. They went through their steps together, and presently he handed Jane back to her brother.

All the while Jane had been thinking how the death of Queen Catherine could be a fine thing for her. What had the poor lady ever done to Jane but take her on as a lady-in-waiting and be kind to her?

As soon as her hand touched Tom's, she turned a puzzled look upon her brother and asked in a whisper, "What do you mean, a fine thing for me?"

Tom smiled. "Isn't it obvious?"

But it wasn't obvious at all, and Jane must wait for an explanation while he handed her back to Norris again and they went through a series of steps quite a while apart, Tom partnering Madge Shelton the whole while.

When Tom took Jane's hand again, she said, "It is not obvious to me, Brother."

Tom looked at her with a wide smile. "But it is clear. The king takes a very great interest in you. You can be his next queen if you but choose to pick up the crown being flung at your feet. What better thing is there for it but to know that his first wife is dead and that there can now be no dispute of your title as queen should you marry him?"

"But . . . what about Queen Anne? Will she not dispute it, should the king decide to do anything half so foolish?" Jane asked.

Inside, as always on this topic, she was divided between disdain and hope. Disdain because she very much doubted that the king would ever choose to court her or marry her. And hope because ever since Queen Anne had laughed at her gift from the king, Jane had wished she could show the queen that she was not a laughable threat.

She knew it was near impossible. And yet she hoped.

But she had to wait while the dance again divided her from her brother. She heard him say something to Madge Shelton, and she heard Madge's foolish laughter, a shadow of her cousin's, just as Madge was.

And then Tom was back, his firm hand on Jane's. "Anne Boleyn will be put away in a convent or some other place. If she doesn't give the king an heir this time, she will be shut away, and no one will view her claim with anything but ridicule. I will remind you, Jane, that the common people call her concubine."

And indeed, they did. Jane had heard it called out to them loud enough when she went out with the queen by litter or coach. Anne Boleyn got called concubine or great whore.

Yet it seemed to Jane that this made not much difference. If such an unlikely time came when King Henry chose to marry

Jane, then Anne Boleyn and her marriage to him would still cast the shadow of illegitimacy over their children.

Jane saw no way out of that and was momentarily relieved that she didn't believe the king had any such intent.

As she thought this, she heard the queen laugh loudly, across the room.

Twenty-three

❧

"DEAR Mistress Seymour," the letter began, "I write to you because, from what I've heard, I have reason to believe you hold my Royal Father's ear and that the king holds you and your opinions in some esteem."

Jane held the brittle paper in her hand and stared at the words—written in a decisive if spidery hand, in black ink—thinking that they couldn't possibly be addressed to her and that there had to be a mistake somewhere.

She read the initial address three times, and she could not doubt it was addressed to Mistress Seymour, nor that the letter had even fewer chances of being addressed to her sister-in-law, Catherine. Because Catherine lived in Wiltshire at Wolf Hall, where Edward had retired, forsaking his duties at court for the sake of keeping his wife company. So, the chances of the dark Catherine Filliol holding any influence over the king were lower than those of Jane Seymour doing it.

Having satisfied herself that she could not have misread the address, Jane looked at the signature. But this, too, no matter how many times she reread it, insisted on saying "The unfortunate Princess Mary, cast away by her father into exile, though she has done nothing to deserve it."

In between address and signature there was a letter that made Jane raise her eyebrows three times in reading it and as many times lay it down atop her clothespress and walk away, only to again take it up and read it once more.

That Princess Mary—or Lady Mary as she was now supposed to be called—was in mourning, there could be no doubt, nor could one doubt that her grief was violent. After all, how should one doubt that any daughter would grieve to loose the queen—or the Dowager Princess of Wales—who had been the kindest of all mothers and ever bent on seeing her daughter at least one more time?

What Jane had trouble believing was what the letter said. Particularly the paragraph that read: "You must believe me to be in very great danger. The concubine has worked for years upon my father to effect my removal—not only from the court but from this world. Unable to convince my father to act that way against his flesh and blood or even against the woman who, with patience and love, shared his fate for twenty years, she has sought and found other means of killing my mother. It is said that when my mother's body was opened, her heart was found to be black like a lump of coal, which no known illness can cause, but which poison may. And you must know poison is an art ever imputed to the Boleyns, and my mother not the first to die at their hand."

Jane read that paragraph again and again. She wished she could say this was mere foolishness and could never have happened. The Jane who had come from Wolf Hall so many years ago would have said just that. Her mouth would have opened wide with shock that English noblemen, the great in the land, could even be suspected of such horrors. And then she would tell herself—and all who would listen—that it was impossible and could not have happened.

But that Jane was long gone, replaced with a woman who had lived at court long enough to know that families had certain reputations, and that the Boleyns might very well have a reputation for poisoning.

She knew, or at least had heard often enough not to doubt it that the king had slept with the Boleyn mother, the older sister, Mary, and now Queen Anne. Any family that could stand that without resentment would be a family bent on success and power at all costs—a family ready to pay any price to be at the top of society. Poison might be the least of it.

But as spine-chilling as that paragraph was to Jane, another one was worse. The one that started with, "Mistress Jane Seymour, I would beg you to use your influence on my behalf with my father. For it is sure that if my father ever would consider anyone's opinion, it would be yours, and if my father but show interest in my well-being, I will at least have a measure of safety. My mother wrote to me of you as someone who was both modest, kind, and properly grateful for any kindness shown to you. For the love of my mother, who was kindness herself, please do not disdain my plea to you."

This paragraph was distressing because Jane could not imagine what influence she could possibly exert for the poor exiled princess, or what kind of power she could bring to bear. Indeed, in her estimation, she had no power at all over the king.

Oh, she knew well enough that if she talked to her brother Tom, he would tell her that she had more power than she thought and probably also, knowing Tom, that she shouldn't exert it on behalf of the disgraced princess.

Tom would tell her it was a fool's game and that her attempt to reconcile father and daughter would bring nothing but the king's fury down on Jane's head. Aye, and Queen Anne Boleyn's, too.

And Jane understood that. Jane even accepted it, as far as it was possible to accept such a strange idea. And yet, if she thought she had the power, she would risk it all for the sake of effecting a reunion between the unhappy princess and her father.

Memories of the queen and how kind she had been to Jane, when Jane herself was but a young girl, alone and away from home, would demand that Jane be kind to Princess Mary. And then there was the undeniable fact that it must be the most painful thing in the world to be born a princess and find herself, overnight, stripped of rank, of power, and even of her father's affection and stamped with the name of bastard.

What Anne Boleyn had done to Mary, also, before she was sent from the court—the physical assaults, calling Mary a cursed bastard, and forcing the girl to carry the train of her infant half sister—all of it had to have left some mark on a girl who, from her mother's portrayal of her, was beautiful but awkward and shy. It had come at the height of Mary's change between a girl and a woman, too, that time when no girl is too sure of herself.

Jane thought if she could, she would do it and be glad. And she would account it not only a service to the daughter of a woman who'd been so kind to her, but a service to the king himself. For it must divide a man from his own soul to be so divided from the children he sired.

A memory of the way he had looked when he spoke of

Catherine and Mary, the distant look in his eye as if he were re-membering past, happier times, confirmed Jane's opinion. She felt sorry for both of them.

But Jane would hardly have the power to do any of this. The king had been kind to her and nothing more. She put her hand down and felt the miniature hanging from her girdle. Even the queen, jealous as she was, hadn't been threatened by Jane's gift. Why would anyone think Jane had any influence over King Henry?

But the messenger from Mary was waiting outside the door. Jane had asked him to wait for a reply, and now she must reply, somehow.

Finding her paper, quill, and ink, she stood at the little desk in her room and wrote hastily in her steady, pointy handwriting:

Dear Lady Mary,

I beg you that you will forgive me the address, since it is the one the king your father decrees, and I would in all, as a loyal subject, do his will.

I read your letter with some distress and completely under-stand your trying circumstances and how you might, per-haps, be under some great danger.

I do not understand, however, how I might be able to help. I am merely a lady-in-waiting to Queen Anne and, though King Henry has deigned talk to me once or twice and has made me a singular gift, yet I do not possess any particular influence over His Majesty's mind.

Please believe that I do not tell you this to avoid helping you. You are right in saying that the memory of your mother's kindness should possess my soul with gratitude and a desire to repay in some manner the gentle treatment she gave me while I was under her authority.

Pray, believe, had I the means at my disposal, I would risk my position and my very life to bring about a reconciliation between yourself and your father, or even just to effect an improvement in your circumstances.

As it is, it is wholly out of my power. All I can do is promise you that should I ever find the means and circumstances at my disposal, I will do all I can to bring you back to court and make you accepted by your father once more.

Your friend and a humble lady-in-waiting,

Jane Seymour

Jane sealed the letter with sealing wax heated over the fire in her room and went to the door to deliver it to the messenger—a sullen boy who, in his everyday life was probably the stableboy for Princess Mary's establishment in whatever castle the king kept her these days.

With it, she emptied her meager purse to give the man a few coins, so that he would not feel justified in extorting the money from his mistress before he delivered the message.

After the man bowed and departed, running at a great gallop down the stairs, Jane realized how much danger she had just put herself into.

Should Queen Anne spot the unusual messenger and ask him from whence he came, should she demand to see the message he carried, how much trouble would Jane find herself in?

At the very least, she would find herself the target of more than mockery from Queen Anne. For she might not be jealous of Jane's power over her husband, but she would never be able to forgive Jane's friendship with Catherine of Aragon's daughter.

Sometimes Jane thought that Anne Boleyn hated the former queen and the king's daughter far more than she loved the king himself.

But most of all, Jane thought of Princess Mary and of Mary's cheerless, desolate life in that lone castle in which she was confined. Tales made it to the court sometimes—tales of an establishment where there was hardly money for new frocks when old ones were outgrown, tales of worn-through shoes, and tales of no wood and insufficient fire to keep warm in winter.

Sometimes it seemed to Jane if only half those tales were true, then Princess Mary must live worse than many of Jane's father's peasants.

Twenty-four

THE day had dawned brilliant spring, the light pouring forth from the morning sky with that look of freshly washed innocence that sometimes made Jane believe she could almost imagine the first day and the world new-created without stain or blemish.

This day might very well be close to it, since it was a day for jousts.

Queen Anne had a great belly. The king wished to keep her amused without giving her any opportunity to exert or tire herself. So he had devised jousts in the central courtyard at the castle. The queen and her ladies would stand—or sit—at windows and balconies, watching while great champions of the joust faced each other and, carrying favors from the ladies, won courtly honor for their patron.

To Jane, this was a moment less for enjoying someone's favor and attention—no knight ever requested her favor to wear—and more to sit back and enjoy great experts at a mad and violent sport attempt to outdo each other.

At its worst it felt cruel and wicked—like Tom shooting the pregnant and tired doe had felt wicked back at Savernake. On the other hand, it could have the same exhilarating feel as of watching a horse race, or two similarly matched dogs fight each other. It was a sport of strength and skill, a brute contest between well-trained men.

They took their places early in the morning, and Jane's was at a little balcony where there was scant any room for anything but herself, standing, slightly bent over the railing.

Joust after joust, contest after contest took place just beneath her in the courtyard. The horses were not those that Jane was used to riding upon hunts or when she had time for a ride. They were a different sort of creature altogether, though doubtlessly housed in the same royal stables.

Where the other horses were thin-legged and tall, with the nervous, graceful look of the Arabian about them, these horses were huge and stocky, and each one alone as thick of body as two of the other horses put side by side. Attired in cloth emblazoned with the colors and device of the knight mounting them, they looked like animate siege engines or, alternately, like great beds on four legs.

The knights who engaged in this pastime, likewise, were for the most part not the gentle knights of the court—though Norris had insisted on jousting and could hold himself, too. Most of the people who engaged in the joust might as well make it their profession, for that was all they did, and they did a lot of it.

You could see, before they mounted their horses, that these knights all knew each other. And you could see from the way they tilted at each other, aiming for this one's weakness, that one's unsteady side, that they had jousted against each other in the past and often, too.

All morning long, the contests were good. Plenty of knights were sent tumbling from their mounts, but the worst injury was a knight who, having fallen wrong, had twisted his leg without breaking it.

And then the king took to the arena. This was neither unexpected nor rare, the king being a great fan of the sport and as solidly built as most of the participants. And a great horseman, beside.

He rode into the courtyard on his horse, enjoying the applause of all the court ladies. He pulled up his visor and inclined his head a little in Jane's direction. At least, Jane thought it was in her direction, though truth be told it was hard to tell when he was bowing within the armor.

Perhaps she was deceiving herself, but just in case she wasn't, she curtsied on her balcony, and it seemed to her—though she couldn't see his face—that the king smiled back.

But then he very properly rode back to his lady wife's balcony and allowed her to wreath his lance with her favor—a sprig of flowers tied with some ribbons.

And then, as his opponent rode forth, the king lowered his visor and his lance for the pass.

The first pass, they each missed the other and by quite a wide margin. The entire courtyard made a sound of disappointment, like a suppressed sigh.

The second time, the king hit his adversary on the side, making him move a little but failing to unseat him. The spectators cheered in acknowledgment of the hit, even if it was less than what was needed to win.

The third pass, you could tell the king was determined and

urged his horse towards his adversary at a speed that left no doubt as to his intent to carry the day.

And then—as their lances met their aim—there was confusion. The sound of metal resounding on metal, the sound of armor and human screaming and a horse's startled neigh.

Jane heard screams of "The king, the king," before she was sure exactly what was happening.

Blinking, she saw the other jouster still on horseback. The man was removing his visor, showing a dark head of hair, and, with the help of his pages, dismounting from the horse, his movements wearied and obviously concerned.

The king lay on the ground of the courtyard. His horse, still attired for the contest, stood a little while away.

Jane blinked again. She'd seen the king tumbled from his horse before, on this type of contest. Every time this had happened, after lying still and dead-looking for a few minutes, the king got up, and his great roar of laughter shook the courtyard and the spectators. And then he would return to the joust.

But this time, he just lay still. Jane waited for him to move, willed him to stand up. Nothing happened.

Some pages and some gentlemen of the court had made it near the king who, from this perspective resembled a fallen giant.

They were pulling him from his armor. The courtyard was as still as a place filled with people and with yet more people watching from every side could be. In the silence each of the clangs of metal on metal as they stripped the king's armor must sound like the tolling of a great bell presaging doom.

Unable to help herself and though her mind gave her all the reasons she should not do this, Jane left her balcony and descended a multitude of staircases to the courtyard.

She must know if the king would live. For . . . what if he would not? Who would reign? Princess Mary, who had so recently been declared a bastard? Or Princess Elizabeth, who most of the kingdom believed to be a bastard? Or the child in Anne Boleyn's womb who, at the moment, might be girl or boy or nothing but a chimera?

A kingdom could not wait, suspended, for a babe to be born and for it to be determined whether it was healthy. A kingdom would not wait suspended.

As she ran down the stairs—with others running along with her, silently, all converging to the courtyard—Jane could well imagine how it would all work if King Henry had indeed died.

The Boleyns would claim the regency on behalf of Anne Boleyn's future child should it prove male, or of Elizabeth, failing that. And the Catholic faction, among them all those who had relatives in Spain or any reason to be loyal to the emperor, would claim the throne on behalf of Princess Mary.

The emperor himself, who had let his aunt be exiled and ignored without moving a finger to stop it, would probably intervene on behalf of Mary—with an eye to marrying someone to his girl-cousin and thus gaining control of England as well as of the large part of Europe he already controlled.

And those subjects who supported the reforms and the declaration of the Church of England's independence from Rome—particularly all those who had in some way benefitted from the partition of the riches of that Church—would follow Boleyn. And all those who favored Catholicism, and Jane believed it was still the greater mass of people, would follow the Spanish faction.

It would all turn to a bloodbath in this nation, which just two generations ago had emerged from bloody civil war.

Jane remembered some of the ballads that dated back to the wars from which Henry VII had emerged victorious to claim the throne of England. She remembered stories of fire and blood, of children killed at their nurse's breast, of old men cut down in front of the fire.

She didn't want it all to happen again, but assuredly it would, with the king dying without a legitimate male heir. Some foolish people might even back his illegitimate son, the Duke of Richmond, Henry Fitzroy, born of Bessie Blount. But in the end they carried no more moral suasion than Elizabeth or Mary.

It would only add a third party to the contest, more dying men to the war.

All this and more was in Jane's mind, the image of a ravaged England, of destroyed fields and burning villages, as she reached the bottom floor and ran across the courtyard to the king's side.

She arrived as they were removing the rest of his armor. He lay stretched on the ground in the padded suit that was commonly worn under the armor. The suit was white linen and, amid all the whiteness, the king looked even more pale.

It was as if all the blood had run out of him, leaving him like a lifeless statue made of wax. When Jane was very young, her neighbors used to deliver votive statues in wax to saints, to request forgiveness for sins or intercession for any great travail. Horses and cows and, sometimes, babes or children sculpted wholly of wax were put at the feet of the saints.

At this moment, King Henry looked like a wax statue of himself, a votive offering on his own behalf. Or that of the kingdom.

Anxious, Jane reached for the miniature hanging amid her skirt folds, and rushed forward, wanting to know how the king was, needing to reassure herself that England did not stand at the verge of an abyss.

Small and determined, she pushed through the crowd and insinuated herself between the shoulders of large males, until she got to the king's side. At the same time that Anne Boleyn made it to the other side of the king.

The two women asked at the same time, "Will he live?"

And looked at each other, surprised, over the king's still form.

Jane retained enough presence of mind to drop a hasty curtsy to the queen and say, "Pardon me, milady, only I was so anxious—"

But Anne Boleyn tossed her head impatiently, as if to say she did not care about Jane Seymour or Jane's worries or even whether Jane was trying to claim Anne's rightful place beside the king. Instead, she looked at the men kneeling by the king, one of them with the back of his hand against the king's neck.

"Will the king live, gentlemen?" she asked. "Lives he yet?"

One of the men, whom Jane remembered was the page of the jouster who had thrown the king down, looked up and nodded. He had a flat face, with the features seeming to rise but a little from the uniform doughiness of it.

Great pale blue eyes looked at Queen Anne, from her elaborate, jeweled headdress and down her body swollen with child, and then he said, slowly, "Aye, lady, he lives. But we cannot wake him."

Water was called for, and some men poured the cold liquid on the king's head, but he moved not. But for the fact that he breathed—his chest visibly rising and falling—it would be hard to believe he was alive.

The king's physician was sent for, and men called to pick him up and to carry him into his chambers.

As they were lifting him, his leg came uncovered, and Jane could see a great gash upon it, which bled copiously onto the courtyard.

"He bleeds," she said in some anxiety and turned to the man next to her—a rough man in the livery of one of the jousters who had come in for the contest. "He bleeds. Could that be why he won't wake? Could he have bled too much?"

The man glanced at her. "No, milady." He had the comforting accents of her native Wiltshire. "No, milady. That's not enough blood to take anyone's life. No. It is a thing that happens sometimes at jousts. You fall the wrong way and twist your neck. Or perhaps you hit your head in a certain manner. In either case, what happens is that though you be alive and breathing, you will not wake.

"Nothing, either good or bad will bring you around." The man shrugged and shook his head, as if by this way commenting on the unaccountable ways of the human body, the impossible will of God.

"And then what happens?" Jane asked impatiently. "Do you sleep forever?" It seemed like something out of a fable.

"No. The human body was not designed to sleep for eternity," he said. "Sooner or later, you either wake or die. But the greater part of them die."

Her heart contracting, her breath caught, Jane wanted to banish the words from her mind, but they seemed to repeat themselves over and over.

She stood, rooted to the spot, while the king was carried away. From the other end of the yard, Anne Boleyn cried, "Oh, please, Lord, someone help me. Help the king."

Twenty-five

I T was as if Jane had been magically transported back to Queen Catherine's court, in exile. For two hours, all of Queen Anne's ladies—and the queen herself—had crowded into the palace's chapel, praying and crying and praying again.

The only difference was that this time Jane felt if God didn't listen to them, if He didn't grant their wish and save the king, then the whole country would suffer and not just the court, or the queen, or Jane.

She was in the middle of fervent prayer when she felt a touch on her shoulder. She looked up to see one of the king's valets—someone she had seen around the king often enough, but never spoken to.

He was gesturing for Jane to follow him. Jane hesitated a moment, but she thought that the page came from the king, and though she couldn't imagine why the page would be calling her instead of the queen, she felt that she should go with him.

She crept out of the chapel after the man, unnoticed by anyone.

Outside in the hallway, the page—a young, blond man of slight build—bowed to her. "Follow me, Mistress Seymour. The king wishes to see you."

"The king?" She felt her heart rush and a smile appear on her lips. "The king is awake?"

The page smiled back as if he'd only been holding back his joy till he could share it. He nodded enthusiastically. "Aye, lady, he's awake, and he's asked to see you."

"Me? Not the queen?" Jane asked, puzzled. They were standing alone in the hallway outside the chapel, all other inhabitants of the palace being presumably at their prayers either within or in their own lodgings. This made the hallway as private a place as could be.

The page looked troubled. He hesitated. "He asked for you."

Jane could not understand why, but she reasoned that perhaps the king wished to make sure that the queen was well, or perhaps he wished to break the news to one of the ladies-in-waiting first, that the lady-in-waiting might break it to the queen without causing that perturbation of joy that can be as difficult for a pregnant woman as the shock of grief.

Jane felt flattered that the king had picked her, that he trusted her with this. She nodded to page. "Then take me to him."

The page seemed relieved she didn't question him further on the propriety of it and bowed to her and led her along the long gallery that linked the queen's apartments to the king's. It was a gallery with windows along it, all of them filled with the morning sun.

Jane blinked in surprise, having spent so much time in the dark chapel that it seemed odd that it would be day out here.

As she got closer to the king's room, she started meeting with gentlemen coming and going, all of them wearing great smiles of happiness and looking as though they could barely contain their joy. They felt, doubtless, as if they had escaped an awful fate, and indeed they had. And Jane had also. As had all of England.

She could barely keep herself from grinning at each of the men she passed. Before she fully realized where she was or what she was doing, she was being propelled through the open doors of the king's room and into the king's apartments proper.

Nothing had ever called for Jane to come into these apartments and see the king's area on her own. If she'd pictured it in her mind at all, it was as the counterpart of the queen's chambers—the queen's room proper and a sort of parlor where she received and entertained the king and his men, and then a gallery along which the ladies' rooms opened.

Insofar as the layout, the king's rooms were indeed the counterpart of the queen's. But the furnishings and decoration were so different as to belong to another world.

As Jane was led past the king's general meeting room, she noted that while the queen's parlor had many small tables and a lot of well-disposed, tapestry-covered chairs, the king's room had one vast table and two benches on either side of it, as if it had been a tavern room.

Against one wall, propped up and arranged as if someone were still inside it, was the king's suit of armor, which should at this moment have unpleasant associations, but perhaps not.

And one wall was taken up completely by swords of several sizes and different styles, mounted in such a way that they could, at any moment, be pulled out.

Past this apartment and into the bedchamber proper, Jane found much more in common with the queen's room. Like the queen's room, it had a vast bed, with embroidered draperies all around it, and a large clothespress—though the queen had several small ones, into which her clothes were sorted—a desk, and a few chairs.

The king's room, however, had one large chair right by the bed, and on that chair the king was sitting, smiling his smile of welcome and triumph. He was wearing only his undershirt, though with that, he was decently clad enough as it came to under his knees and left exposed only calves covered in blondish red hair and large but well-shaped feet.

On his leg, in the place where Jane had seen the wound before, a wide cloth bandage was wrapped.

"Well, Mistress Jane," the king asked, "how do you find me? You look happy to see me . . ."

Jane recalled herself enough to curtsy and nodded, feeling tears of relief come to her eyes. The king would live and, God willing, would sire a boy, and until the boy attained majority, the king would be alive. There would be no more war, God willing, in England, or not for a long time.

"I am happy to see you, Your Grace. I am. We feared the worst, and we've been praying for your swift recovery to the good Lord."

The king laughed, a loud and satisfied laughter. "I'm glad of your prayers, and I'm sure they won't go to waste, but you shouldn't have worried on my account. I have a great Tudor head, so hard it would take more than a little knock to do any permanent damage." He grinned at Jane. "But you are a sight to see, and I am glad I am alive to behold you. Come here, Mistress Jane."

Jane would normally have held back. Even in this moment,

she thought that she was in a married man's room with him, and he wearing only his underclothes.

But the man was the king. And he'd just recovered from life-threatening injury. And Jane was so grateful for his recovery that she could cry. And the king had never, in Jane's life or experience with him, done anything to make her believe that he would treat her with less than respect.

She approached him slowly and stopped right in front of him, ready to drop another curtsy.

He was smiling at her, a fond and indulgent smile, and his eyes had the oddest expression in the world, as if he were looking on something out of his dreams and not directly at Jane herself.

He looked at where her hand, out of habit, was holding the miniature of him that she had clipped to her girdle.

"I see you wear my gift," he said.

She nodded. Her mind whispered that she should tell him it hadn't been altogether proper for him to send her a gift, but doubtlessly the king knew that, and what could mentioning it do other than bring him distress?

Instead, she said, "Are you quite well, Your Grace? You do not feel faint or weak, by any chance?"

King Henry laughed again. "Weak?" he said. "I'll show you who is weak."

He reached down. Jane felt his hands on her waist. She felt herself lifted effortlessly, as if she'd been a toy or a small child.

"Milord!" she shrieked. "Your Grace!"

But the king, still chuckling, had lifted her clear and sat her on the knee of his good leg, like a man might hold a toddler. He moved his leg up and down beneath her and held both her hands behind her, one in each of his great hands. "Weak, you say. Now tell me who is weak."

"Your Majesty must let me go," Jane said. "This is not right. It is not proper . . ."

The king held her and pressed his face against her neck, his beard tickling her. "Oh, forget proper for a moment, Jane."

And on those words the door between the bedroom and the meeting hall, which had somehow gotten closed without Jane's noticing it, now flew open. And in the opening, Anne Boleyn stood, looking incredulously at the king, at Jane.

Jane, feeling heat climb her cheeks, struggled to climb down from the king's lap, but the king only held her hands tighter and pulled her closer to his body, till she could feel his chest against her back, through the thin shirt.

"Jane Seymour," Queen Anne said. She said it as though Jane's name were unbelievable. Some formula dreamed up by insane alchemists or perhaps the name of some fantastical food brought from overseas by explorers, in the belly of a boat. "Jane Seymour."

Her face drained of color so slowly that she might have been turning to salt like the wife of Lot, who looked back at her destroyed city. She opened her mouth and closed it, gasping for air.

Jane's heart beat near her throat. She tried to find words, but only a stammer came. "You must not think—" and "You must not believe . . ."

But the queen, pale as death, found her footing. She stood in between the doors and took a deep breath. "You . . . hypocrite," she said.

It was a word full of feeling and meaning, but Jane could not tell to which of them Anne Boleyn was speaking. "You betrayer. You . . . serpent. How dare you humiliate me thus, and in front of the whole court, too."

Indeed, as the queen screamed, more and more people had

massed behind her, rank on rank, males come from elsewhere within the king's quarters and females, doubtless called from the chapel by the screams.

"While I was praying for your recovery, you sent for this pasty-faced bawd, this hapless slut to come and do your bidding."

The queen stepped forward, her long, elegant hands like claws, aimed at Jane's face and head. Again, Jane tried to wriggle away and this time succeeded in spilling herself from the king's lap and falling sideways onto the floor beside him.

The queen made for her, with extended fingers. And met with the king's arm firmly blocking her path. "Mind your manners, madam," he said. "And your thoughts. For nothing has happened here that can give you injury." He paused for a moment. "Yet. Mistress Jane Seymour was simply testing my strength after my injury."

"Testing your strength," Queen Anne said, her voice dripping with derision. She fixed King Henry with a withering stare, then spat in Jane's direction. Because she was so far away, the spittle fell short and only landed on the floor at Jane's feet.

"I didn't mean—" Jane said, her mind a whirl of confusion, of shame, of guilt, of embarrassment. She should never have allowed the king the familiarity. Only she'd been so afraid for him, so relieved to see him recovered that she'd forgotten herself. "I forgot myself," she said.

"Forgot yourself," Queen Anne said. "Remembered yourself is more like it. The Seymours have sought to place one of them high enough at court for quite a while now. I wager they never thought it would be the ugly sister." She turned the glare of her sparkling dark eyes onto the king. "And you! I no longer amaze myself when I find your betrayals. But how could you find it upon yourself to stomach even touching such a plain and insipid creature?"

The queen's voice had grown in volume, as it did whenever she was in one of her fits, and when she said this last, it seemed to Jane as if the whole court must hear it, the whole court must be aware of it.

Her face burning with shame, she covered her eyes in her hands, as if, if she could only avoid looking at the shocked faces of courtiers, they, too, would cease to see her.

"Pack your luggage and leave, Mistress Seymour," Anne Boleyn said. "I want you out of the court and back to that Wiltshire hellhole from which you hail by sundown."

"No," the king intervened. His voice, loud and booming, drowned out the echos of the queen's screams. "She'll go nowhere."

"You expect me to keep in my court a lady-in-waiting who is playing me false with my own husband?" Anne asked in tones of great incredulity.

"And why not, madam?" the king said. "Since your betters have, before you."

"You're comparing me to the Dowager Princess of Wales?" Anne asked. "She was never your true wife. Great wonder she didn't feel like a proper one."

Sitting on the floor, her side against the cold stone wall, Jane heard their screams cross in the air above her. She had some dim idea that the queen wanted her away from court and that the king had ordered her to stay and was defending her.

But all Jane could think was that she'd been caught in a compromising position with the king. And that it couldn't be real. Any of it. The king, with a court full of beautiful women at his disposal, couldn't really want plain little Jane Seymour, with neither looks, fortune, nor connections to recommend her.

No. He'd probably planned to be caught. He'd sent someone to the chapel to call the queen immediately after he'd sent for Jane. She recalled how he'd held Jane's hands and prevented her from leaving his lap when the queen entered.

King Henry had no regard at all for Jane. He probably agreed with the queen that Jane was plain and insipid. Jane was only a weapon in his silent war against Anne, in his effort to get a reaction from her, a reaction that would tell him she still loved him.

In the end, Jane was no more to King Henry than she'd been to Thomas Wyatt, who'd used her as a means to unnerve Anne Boleyn. Only King Henry, the greater man and probably the more intelligent one, too, had succeeded where Wyatt had failed.

But in either case, Jane was just a thing—a means to make the queen jealous.

With a whimper of humiliation and frustration, Jane got up off the floor and ran blindly towards the door and out of it.

Behind her, she was aware of the queen's shriek becoming a formless scream of pain, climbing up and up and up in the cool morning air.

Twenty-six

"SHE may be miscarrying her savior," Thomas Seymour told Jane across the length of Jane's room at court—a narrow room outfitted with a narrower bed, a clothespress, and a desk at which one must stand to write.

Jane stood by the bed, having thrown all her clothing and belongings into a great package. She meant to leave by sunset and be out of court by nighttime.

All the while, the screams of Anne Boleyn, thrown into premature labor by the shock of finding Jane on her husband's lap, reverberated through the palace.

"What I don't understand," Tom said, "is why you're leaving or where you think you're going when your star is on the ascendant and your fortune assured."

"Oh, talk not of fortune to me," Jane said. "What fortune is there in this? I was humiliated before the whole court."

Tom looked at her with the blank stare of one who refuses to understand. "How humiliated, Jane? You were not found in dalliance with the stable lad but with the king's majesty. What is the humiliation in this, pray?"

Jane glared at Tom. It was unlikely she'd ever be able to explain it to him or to anyone else of the male gender, for that matter. Or even to people like her mother.

There was a certain kind of people who thought in clear, straight lines and could not or would not understand that people's motives were not always the ones they proclaimed. Just as Jane's mother had seen Thomas Wyatt's interest as an interest in Jane for a wife, and not an interest in using her for his own ends, Tom would refuse to understand any possible duplicity in the king's meaning.

"There was no dalliance," she said tiredly. She lay her hand upon the sheet she had used to wrap her apparel, and toyed with the string. "There was nothing resembling dalliance. He picked me up as one would pick a child, only . . ."

"Only?" Tom asked, his eyebrows rising and his whole expression proclaiming that he hoped Jane was finally beginning to see the light.

"Only I think he did it to get the queen's attention. Why I don't know. Perhaps because he was angry that she did not stand at his bedside when he woke. But I am sure, from his holding my hands, so that his queen might see us fully in a compromising position, that he did it only to show the queen up. Which you must believe is a humiliation to me—being used as a pawn in their games."

Tom crossed his arms on his chest. Today he was wearing black—subtly lustrous black velvet, exquisitely tailored to mold to his muscular stature and the breeches pleated and ornamented with bits of glass along the length of the legs. On his head was a hat that rather resembled a flat cake, ornamented with black plume at least Tom's height.

"Perhaps he did hold your hands. Perhaps he did want Anne Boleyn to see you sitting on his lap. But why must it follow that it was to use you only as a toy, a pawn in a game played against the queen? Couldn't it be that he is tired of her and looks onto you for a replacement?"

Jane looked at her brother a long while but failed to detect any hint of mockery in his speech. Instead, there was only his annoyance and his clear-eyed stare at her.

She took a deep breath. The queen's screams, now having attained an edge of desperation, cut into Jane's very thoughts.

She stepped away from her bed and her bundle of clothing and towards her brother, and she opened her hands outward in his direction. "How is it you fail to see what is before your eyes, Tom?" she asked. "Can you not see that I am a plain woman, lacking any great personal charms? See you not that the king is surrounded by beautiful women, and that I have nothing to offer that other women can't give him and better?"

"Oh, I don't know about that," Tom said. To Jane's surprise, he seized her hands in his and pulled them away from her body. He fixed her with an observant stare. "You have a comely enough body, and a womanly one," he said, letting go of her hands.

"And there's more you're not thinking of," he said. "The king fought for many long years to get a very beautiful woman into his bed. He tore the kingdom apart for the love of Anne Boleyn who, once married, has done nothing but bully him, order him about, and demand that he do all manner of things for her. Is it not possible that he thinks if he marries another woman simply for her beauty, she will—like Anne—make his life a living hell?"

Tom shook his head and looked at Jane as if she were

deficient in reason. "Why should he not look for a woman who is kind and accommodating, a woman who cares for him above all things and who gives him care and joy in all things? Why should he not, Jane?"

But Jane shook her head. "I do not look to step into the queen's shoes," she said, and in saying it she knew she was lying. She had wanted to step into Anne Boleyn's shoes, displacing her if needed, ever since the queen had mocked her over the gift from King Henry.

"Oh, come. Someone will. It is clear the king is tired of her and longs to have her gone. He will dispose of her and put her aside. It won't be so difficult, considering her conduct. And then he will look for someone else." Tom smiled at Jane, a little, crooked smile. "I think that you are too kind to let the king fall prey to some woman who cares not for him or his happiness. I think for the sake of the king's peace and the country's future, you will consent to be his in the end.

"But mind you, Jane," he stepped close. "Your modesty does you credit. You should indeed, as you are, make yourself scarce to our king. Tell him that you have your virtue to defend and protect. Do not, again, let him take the liberties he took today in his room."

Jane felt her cheeks redden. "I was confused. He had been near death's door. I was only grateful he was awake and well, and he said he wanted to show me how strong he was. I did not think—"

"You must think, Jane," her brother said. "You must preserve your . . . honor, as you preserve your life. Do not let him touch you, let him not have unwonted liberties of any sort with you. Remember, King Henry is a king, and kings get used, very early, to getting all they want handed to them by all-too-eager servants. It is the denied that fascinates them."

Jane understood, with a start, that Tom was not instructing her for fear of her virtue but rather because he thought that she had a better chance of snaring the king if she played the virtuous maiden. She looked up at Tom, suddenly shocked. "You can't mean it," she said. "You can't mean what you've said. Mean you that I should use my virtue as a snare to capture His Majesty?"

"Why not?" Tom asked. "Anne Boleyn did it, and if stories of her at the French court are true, she had far less virtue to protect than you do."

Jane tried to understand her own feeling of revulsion and shock at the thought. Oh, she'd known long enough that this was how Anne Boleyn had snared the king—though she often asked herself whether Anne knew it. So why feel so outraged at the idea of using the same means? "But . . ." she said, and groped for words. "But I'm not her," she said. "I am not Anne Boleyn. I do not . . . She is beautiful and cruel."

"So, be gentle and kind," Tom said with a grin. "After marriage you can be as kind as you ever wish to be to the king. You can give him all he wishes and be his true and obedient wife." He chuckled. "I'm sure he'll appreciate the change. But while you're yet unmarried, do not let him touch you. Surely you don't need any justification for this. Surely you don't think this is evil."

"He is my king," Jane said in confusion.

"Oh, yes, but there is a God above him. And God's law commands him to respect your maidenhead, and you to keep it intact till marriage. Further, your respect to your father and your family demands that you not dishonor us with a bastard."

"I think you're wrong," Jane said. The whole conversation had been working itself through her mind, to the counterpoint of the queen's screams, and it seemed to Jane that she had to think on every point again and again, because it all still seemed wrong to her. The seeming of the thing was not the same as the true thing.

"You think our honor demands bastards?" Tom asked, looking so confused that Jane almost laughed despite her distress.

"No, Tom. But I think you are wrong about the king wishing to set the queen aside, and his looking about for a new queen. I think that though Queen Anne is difficult to live with, the king is so fond of her he will stay with her despite all. Oh, he will stray. He strayed from Queen Catherine, too. But he had in Queen Catherine a good and obedient wife, and he left her for a slip of a girl who retorted wittily to each of his thoughts and who would not let him have peace lest she be satisfied. Why think you he'd leave her now?"

"Because what's endearing in a mistress with whom you steal an hour now and then is tiring in a wife with whom you live every day at close quarters," Tom said.

"But there are men who enjoy that, are there not? Do we not see them about court every day? And even at home, did we not know burghers and gentry where they fought and disputed every day and loved each other all the more tightly for that?"

Tom shook his head. "There are men like that, I will grant you. But King Henry is not one of them. He's used to obedience, and he demands it. He cannot understand why he should not get it. He endured Anne Boleyn's retorts and her disputes because he lusted after her, and she would not let him touch her. There was to it no more than that, that his unsatisfied lust led him by the nose into this marriage. But after marriage she did not change, and he, having sated himself on her charms, no longer was willing to endure all for her sake."

Jane thought of Thomas Wyatt, on that day long ago, saying in that melancholy voice of his that the king was finding the craving was better than the possessing. "But . . ." she said. And shook her head.

Did she want to play for such high stakes? Did she really want to be the queen to this king, whose satisfaction never equaled his cravings?

"No," she said. "No. These tumultuous court rivalries and disputes are not for me." She reached for the bundle on her bed, grabbed the bit of twine she'd used to tie it together, and lifted it. "I said I would be gone by sunset, and I will be gone by sunset."

"And where will you be gone?" Tom asked. He stepped back, out of her path, to allow her towards the door. His arms, in their resplendent velvet sleeves, slashed through to show satin as black as the velvet, remained crossed on his chest, but a very small, wry smile played on his lips. "Where will you go, Jane? Think you our parents will take you back? I've apprized them, and Edward, of your prospects all along. Think you not that they will send you back to court to seek your fortune? And else, where do you think you'll go?"

Jane stopped at the door, her clothing bundle dangling from one hand. She wished she could say her brother was ex- aggerating, but she knew her family too well. Her parents, who had despaired of ever marrying off their plain daughter, would not want her back with the taint of being one of the king's flirtations.

However, they would have no objection at all to her being one of the king's mistresses, much less the queen. For that, they would urge her back to court that she might further her state by either attaining a crown or furthering her infamy, either—a queen or a royal bastard in the family—improving the family's standing and reputation.

This thought further disgusted Jane. She could feel her lips setting disdainfully as she said, "I do not care where I end, Tom. I will go and throw myself at our parents' mercy, and if they turn me out, I will seek the first convent or charity home that will have me."

Always, the convent presented itself as an option, and Jane could see the look of surprise in her brother's features as she pulled the door to her room open.

And found herself facing a crowd of courtiers. There were ladies-in-waiting, and pages, minor courtiers whose faces she did not recognize at all. Among them, the only faces that stood out were those of Sir Nicholas Carew, the king's master of the horse and a great jouster. And Sir Francis Bryan, his kindly face trying to show grief but showing instead a sort of amused gratification as he looked at his young protégée.

He was the first one to address her. "Are you leaving, Jane?" he asked in a light tone that implied she should do no such thing.

Jane did not know what to say. She had done many things against the expectations of her family in her life, but she'd never gone against their wishes. She had contrived to live her life at that small margin that left her still an obedient daughter but allowed her to have thoughts and desires of her own.

How could she tell Sir Francis she was leaving the court, against what was sure to be the explicit wishes of her parents and family? Behind her, she could feel Tom glowering triumphantly at her back, as if to say that she would now see the untenable quality of her position.

In her moment of frantic confusion, she realized that Queen Anne had stopped screaming. Jane did not know what she hoped for—that the babe had been preserved and remained in his mother's womb, something Jane had heard of being achieved by means of draughts or skillful manipulation, or that the hope of pregnancy was all gone.

She wasn't sure what she wished, either, or not fully. To retire into decent obscurity or to become the next queen, should the king put Anne Boleyn aside? It seemed to her that the second was a fantastical wish, no more likely than wishing upon a star and expecting it to come true. And so the first it must be. And since that was the path left open to her, she must side with her own better Christian nature and hope that Anne Boleyn's child would live to be born in his proper time.

Jane curtsied and looked down at the floor in considerable modesty. "I thought I would absent myself from court, good cousin, while the queen recovers. And the king, too. Perhaps I'll return when our prince is born."

"There isn't going to be a prince," Sir Carew said. "The queen has miscarried of a man-child."

Jane addressed this newcomer. "The queen has miscarried before, but she has also borne our Princess Elizabeth alive and hearty. And the child thrives. This means the queen can produce a son as well. If not this one then the next, and I'll return when that happy event takes place that makes the court more settled."

"There will not be a next one," Sir Francis said. "The king has said that the queen will have no more sons by him."

"This is true, milady," Elizabeth Exeter said. She was very young, all of fifteen or so, recently come to court, and very pretty. "He came upon her, in her blood, still grieving over the lost baby, and he told her she killed all his sons and she would get no more sons from him."

She spoke nervously, through trembling lips, then curtsied hastily towards Jane. Both the curtsy and her having addressed Jane as *milady* gave Jane an odd feeling of walking through a landscape of madness.

Elizabeth Exeter was a true lady, the honor of whose birth

so overshadowed Jane's as to leave Jane Seymour fit for nothing but serve in her household. That this noble-born, graceful lady was curtsying to Jane and calling her "milady" could not be all an error or a mistake.

Oh, surely, the bloodstains on the lady's gown spoke of Elizabeth Exeter having spent a considerable amount of time in the birth chamber trying to help her current mistress. And the tears in her eyes when she described the king's cruel words spoke very feelingly of her sympathy for Anne Boleyn who, indeed, had never been very good at attaching the affections of any woman.

But a lady by birth simply does not make the mistake of treating those inferior to her as being above her in rank. It was not done. It was impossible.

Jane was overwhelmed with the thought that court habitués and steadier heads than her brother Tom's were treating her claim to the king's affections as having some worth, and her possibility of occupying the throne as being real.

The thought overwhelmed her. She dropped the bundle from her hand and, feeling faint, reached for her door to steady herself.

"Jane, are you well? Jane?" Sir Bryan's voice asked.

Other voices drowned his in tumultuous confusion.

"Mistress Seymour, do you need anything?"

"Mistress Seymour, I shall fetch you water."

"Mistress Seymour—I have some fruit recently sent to me from my estates. I think some will revive you wonderfully. I shall send for it."

A fine linen handkerchief was pressed against Jane's brow by a gentle hand, and someone waved vinegar beneath her nose.

Through the confusion, Jane was aware of Tom's picking up her bundle of clothing and returning it to within the room.

From the sound of opening and closing a heavy lid, he'd dropped the bundle, entire, into her clothespress.

Someone brought her a glass of claret to revive her spirits. Jane could not even tell who or which hand had proffered the crystal goblet.

Sipping the sweet wine, she knew that the court had shifted directions. She'd seen this happen before when it had become obvious that Anne Boleyn would press her claim and become the next queen, having succeeded in putting her rival away.

Jane had seen courtiers flee the waning protection of Queen Catherine's favor for the newfound sun of Anne Boleyn's ambitious power. And now she was to be surrounded by the same fawning attention.

She wondered, even if they were right and she had some claim on the king's attention, why would she want such a fickle favor? But at the same time something within her was gloating—because plain Jane could command a king's interest and the courtiers' devotion.

Twenty-seven

❦

IT couldn't be said that Jane had a court of her own. Not yet.

But Queen Anne was immured in her room, still recovering from a miscarriage more than a week past, and possibly from the king's cruel words. And the life of the court turned slowly towards Jane.

Courtiers and old favor seekers, of the type that always clustered about looking for more lands or a favorable decision in some century-old dispute, clustered around Jane now.

Her small room daily overflowed with flowers and fruit and gifts of jewels and books and she knew not what else, till she wondered about the wisdom of people who would divest themselves of all their riches to seek new ones. Or perhaps to seek honor, that most elusive of goods in which the court traded.

She'd seen the king, twice, in the normal processes of the

court, and both times he had asked after her health and how she was doing, as he had heard of her swoon.

He seemed wholly unaware that, a few doors from him, a woman—his queen—lay in far greater distress. And this, together with everything else, gave Jane a great disgust for the court and all of its habits.

Today, a raw and inhospitable early February day, while she sat in her room, always small and narrow and now overcrowded with baskets of delicacies and of flowers forced out of season in some hothouse on the coast of France, she felt she must leave the court or go insane.

She knew all too well, and had perceived it all too well, from the courtiers' behavior and from the king's demeanor that she would never be allowed to leave permanently. But she must leave at least for a moment.

And it came to her that when Catherine was queen, she'd often gone praying to some chapel or other, reputed to be blessed by some particular saint and that the same dispensation might be allowed to her.

Oh, she'd never gone out of the court on her own. She'd never commanded the means to be transported elsewhere in the city—litter or horse or even carriage. But she suspected this, as so much else, must now be changed.

She opened her door and found, loitering about outside, the same crowd of people who usually hovered about these days, bringing her good wishes from this person, or a gift from the other, or else simply to be seen in the company of the king's new interest.

Their faces, all eager, their interest, all turned to her the minute the door opened, were part of the reason Jane wanted to get away. But she could say no more than, "I have a great wish to pray at a shrine devoted to Saint Catherine." She chose

the saint with good intent, knowing that, the last queen having been named after the saint, there was a good chance there
was, in the city, at least one chapel devoted to her. And probably several.

Of course, the chapel might or might not have its shrine and
saint representations intact. The break from Rome progressed
unsteadily enough, tilting and swaying this way and that, but
many strict devotees of the Protestant religion had long ago
seized the power to strip chapels of their more obviously Papist
adornments. They were aided and abetted by Archbishop
Cramner and Cromwell, the king's dark shadow and the mas-
termind of his secret services whose sympathies lay with
Protestantism.

Jane knew all this, but she also knew that she was considered a woman of conventional devotions, of whom no more
was expected than that she should bow to the saint statues
she'd learned to venerate in her childhood. Whether she was
that, she didn't know. She'd never examined her religion, beyond knowing that she believed in God and obeyed her sovereign and that she found some comfort in old rites performed
the ancient way.

"There is one," a young woman spoke. She was a lady-in-
waiting, but so new to court that Jane had yet to learn her
name. She had arrived sometime while they were all embroiled
in this confusion over Queen Anne and her miscarriage. "It is
towards Cheapside, near the cross." She hesitated. "It is not
much of a place, madam, but the statue of Saint Catherine
there is venerated and accounted most miraculous."

"Thank you," Jane said. "But I must beg of someone the favor of a conveyance, since I have none at my disposal here."

In that moment, almost before the words were out of her
mouth, several were proffered for her use: carriages, litters,

and palfreys said to be most gentle and suited for a well-born lady.

And thus it happened that an hour afterwards Jane was on her way to this shrine. She found herself most comfortably ensconced within a litter with sturdy curtains, carried by two gentle palfreys, all of it belonging to one of the premier families of the realm. It was accounted a great honor to them that Jane had chosen their conveyance.

Which must rank within the realms of foolishness. The privilege of birth, power, and gentle pedigree were all overthrown by a king's preference, not even yet shown truly as such.

It made Jane very happy to be away from court if even for a few hours. She was alone within the litter, though outside two pages mounted on horses escorted her, making sure nothing untoward happened to her while out.

And Jane, who'd picked the litter over carriages because they could transverse the narrower alleys in town, peeked between a crack in the curtains to watch that daily life of which she saw so little.

On this raw February day there was not much of it abroad. Only here and there, an urchin running, often barefoot on the half-frozen mud of the streets.

But as they passed tavern doors, the doors would be open, and from within them came the sound of song and talk and laughter, and it told Jane that there was indeed a kingdom out there, beyond the confines and the corrupt affections of the court.

Had she more courage or less regard for her own honor and her family's decency, she would have asked that the litter stop and that she be allowed to get out and enter one of those taverns and look on at the real people, living their real lives, ignored by the court and in ignorance of it.

It seemed to her that such an action, being such a great departure of everything expected of a courtly lady, might well lose her the attention of the king and thereby solve at least one of her problems.

On the other hand, she had come to see, as Tom had told her, that if she didn't become queen over Anne Boleyn's disgrace, then someone else would. And Tom was right about one thing—thinking of the king's face, the wrinkles of grief starting to etch themselves into the corners of the royal mouth and eyes—she cared about the king too much to allow him to make another match that would bring him nothing but grief.

Oh, he was callous with his current wife—but how could it not be? It wasn't the babes that had been born dead or simply producing the one, single princess. Jane had witnessed, day to day, how Anne had tried the king's patience and tried to dominate him by every means available. How could the king not resent that?

It was as though Queen Anne had set out to kill their love, day by day, with unkind word and deed.

As Jane was immersed in these thoughts, and looking out into the world where rain and sleet now fell mingled, deflected from her only by the cloth roof and the heavy curtains of her litter, she saw a man seated at a tavern's door.

He was singing something. So many itinerant singers, or beggars—the distinction not always being immediately obvious—did sit at tavern doors and sing, seeking not only the tips of the patrons passing to the warmth and comfort indeed, but often looking to a meal or two tended in gratitude by the tavern keeper, for drawing patrons forth with their sweet song.

This man's voice was indeed sweet. High for a man's, it rose in the frosty air with brittle beauty, as though the ballad he was singing were woven, itself, out of frost and would break at the least inconsiderate touch.

The subject matter of the ballad, on the other hand . . .

Still a little while away, it seemed to Jane she heard her name, and then again. As the litter reached the man, she was trembling, for she had understood the subject of the verses. They aimed at nothing else than at recounting the incident at court, with Queen Anne finding Jane on the king's knee and how "Thereby, in mortal shame and pain her womb was opened."

Trembling, Jane put her head out of the litter and asked that they stop. She got out, picking her way, with her new boots, amid the sleet and mire on the street.

Sleet and rain combined fell on her, soaking her headdress and her expensive, velvet dress, one of the few good dresses she'd had in her life. She cared not. She rushed to the man who was singing at the tavern door, sitting out of the rain beneath a little roof that covered the door.

"Play your song again," she said, wishing to know in full the worst of it.

The face that turned towards her was one of those odd faces that look young and old at the same time, so that it is impossible to tell their age. There was a sleek, unlined look to its features, but the hair above was the purest white. And the eyes, which turned in Jane's direction, would not be able to see her. A blue so pale they were almost pure white, they looked as opaque as a boiled egg. The man was blind.

But the face remained turned towards her—all in ignorance of who she was. Jane understood. She dug into her sleeve for her purse and extracted a meager coin from it, which she dropped into the man's lap.

The man grinned in her general direction—showing a

mouth almost devoid of teeth—and touched his forelock in acknowledgment before plunging into his song again.

It was the most scurrilous collection of lies. Jane's mouth dropped open in astonishment on hearing it. Not only did it presume her to be already the king's mistress, sharing his bed and probably already delivered of bastards by him, but it called her beautiful, comparing her face to the shine of the noonday sun.

Under the rain, anonymous in a London street, Jane would have laughed at it all, it was so fantastical. Except that to this tissue of lies her name was linked—her name bandied about all of London and, if she knew how this went, soon to be bandied about all of England, as a bawd and a seductress.

She felt her faintness come upon her again, as the song described how much the king enjoyed her favors in the secret of his bedchamber. Would people believe this? Why shouldn't they?

She shook and was aware that the two pages were now on either side of her.

"Hey, there, old man," one of them said. "Stop that. The king will have you hanged, should he hear of it."

And the other one offered Jane his arm and said, "Mistress, you are not well. You shouldn't stand about in the rain. You will catch your death of fever."

Jane could only find enough voice to whisper. "I am well," And to the other page. "Leave the singer alone. I asked him to repeat it."

She turned again to the man on whose arm she leaned, "Only, please see me back to court, for I think you are right, and it is too cold for me to be about the streets."

Twenty-eight

JANE came back from her expedition streaming wet, her dress dripping blue-tinted water onto the floor.

She hastened down the back passageways of the palace, where the servants usually moved. She didn't want to meet anyone, didn't want to speak to anyone. The bawdy words of the street song went around and around inside her head. She could not bear the thought of how many people might have heard them, and how many must laugh behind their hands when she passed and imagine that she was delighting the king with forbidden pleasures in his bedchamber.

Her cheeks flushed red, her gown in ruins, she made it to her room. But at the door was clustered the now usual crowd, all exclaiming in great distress at the state of her gown, all muttering among themselves of how she could have got that way and what misadventure might have befallen her.

She heard talk of highwaymen, and talk of an assault on her by envoys from Anne Boleyn.

Ignoring all comments, she ran past and opened the door to her room and was about to close it, when a man forced himself into the room after her.

"Please, leave me alone," she said. "What do you mean?" she asked, her door still opened, the man framed in the doorway.

The man bowed. Jane realized now that he wore the livery of the king's own servants. "Madam, I cannot delay, for I come with a gift and a letter from His Majesty, King Henry. I have been waiting for you long."

"A gift?" Jane said. "From the king." She heard the shock in her own voice, and she covered her mouth with her hand. In her mind was the ballad and what the common folk would think she'd done to deserve gifts.

"It's some coin for your expenses, madam," he said. "And a letter."

Jane could feel the eyes of all on her, from outside the room. They looked past the messenger at her. There were faint murmurs of approval from out there. The self-congratulatory exclamations of courtiers who'd backed the right rising star and expected much reward and success from it.

And Jane shrank in horror from what they thought of her. What they imagined she'd done or would do to secure the royal favor. What else would they think when it was common knowledge that she had been caught sitting on the king's knee by Queen Anne? She would be judged by the common folk a more abandoned debauch than they'd ever imagined Anne Boleyn—with her knowledge of the French court—to be.

But what could Jane do? She could not turn back the king's gift, could she? Not without some great repercussion. Perhaps not without turning his fancy from her altogether.

And yet if she accepted the gift and allowed the belief that she was the king's mistress to go on, wouldn't the king come to think of her as no more than a very ambitious woman, like Anne Boleyn? Wouldn't she be securing her own disgrace?

No. She must keep her reputation, for that would serve her, no matter what else she lost by it.

"Give me His Majesty's letter, please," she said. She pronounced the words slowly, distinctly.

She felt cold and as if she were signing her own death sentence. In the crowd, she could discern the face of her brother Tom, looking on her attentive and unsure, as if he could not tell himself that she would do the right thing. Jane wondered what Tom thought the right thing was. Surely not what she was about to do.

She took the royal letter in her hand, marking the imprint of his signet ring upon the wax and the marks of a dark, decisive handwriting visible through the paper.

Falling on her knees, with the letter in her hand, she heard a gasp from the audience out in the hall. One or two people rushed towards her, thinking she had swooned, but before they reached her, Jane took the king's letter to her lips and kissed it, then caressed it with her hand, and returned it to the messenger, unopened.

"Pray tell His Majesty that I thank him, for his thought and attention to this maiden," Jane said, as clearly as she could manage. Her voice trembled, both with cold, because she was still wet through and the cool air of the great, stony hallway seemed to insinuate itself through the fibers of her gown, and with fear because she did not know where this step of hers would lead. And she suspected where it might lead depended more on the king's mood when he heard what she had done than on any merit of her behavior.

But all the same, she'd do what she must do. "Pray tell King Henry that as much as I prize his words and his attention, I am but a poor maiden, born to an ancient and honorable but not wealthy family. I have nothing but my honor to entice some eligible gentleman into matrimony, and I beg the king that he would not give rise to rumors and talk about me, with his generosity and his great gifts. I understand these come solely from his well-meaning heart, but I cannot, in propriety, accept them. If he should wish to make me a gift, I must ask that he reserve such for such an occasion when it please God to send me a good marriage. And then shall I be very glad to have it as my dowry."

She heard shocked gasps from the hallway and, raising her head, saw that Tom looked very shocked indeed, and perhaps a little afraid. In fact, the courtiers out there seemed to all step back from her door at the same time, receding in a great wave of fear of displeasure.

The messenger, looking bewildered, bowed to her. Letter and velvet purse in hand, he left her room like a man who scarce knows what he does.

Jane rose to her feet slowly.

"Jane," Tom's voice said from amid the crowd. Jane pretended not to hear. She barely waited till the king's messenger was gone before she closed her door.

From outside in the hall, she could hear murmurs of consternation and dismay. She retreated blindly into her room and set about removing her soaked clothes.

She didn't have the queen's favor, and she might just have squandered the king's. She did not know what to think of her own actions, nor was she sure that the next message from the king would not be a request that she leave court and never return.

But if such should happen, if she were forced to leave, Jane knew that she might leave without jewels, honors, or money. She would certainly leave without the great cloud of sycophants who had recently surrounded her.

But, no matter what wretched reception might wait her in Wiltshire, she knew that she would leave with her honor intact.

Twenty-nine

"You are a genius," Tom spoke in a fever of admiration. He had just closed Jane's room door, but not so fast that Jane didn't see that, outside that door, the crowd of people remained, unabated and perhaps a little augmented by fresh courtiers.

Jane sat before the fire in a fresh linen gown, wrapped about with a blanket which, as yet, had failed to banish the chill she'd caught in her ill-advised foray in the London streets.

Tom was fully dressed in one of his resplendent outfits, this one dark red velvet, with strips of metal and jewels sewn all over, each of them rivaling the other to glint more fiercely by the firelight.

He gave, more than usual, an impression of force, of unbridled energy barely contained in his human body. He paced and stomped, and grinned maniacally at his sister.

Jane, by the fire, endured it all, the effusive congratulations, the mad and repeated peals of laughter. She understood very little of Tom's mood, save that her actions had, somehow, failed to utterly disgrace her in the royal eyes.

"I understand then that the king was not offended by my refusing his gift?" she said hesitantly.

Tom grinned at her. "Offended," he said, and chuckled. "Indeed not, as you well know." He stooped and kissed Jane's hair in an outburst of brotherly affection such as he hadn't shown since they were both children in Wiltshire. "I must say, little sister, that even I who have always had a high opinion of you, your abilities, and your wiles, am amazed by this, your latest success."

He paced from one end of the room to the other, as if unable to contain his emotions and forced to walk to keep them from bursting forth from him and perhaps cause him to explode. "Even I thought the king would be offended. After all, who are we all but the recipients of his gifts and largesse, and why should he not resent that the daughter of a mere Wiltshire gentleman should refuse his gifts?" He turned around and started walking towards her, managing to give the impression he would presently break into mad dance. "But you outfoxed us all. You must have taken to heart my injunction, these many months ago, that your attraction to His Majesty was the fact that you were in everything so unlike the current queen."

He turned again. "And look how well you played your cards. Anne Boleyn accepted all gifts from the king, but you refuse them. Anne Boleyn did not disdain his largesse and corresponded with him while he was still married, but you will not do so, in great fear for your maidenhood and reputation. And what does that get you?"

Jane looked steadily at her brother's expansive grin. Just looking at Tom was tiring. She imagined the news was good, because Tom was like a child, ever bursting at the seams with happiness or wallowing in a dejection of grief. She suspected if the news were not good, or not very good, he would be acting as though both their lives were in peril.

But knowing that Tom considered it good news and knowing what it was came to quite different things. Nor were Jane and Tom always of a mind about the meaning of some court event. And particularly not when it came to the king's interest in her.

"What does it get me, Tom?" she asked impatiently. "You must speak now, for I have no more patience for your crowing and triumphing without my knowing exactly what you might be crowing and triumphing about."

"You mean you don't know?" Tom asked. "Well, then, you're the only one at court who doesn't."

"It all only happened less than an hour ago," Jane said. "My clothes are still wet from the rain."

But Tom only grinned at her. "An hour is more than long enough for everyone at court to know news. Particularly when the news is so startling as this."

He paused. "You must know that the word abroad and in all mouths was that you should be gone by morning, after you refused the king's gift. We all thought he would be much offended by your turning down his largesse, as if somehow his favor might taint you."

He stood by the fire next to her and extended his hands palms outward, towards the flames to warm himself. "But it turned out you know the king better than we know, and are a more consummate courtier than all the old hands who've long played at court."

"Tom," Jane said with some impatience. "I am no such a thing. I refused the king's gift to save my reputation, for already there is abroad a report that I am his mistress and that it is for this that the queen has miscarried. Imagine if I should accept money from him! It would only add to the scurrilous rumors."

Tom frowned briefly. "The king has heard of the ballad himself," he said. "And he begs you not to distress yourself over it. He says he has even now given orders to Cromwell, his secretary, to find the author of those disgusting verses. He will be found and punished to the full extent of the law, paying with his life for slandering your name."

"Oh, no," Jane said, and half rose from her chair. "Oh no. You must tell His Majesty I implore him not to do that. I do not want blood shed in my name."

Tom looked confused. "La," he said. "You are so strange."

"No. I mean this. You must beg him—"

"I will let him know you wish the scourge to live who has slandered you. To me it seems like the sheerest lunacy, and I expect the king will think the same, but perhaps I am wrong, since I did not expect his reaction to your turning back his gift."

"A reaction you have not yet told me of," Jane said.

Tom crossed his arms upon his chest, and his mouth curved upward in a very self-satisfied smile. "Our brother Edward is to be a privy counselor," he said, "and move to London."

Jane's mouth fell open. "What can that have to do with my refusal of the king's gift?" she asked.

"Why, everything," Tom replied, his grin all the more expressive. He bowed to her. "You are the mistress and architect of it all."

"When the king was told of your reply," he said, "he said that you were all that was correct and proper and a model for every young maiden in every corner of our fair kingdom. He said that you had acted most correctly and better than he did, who is used to abusing common behavior rules by virtue of his royal power. From now on, he said, he would do nothing to endanger your reputation. He'll never see you unless you have a proper chaperone of your own family nearby to keep you safe from his lusts and from the wagging of tongues." Tom grinned. "And so Edward is to come to town, with his wife Catherine and the children. They are to have very fair lodgings in Greenwich, which were volunteered by the king's secretary, himself. And I must congratulate you on securing Cromwell's alliance, for he's one of those men you do not wish arrayed with your enemies."

"I did not secure—"

"Perhaps not on purpose," Tom said. "But he is on your side, and this is something to congratulate yourself over. He has vacated apartments, which are even now being prepared with the arms of our family, so that Edward and Catherine may occupy them. And you're to reside with them and there receive the king in all propriety. Only it is better than that."

"It is?" Jane asked, awestruck but pleased that she could have effected the advance of her deserving brother, Edward, who, for many years now, since his marriage, had been living in Wiltshire, quite forgotten by His Majesty.

"Yes, for you see, secret tunnels link the palace to those rooms, so—though the king will see you in all propriety and escorted by your own family, the king need not even be seen when he goes to visit you, thereby allowing him to visit as often as he wishes without causing any scandal."

Thirty

EASTER Sunday Edward Seymour and his wife moved into their new lodgings, with their sister Jane Seymour, whom they were expected to chaperone.

The months in between had been a whirlwind of activity and favor for Jane. The king had not tried to repeat his gifts, nor even to see her alone. But he had contrived to see her as much as possible at court.

Only, in such confines and while Queen Anne, finally risen from her bed, presided over the ritual festivities and dances, the king could not do much more than smile at Jane Seymour.

Smiles were enough though, for those used to reading the events of court like a book and divining from them which way they should lay their fortune. Jane had been sought as never before, and while not receiving presents from the king, had received them from practically everyone else. Ladies-in-waiting had sent her clothes. And—once it had become known that she was very fond of the meat of red buck and quails—gentlemen sent her portions of game, which Jane insisted be cooked and prepared for the entire company of ladies-in-waiting.

Though Jane still sat by the fire to work her embroidery while the queen and other maids took their place at gaming tables, now it was the gaming tables that appeared a place of exile. The other maids, and often the king's gentlemen, if any were present, would all gather around Jane and comment on the delicacy of her needlework and her ability, as though they'd never before seen a woman capable of sewing and embroidering.

Jane was not yet used to this, not yet used to receiving courtly poems and compliments from gentlemen who, seemingly against the evidence of their eyes, called her fair and pleasing. And she lived in continuous fear of Queen Anne's temper.

But the queen appeared much changed, quiet now and subdued, enduring Jane's ascendance as Catherine had once endured Anne's. And it seemed to Jane there was more praying done at court and fewer contests of poetry and song to praise the queen.

When the queen herself took up her lute, as she did now and then, it was to play some melancholy song, the word *death* never far from her lips. In fact, it seemed as if she went around shrouded in melancholy and in daily expectation of death.

Jane wondered at this, imagining that Queen Anne suspected Jane of wishing to poison her, but she could not imagine any such calumny and, in reaction to the other woman's perceived fear, Jane spent much of her time appeasing her rival and reassuring her that all was as well as it could be between them.

It led to an atmosphere of chilly courtesy in the court,

quite different from the epic battles of wits and voices that had raged between Anne and Catherine.

But still, there was great tension, and for that, Jane was glad to officially abandon the court for the Greenwich lodgings.

Edward was glad, too. Jane had not seen her eldest brother in some months and was amazed to see him now smiling so greatly and pleased. "Ah, Jane," he said, as he entered the rooms for the first time and looked in wonder at the great salon with its carved oak ceiling fashioned with the Seymour panther and many cunning devices. The windows, too, great mullioned windows partitioned by strips of lead, bore his family's arms and his initials in bright stained glass. "Ah Jane, you are a miracle worker," he said and, undemonstrative man that he was, yet seized his younger sister in his arms and kissed her effusively.

"Yes, Jane," Catherine, Edward's wife, said. She was a dark woman, a beauty with the sallow complexion that betrayed some Mediterranean ancestry in her line. "You are indeed a miracle worker, for I thought I would go mad in Wiltshire, without an establishment of our own. Of course, it must be said that this might be best accounted your establishment than mine."

"But it is not," Jane said. "It is just judged, by His Majesty the king, that Edward, the newly appointed member of the king's privy council, should have rooms worthy of his rank, for when he comes to town."

Edward gave her a long look, as though trying to evaluate whether she truly thought what she was saying or whether she said it out of a wish to play the innocent.

In fact, it was neither, and Jane met his gaze with level calm. She meant what she said in that she neither wanted the responsibility of maintaining this lodging nor the honor of ruling over it and was quite glad to see Catherine undertake it.

At the same time she was not so foolish that she didn't realize that her brother had been made privy counselor not out of some great deserts of his own, some great wisdom he might impart to the king, but because he was Jane's brother, and the king needed someone to chaperone Jane.

Jane was simply glad of the chaperone, the appearance of propriety which would keep her safe from wanton tongues. She remembered the hours when the king had lain unconscious, and everyone had been in expectation of his death.

Should the same happen now, she did not wish it bruited about that Jane had been his mistress, nor did she wish her reputation sullied. It was unlikely that anyone else should offer marriage to her, even were she accounted the purest maiden to walk the land, but at the same time Jane knew that the king's preference conferred on her a certain value. And should the king die, there might be those glad to marry the king's affianced bride. Volunteers to marry the late king's mistress, on the other hand, usually required a great deal of money and honors, neither of which Jane had.

But all this was fantasy. The new setup might guarantee Jane a place to see the king in some almost privacy and in a decent manner. But it did not grant her that one thing without which any talk of her being queen was fruitless. And that was that Jane still couldn't understand how Anne Boleyn was to be set aside—how her marriage to the king was to be revoked.

Oh, the king had revoked his marriage to Queen Catherine by invoking her previous marriage to his brother. He had the same, if not more clear call to reject his marriage to Anne Boleyn, with whose mother and sister he had openly fornicated. But Jane guessed that the country, that great mass out there in the streets of London and beyond, in every hovel and village of the land, among the rolling hills and the forest groves, would laugh at the king again claiming consanguinity as his reason for dissolving a marriage. And the king could not wish to divide his country.

As much favor as Jane had, of late, commanded, and as much attention as she'd gotten from courtiers, it was still possible—perhaps likely—that with time and Queen Anne's newly humble disposition, the king would give up on his intent towards Jane, return to the marital bed and, Queen Anne being yet young, perhaps sire a son by her.

Jane played her cards accordingly and, rejoicing in her brother's new position and in his gratitude to her, she maintained that it was all due to her brother's own merits and that Jane had nothing to do with it at all.

Thirty-one

"How like you your new rooms?" the king asked her. He had come along those passageways that Jane had heard rumored and been admitted through a secret door at the back of Edward's new study.

This subterfuge had allowed him to visit without all his gentlemen in attendance. It was just King Henry, and he'd dined with them, with the necessary attention to his rank, but as if he were no more than a family member, without his court about him.

And now, after dinner, he and Jane walked in the gardens at the back of her new lodgings—extensive gardens and furnished with a corner for roses, which were now in bloom, releasing their perfume to the warm night air.

"As you see," the king said, "I remembered you liked gardens."

"Your Majesty's generosity knows no bounds," Jane said, and curtsied slightly.

The king looked at her with an expression that resembled hunger, and Jane thought that, but for the presence of her sister-in-law, who sat embroidering under a nearby tree, under the failing light of the setting sun, Jane might be grabbed again and most improperly held in the king's great arms.

Was it improper of her that she almost desired it? That she thought of him as a man and not her king? Or was it merely her gratitude that he looked on her as a woman and a woman worth possessing? No one had done that since William. Even Sir Thomas Wyatt in his prolonged, unconvincing courtship had never managed to make her believe he wanted her as a woman. He might have wanted her as a companion or a friend or simply as a being whose affections he thought were his. But not as a woman.

However, King Henry's look was undeniably tender as he reached for Jane's hand and held it. "It is not generosity, Mistress Jane. You deserve it all and are fully worthy of all honors."

Jane cleared her throat and pulled her hand away and made to ask a question about her prospects without ever intimating they were her prospects or that she was anxious for them at all. "And the queen, how is she? Is she fully recovered?"

King Henry gave Jane a dark look that almost seemed like anger but might be a look of disgust or distrust.

Jane stepped back, surprised by it, then realized he was not disgusted or angry at her but at the subject of their conversation as he said, "Mistress Anne Boleyn might do as she well pleases. I do not know of her health nor have I inquired in a long time."

Jane's face might have betrayed something of her inner feelings. Even though she had determined to replace the queen, yet to hear her talked about in this way by a man who had done so much to possess her, and lived with her as a husband for three years, and sired children upon her, seemed shocking and cruel.

"You are amazed," the king said. "At my cold heart no doubt." He looked away from her and over the trees, at the sun that was setting in red splendor.

"Oh, no, Your Grace. I would never presume."

He looked back at her and smiled, a quick flash of a smile, quickly vanished. "No. You wouldn't presume. But I must explain my contempt for the woman I loved so long and so well."

"You must explain nothing, Your Grace," Jane said, knowing what a difficult business it was to ask the great for explanations and having guessed, from her long acquaintance, how little King Henry liked holding himself in the wrong and exculpating himself for his actions before anyone.

He lowered his eyebrows over his eyes, while his mouth smiled, an expression of confusion and deep thought. "No," he said. "But I want you to know why I might seem cold and distant towards Anne Boleyn. I wouldn't want you to think that was the quality of my heart when, in fact, I have a heart as warm and affections as tender as ever any troubadour sang of. I want you to know my affections are reliable and ever to be counted on." He smiled at her.

"But I also want you to know that there is good reason to believe Anne Boleyn brought me to marriage by means of incantations and dark witchcraft."

Jane stared at him, for a few moments, in shock. That there was witchcraft, she did not doubt. She was a country girl and had grown up with stories of the evil eye and of old women who could look on sheep and make them fall dead. And there were other, older stories, of witches of great power who could summon storms or blight the crops in an entire area around. Jane did not doubt these because she could not. Every farm girl had heard too many stories of it to doubt it.

But Anne Boleyn a witch? Anne Boleyn having brought the king's affection on by some love philter?

"Oh, my marriage with Catherine was invalid," the king said. "And I had doubts for many years about the validity of it. That all our sons died seemed to me a bad omen and a sign that I had done something to displease the Lord our God. But I loved Catherine of Aragon well. I would never have been able to set her aside, never have been able to see her die, alone and in pain at Kimbolton, but that I was under a spell."

Jane could not gainsay it. She remembered the king's look on the day of his first wife's death. That brittle joy that had caused him to dress all in yellow and put a feather in his hat, when all the while he looked haunted, as if his joy were but a means of denying a great suffering.

"There is reason to believe," King Henry continued, "or so Cranmer and Cromwell and their spies tell me, that Anne has witchcraft in her and that she made that pact with dark powers that witches often make, by which she secured her rise in the world and my affections." While speaking, he crossed himself with superstitious fear. "And in that manner, she became queen and secured that I would do everything, including damn my own soul for her."

"But . . ." Jane said. "That is dark indeed, but if she has that power, and if she can call on such forces, how can she not have delivered a son yet?"

The king patted Jane's hand. "It does you good, Mistress Jane, to be so fair and to have doubts about the queen's guilt. To a heart as good as yours, such corruption must seem unimaginable. But you see, there is a history to these dark pacts, to these contracts with the prince of lies, and that is that he always betrays those who seek favor through him." Again, King Henry crossed himself, as though the gesture would stand between him and the evil he spoke of. "And in that way he mocked the queen and her dark arts, giving her a child but not a son, and then he claimed the lives of all my boys, in payment for his assistance to her."

Jane was speechless. "That is monstrous," she said.

"Indeed," King Henry agreed, nodding. "And this is why I have determined I will not give her another son whose soul the dark one might devour before the babe is ever born. I have determined she will be put from me." He looked away from Jane and at the sky from which light had faded to the extent that it showed only dark blue and purple tints, like the vestments of priests at Lenten Masses. "And there are other . . . intimations, which might mean that our marriage was never such, that our union is invalid, that I am a bachelor."

"Milord," Jane said, in some confusion.

"No, I will not speak of it," the king said. "Nothing of this is known, outside, not even the witchcraft, and I trust your discretion and that of your family to keep it a secret. And I will not speak of other things that are yet under investigation, but . . . Lady Jane, if it turns out that the queen played me false in some way and that my marriage was never a true marriage, will you have me? Will you take my hand and with it my kingdom?"

Jane looked down in confusion. It seemed she was doomed to unconventional proposals. The proposal from William hadn't been one. Instead, it had been a meandering conversation that had ended with her telling him that they should marry and his not disagreeing with it. And this one was a very odd proposal indeed, made by a man who was married and who had just told her he had grave doubts not only of his wife's honesty but of her soul.

"Milord," she said.

"Indeed, indeed," King Henry said and grinned as if she had given him an answer and more, the answer he wanted to hear. He patted her hand again, his hand large and soft against her own little hand. "You are as always propriety itself, and no fault can be found in your behavior," he said. "It is I who am impatient and must always anticipate myself in my wish to secure you. But Mistress Jane, you must know that I have long thought of you as modest, kind, and obedient, and exactly the type of lady who would suit me for a wife and my kingdom for a queen. And I dare expect, from your looks and your kind demeanor, that you would not scruple to keep company to this man, so much older than you, and perhaps to bless him with children?"

Jane felt herself color violently. But she felt it was not a question to which she could any longer avoid making an answer.

Clearly she realized that the king wanted to know before he acted against his present queen what the prospects were of getting Jane's affections. And her hand.

But it all confused Jane, because if Queen Anne was guilty, surely the king would want to part from her in any case. And yet he acted as though whether he put Anne Boleyn away or not were all dependent on Jane's response.

But perhaps Jane read it all wrong. Perhaps the king truly loved her and simply wanted reassurance that his love was returned.

Her lips trembling, she inclined her head. "To be Your Majesty's queen," she said, framing her reply carefully. "And more, to be your wife and the chosen partner of your days and mother of your children, is such a signal honor I cannot imagine any woman refusing it," she said. "Save that perhaps, some, such as I, must find it too much for them, and too high an estate for them to aspire to."

She looked up to see the king smiling broadly at her.

He reached out and plucked a red rose from a nearby vine. "I hope you like roses, Mistress Jane," he said. "For as you know it is the symbol of my family."

Thirty-two

PHOENIX TRIUMPHANT

 "MARK Smeaton has been arrested," Edward said at supper.

He looked intently at Jane while he spoke, and Jane remembered the talented musician and deft dancer who had always been such a great favorite with the king and wondered if Edward could, at his most deluded, imagine that Jane had anything to do with the man or owed him any sort of feeling.

Instead, she could only look her surprise. "Arrested? For what?"

Edward smiled. "For depravity beyond your understanding, Jane. It is said he has confessed to lying with the queen, in an attempt to bring about an heir for our kingdom."

The piece of mutton that Jane had been chewing—and which had been too dry and heavy for her taste to begin with—seemed to turn to leather in her mouth. She managed to swallow it, but only with difficulty, and she looked up at her brother in astonishment. "But that might have put a bastard on the throne," she said.

"Exactly," Edward said, beaming on her as though he were a good teacher and she his favorite pupil. "It could have. And because of that it is high treason on the queen's part. But there is worse."

"What can be worse?" Jane asked. In her mind she reviewed whether there had been opportunity for the queen to commit such great infamy.

It seemed that everywhere she went, the queen was surrounded by a mass of her ladies-in-waiting and her attendant gentlemen. Jane could not imagine how it would be possible to find time for dalliance with a simple musician like Mark Smeaton without having alerted the whole court.

"Well, there are gentlemen implicated in her dishonor," Edward said. "But really it is not for your ears, Jane."

"What else can be for my ears, when it must so nearly impact my prospects?" Jane asked sharply. In her mind was the thought that if certain gentlemen, the ones who were always with Anne Boleyn—Norris and Wyatt, Weston and Anne's brother, Lord Rochford—had been complicit, then it might be possible that Anne could have managed an affair with Smeaton.

Edward was looking at Jane and clearly making some effort to speak, but he could not manage it, and Jane thought it would be more quickly forthcoming that he would embarrass himself to death than tell her the truth. No, in this matter, if she wanted to hear more, she must ask Tom. Tom had always had problems mustering discretion, and he did not think that Jane was a frail plant, which would dissolve were she to hear things that shocked her.

But meanwhile, and to allay her own suspicions, she asked, "And Thomas Wyatt, has he been arrested?"

Edward looked at her seriously. "Yes," he said. "Jane . . . our mother told me . . . If there is any precontract between you and that gentleman, pray tell me so that I—"

Jane shook her head. "No precontract. He used me to get the attention of Anne Boleyn when she seemed not to care for him at all, but I am not the kind of woman that attracts him, for he must have them cruel."

As soon as dinner was over she rushed to her chamber and summoned her brother Tom with a letter.

Tom came, dashing in purple silk, and bowed to her and grinned. "There stands Mistress Seymour," he said. "One step closer to the throne."

"Do not talk nonsense," Jane said. She'd waited for him in the garden, with her embroidery. Edward, who was quite capable of trying to curb Tom's tongue, was within, occupied with something in his study, and Catherine had left, bent on some errand of her own. The children were with their nurse, and the garden was, therefore, all Jane's and Tom's.

"You think it is nonsense that you will soon be queen?" Tom asked.

Jane shrugged. "I think it is nonsense to greet me with such elaborate pageant. I have need to talk to you. Edward will tell me nothing. Am I to understand that gentlemen have been arrested, accused of . . . carnal knowledge of the queen?"

Tom nodded. "The queen herself was arrested," he said. "She's in the Tower now."

"Put to the question?" Jane asked, startled.

Tom shook his head. "No. She is still the queen. I understand she occupies the very same apartments she occupied at her coronation. But her . . . associates have made many accusations about her, and it is enough to send her to the Tower."

"What gentlemen were arrested and accused?" Jane asked.

"Why, Jane? Did any of those gentlemen call your eye or your loyalty?" Tom asked.

"No," Jane said. "Only I would know who they were."

"Why?"

And there, it was another of those questions that Jane probably couldn't help answering. Because if she didn't answer, Tom might very well think she did have an interest in some gentleman or other, and Tom had an intemperate tongue and was not intelligent enough not to speak, even when speaking would clearly hurt both his cause and his family.

Jane bit her lip in annoyance but spoke quietly enough. "I must know so I can judge the veracity of these charges. Surely, Tom, you realize even when a woman is considering the king for her husband, she must yet realize that he is a man. And she must make sure of her safety." She pulled the thread too tight on her embroidery, and it broke, forcing her to start anew, with a freshly knotted thread.

Tom frowned at her. "You would doubt the king?"

"Tom, when it comes to marriage, my heart, and my safety, I might very well doubt a saint. And this is just between us, brother and sister," she emphasized. "You will listen to me, please, and be quiet about it to any strangers."

"The gentlemen implicated with the queen are Mark Smeaton, Henry Norris, Francis Weston, and William Brereton. Also her brother, George, Lord Rochford."

"Thank you, Tom," she said, even as her mind tallied over those gentlemen and realized those were the ones who were always with the queen. They and Madge Shelton would have seen any adultery going on. But if they were all complicit . . .

She couldn't imagine any woman's appetite running to all those men, but then in her mind she saw Anne Boleyn as she looked when her face was distorted in one of her rages, and she recoiled. Anne Boleyn had always been such, so incapable of denying herself any pleasure, so determined to fully feel and revel in any pain, that it was probably not surprising if she would also want many men in her bed.

"Her brother, Tom?" Jane asked very steadily. "How can any believe that?" Jane herself recalled the good-humored Lord Rochford, who was never as boisterous as his sister, never as cruel. It seemed hard to imagine such a thing of him.

She looked steadily at Tom.

Tom sighed. "They were denounced by Lady Rochford, who surely would have some knowledge of the matter, since she's married to Lord Rochford. Apparently Anne Boleyn was determined to conceive an heir for the country and perhaps pride in her own race and place . . ."

Jane's mind still recoiled from the thought, and the horror must have shown in her eyes.

Tom sighed again. "There is more. They say that she had the Lady Catherine, the Dowager Princess of Wales, poisoned or bewitched. They say when Princess Catherine was autopsied, they found that her heart had turned all black, and that could either be the result of witchcraft or some arcane poison."

Confronted this way, a fact that she had only before encountered in her private correspondence from Princess Mary, Jane felt as if everything must, perforce, be confirmed. It was all true. Anne Boleyn had not been content with seducing the king and tormenting him into sitting her on the throne. She had also poisoned people and committed adultery.

"It is passing horrible," Jane said.

"It is," Tom said, but he smiled a big smile as he said it. It was hard for anyone of Tom's stamp to view the world as being horrible or filled with darkness. "It is. But let us be glad not all her plans succeeded. They say she also planned on poisoning Princess Mary and the Duke of Richmond. We must be glad she didn't succeed in that."

"Yes," Jane said. "Yes. We must give thanks for that to God."

That night, in her dreams she saw Anne Boleyn as a Circe, a dark enchantress, muttering incantations over a dark cauldron. It seemed to Jane as if Anne Boleyn's eyes looked directly at her, then down at the cauldron. And, as though reading in the cauldron some fact of Jane's future, Queen Anne threw her head back and laughed, that loud, ringing, intemperate laughter of hers.

Thirty-three

"ARE you quite contented here, Jane?" Sir Francis Bryan asked her.

Her kindly relative looked genuinely concerned, but Jane was not sure why. Two weeks ago the king had requested of Jane that she remove to the house of Sir Nicholas Carew, some seven miles out of London.

It was a pleasant house, looking down on vast gardens that led by steps down to the river. Sir Nicholas and his wife had treated Jane as an honored guest without stifling her, and she'd been allowed to spend much of her time in the garden, planting and weeding and watering to her heart's content.

Sir Francis Bryan had come to find her at the bottom of the garden, occupied in pulling up the bindweed that had grown thick around the roses. She was on her knees, the smell of fertile loam in her nostrils and her hands stained with green and garden soil.

At Sir Francis's question, she rose, dusting her hands one against the other to remove the dirt. "Should I not be?" she asked her older relative. "Should I not be contented?"

Sir Francis smiled at her. "Some young women would resent being sent away from the court, just when everyone had expectations of their becoming the next queen. They would think they were being sent away from the joy and homage of their followers and imagine themselves in exile here, working in the garden."

"By some young women you mean Anne Boleyn?" Jane said, giving Sir Francis Bryan a steady look.

Sir Francis sighed. "Aye. Anne Boleyn. And many others."

Jane shrugged. "I like gardens, and I do not miss the confinement of the court, where everyone watched me all the time till I felt like a curious animal on display to the courtiers. I felt sometimes that they would next poke me with a stick to see if I moved."

Sir Francis laughed, as if surprised at her response, then he smiled. "The king sends me to tell you that you are still very much in his thoughts, and you should not listen to any gossip to the contrary. He wants you to know that he waits only legal sanction so that he can make your engagement official."

"You mean Anne Boleyn's death?" Jane asked.

Sir Francis Bryan looked alarmed. "You could become a very uncomfortable woman, Jane, should you follow this habit of saying exactly what's on your mind."

"Why should I not?" Jane asked. "If Anne Boleyn was an adulteress and a witch, and if she planned to murder the king our sovereign and his children, why should I not talk of her death as something to be expected and looked forward to? The king tells me it will be accomplished soon enough."

Sir Francis looked quizzical and concerned. "Will you take

a turn with me around the garden, Jane?" he asked and offered his arm.

"Sir Francis, I have soil on my hands still," she answered, rubbing her hands one against the other but still showing a fine coating of dirt on the pale skin. "I will stain your fine doublet."

But Sir Francis shook his head, showing disdain for his doublet, which was very fine indeed, a thing of flame-bright velvet slashed through to show sky-blue satin beneath. "Never mind the doublet, girl. I must talk with you."

And on those words, he offered his arm again. Hesitantly, Jane put her arm through it.

He started leading her around the garden, which was large and gently sloped, leading down to the riverside. At this time of the year, the beginning of May, the river ran swollen by spring rains and made a fine music, which seemed to light up the entire landscape of gently rolling green lawn and flowers. The trees above were full of leaves and birdsong. And from somewhere came a steady buzz that made Jane think of bees drowsing in the sun.

They were the only ones in the garden. Oh, Jane doubted not that there were people in the windows above, watching them walk, and that anything irregular happening between herself and Sir Francis would be speedily reported to the king. But they were as free of speech as they were likely to be anywhere.

Which Jane understood as Sir Francis said "Jane, what is Anne Boleyn's guilt?"

"Adultery," Jane said quickly. "And witchcraft and attempted murder."

Sir Francis was quiet a long time. "Have you ever wondered," he asked at last, "how she could commit adultery with so many men, in the court where, as you say, the queen or even the future queen is watched all the time, like a curious animal in a cage, and perhaps sometimes poked, to see if she will move?"

"I thought about that a lot," Jane confessed, "when I first heard of the charges. But then I realized that all the gentlemen implicated were the same men who were always about with her, all the time. They, and perhaps Madge Shelton. And Madge Shelton wouldn't tell on anyone for debauchery. It is often rumored that there is no male at court who hasn't tried Madge, from the stableboy onto the king himself."

"Yes," Sir Francis said, but the word was long-drawn-out and not a quick admission of Jane's excellent reasoning. "But, Jane, think on this—all of them? Together? At the same time? You might believe Anne Boleyn abandoned or a witch, but do you believe her that shameless?"

Jane thought back on the queen's brittle dignity and wasn't sure. Oh, Anne would often have gentlemen around her, at her rising in her chamber. But she always made sure not to expose herself till she was decently covered, often dressing within her bed curtains and poking her head out only to engage in badinage with her companions.

"And the witchcraft, Jane . . . If she's a witch and so powerful, how come she has allowed herself to be ensnared? How come she's not even now flying out of the Tower window and harkening to freedom in some cursed glade?"

His words were so compelling that Jane did look up at the sky, as if to see if her rival had indeed taken wing. But the sky was empty.

"The devil does eventually desert all those foolish enough to make a pact with him," Jane said, repeating what the king had told her. But her voice came out with no force at all.

Sir Francis sighed. "I am not saying it is not so, Jane. Sounder heads than I, and greater scholars have said just that.

But perhaps, just perhaps, no one would be foolish enough to make a pact with the devil, were his protection so slim, his loyalty so feeble?"

"Sir Francis . . ." she said.

"And there's no proof at all of her conspiring to kill anyone, save that some maids said they sometimes heard her swear she wished so and so was dead. Now, you might not have ever said such a thing, Jane, as you are a sweet and quiet girl, but I assure you hotter tempers than yours say those words quite frequently and mean nothing more by them than that they are vexed at one of their acquaintance, relatives, or adversaries."

"Sir Francis," Jane said, the import of what he was saying sinking heavily into her mind, "are you telling me that you believe Anne Boleyn to be innocent?"

Sir Francis looked shocked. "Why, no, girl. What could have put that idea in your head? No indeed. Anne Boleyn is guilty as sin and deserves to die for it." He was silent a while as they walked along the path some more and down by the stables, from which the whinnies of horses reached Jane's ears.

"Then what are you saying? Speak not in riddles. My reason is not strong enough to understand them."

"Your reason," Sir Francis said, "is strong enough to understand anything. And to regulate your conduct accordingly. Which is why I must talk to you."

"Anne Boleyn was guilty, but not necessarily of witchcraft and adultery or even attempted murder. No, her crime was more severe and must bring a more immediate and unappealable punishment." He was silent a moment. "You know I've known the king since my youth, Jane?"

"Yes, milord," Jane said.

"Jane, please attend, what I have to tell you could see me hanged three times, and drawn and quartered, too, and no mercy shown to any of my heirs, yet I prize your life and you, yourself, whom I have known since childhood and whom I've watched grow with some interest and always valued above what your provincial family could discern in you and for you. I'm not going to ask if you love the king, Jane."

"But I do, milord," Jane said, surprised as her own voice came out tinged with tenderness.

"And so your danger is yet greater," Sir Francis said. "I think Anne Boleyn loved the king, too. Or perhaps hated him, the two sentiments being not so far from each other as one might wish to believe. From love comes jealousy, and from jealousy, in a woman of Anne Boleyn's fitful and untrained disposition, there must descend scenes and screaming and many attempts to get attention from her beloved when he seems to stray."

Jane nodded. She had often seen Queen Anne's fits and been horrified by them.

"And from love," Sir Bryan went on, "comes a great wish to have your beloved see you as an equal and recognize you and love you as you love him—as a complement and part of yourself. This is normally pleasing and a good trait. But not when your husband is the king, who must always be regarded as being above yourself and whose word represents the law of God in these isles.

"Do you understand, Jane?" he asked vehemently.

She looked at him, puzzled.

Before she could open her mouth to question him, Sir Bryan said, "Anne Boleyn is guilty of trying to be equal to her sovereign and of making his life uncomfortable and his conscience uneasy with her fits and her demands. In a way, when you consider that the king's will is the will of God, she is guilty of heresy."

"But—"

"No, only think. God appointed the king over us as our sovereign lord and gave him power over our whole lives, did He not? We live and die when the king commands it, and those of the nobility marry or not as he wishes it. Is that not then that God has delegated His power upon the king and that for us the king's will must be the will of God?"

Jane inclined her head. "When you tell it that way, milord."

"I do tell it that way. I mean it that way. Now, listen, your great and strong king, before you knew him—before you were born, before your parents were married—was the merry and laughing younger son of a great house. He grew to maturity in the shadow of his esteemed and great older brother."

"Was Prince Arthur really that perfect?" Jane asked.

Sir Bryan shrugged. "In my estimation, no. But I was a callow youth, and I saw in Arthur nothing but a bookish boy, forever reading on this and that, spending time debating with this ambassador and that priest. I understand he was learned, though, and wrote in passable French and decent Latin." He shrugged. "I would not know. As I said, I was just enough younger than him to regard his accomplishments with equal degrees of indifference and misunderstanding."

He took a deep breath, and his walk slowed. He looked away from Jane towards the sky, and his voice acquired that faraway, reminiscent tone of an older man speaking of his youth. "My friend was merry prince Harry, the Duke of York, who, removed from the need to be the serious, grave heir to the throne, amused himself as he best pleased, running through the streets and enjoying a liberty not often permitted to those who are believed to have a chance of becoming king someday. Yes, we were merry then. And Henry excelled at dancing and hunting and horse riding." He took a deep sigh. "He was suffered to grow wild, you understand. His father did not bother with him, so sure was he that Arthur would succeed him and that Arthur would, as the name implies, restore the glories of Britain." Sir Francis shook his head, as though at the folly of humanity in general. "He was at the same time a happy young man and pleased to chart his own path in everything, and a boy who longed deeply for notice from the father who never gave it to him."

A deep breath that sounded like a sigh entered Sir Francis's chest, and he looked at Jane, his eyes full of sadness. "And then Arthur died, and the king, where he once had ignored Harry, of a sudden became all too interested in him. But the type of attention he devoted to Henry was the worst possible. Henry was a sensible boy, even if wild, and he would have understood dynastic need or speeches about his value. Any proof at all of his father's confidence in him would have overjoyed him and made him wish to do everything to make his father and his family proud.

"But King Henry VII, great general that he was and great at evaluating soldiers, was not so brilliant at evaluating boys, particularly not those related to him. He looked at my friend with his merry, unguarded ways, and he became fearful. He thought him too much like his maternal family, the Plantagenets—handsome men, too fond of their food, their women, and their amusement. And in that spirit, the attention he gave Henry was to make him a prisoner and watch his every step for fear Henry should disgrace him. Henry was only suffered to sleep in a room beyond his father's room, where he could not escape without passing through his father's room. And he was only permitted to spend his day in serious study, and only with those friends that the king sanctioned. And no women were allowed near Henry for fear

Henry would form a wrong attachment. Thus Henry lived to the age of nineteen.

"The sweet freedom of his earlier years, the too great confinement of the later years made Henry like his pleasures very much. More so than he might have, with just the inclinations of his mother's family to account for it. He enjoys his food just the way he likes it, and his wine just the way he likes it. And his women, too, are supposed to be just as he likes them and give him no problems at all."

"Queen Catherine, whether or not Arthur consummated their marriage—"

"Would she have lied about that, milord? She was a pious woman," Jane reminded him. In fact the king's insistence that the queen's first marriage was valid and that therefore her marriage to him wasn't had always disturbed her. She remembered Queen Catherine at her prayers. She remembered Queen Catherine swearing in God's name she had come to the king a virgin, and she thought that doubtless a woman so pious would not lie. And about something so important, too. And in God's name.

"Yes, but even a pious woman might account a lie not a sin when she was lying on behalf of her daughter's standing in the world," Sir Francis said. "And then, you know, the pope had given them dispensation for their marriage so, in the queen's eyes, it would always be a proper and valid marriage. And then again . . . well, she was so young and so was the prince. Who knows what took place between them, in those nights together? Perhaps he was wholly unable to consummate their marriage, and perhaps he was not. Perhaps what took place was so strange and painful and disturbing that she blotted it completely from her mind and did not know she lied in later years when she swore that nothing had happened. The human mind is a great mystery, Jane, and I do not propose to interpret it for you. I just want you to understand the king, so you, too, will not make a mistake and be put away."

"I understand," Jane said, "that to please the king I must give him a son. I understand it is my greater duty and obligation to provide England with a prince, and I'll endeavor to do so."

Sir Francis gave her a nervous smile. "I am sure, Jane. I am sure you will try to do so. But you must listen and listen carefully. Whether you give him a son or no, and I agree with you that it would be best if you do and quickly, too, you must learn to act in a way that will please the king."

"You mean . . . in bed?" Jane asked in some alarm, feeling the color rise on her cheeks and feeling a sudden sense of panic. Because, of what went on between man and woman in the marriage bed, she knew very little. Only what she had gleaned from gossip at court, and since she tended to change the subject and think on other things when such came up, that was little at all.

But Sir Bryan made a dismissive sound in his throat. "No, Jane," he said. "In life. I know Anne Boleyn thought she could enthrall him with some tricks or knowledge she learned in France. She thought that would keep him satisfied, but that wasn't so. King Henry is a simple man. If he wants a whore's abilities, then he seeks a whore. His wife he wants modest and wholly subdued to him in bed and . . . in the rest of life. Do you understand, Jane?"

It seemed to Jane she did. And since Sir Francis had exposed himself so far, she dared say it. "Sometimes, when Queen Anne was raging," she said. "I looked at the king and thought I saw a little boy. A little boy who did not like to be scolded and wanted to be comfortable and easy in all things."

Sir Francis laughed. "You have the right of it, Jane, for in many ways all men are little boys. But this little boy has power of life and death over other people. And he has long been used to having it and thinks that is how life should be. Do you understand?"

Jane started to open her mouth to say yes, she thought she did, but she heard running steps behind them and, letting go of Sir Francis's arm, turned around to see Sir Nicholas Carew approaching.

"Sir Francis," Sir Nicholas said. "You'll pardon me only now coming to you, but no one had informed me of your arrival before."

Jane took this to mean that Sir Nicholas thought Jane had spent enough time in conversation with that old reprobate Sir Francis and that it was time to break up their tête-à-tête lest the future queen learn something of which King Henry might disapprove.

But Sir Francis pretended to believe it and smiled benevolently. "That is fine, Sir Nicholas, for you see I brought Mistress Jane news of the king and reassured her of his affection, and she was just giving me all her wishes and thoughts that I might transmit them to the king. It seems"—he gave Jane a sideways glance, as if daring her to disagree with him—"that Mistress Jane thinks on nothing but the king and on that happy day when they shall be united in matrimony."

Jane's color rose quite naturally at those words, and she looked down at the ground at the same time.

"Is that so, Mistress Jane?" Sir Nicholas asked in a kindly, joking tone.

"Oh, yes, Sir Nicholas," she said, her voice coming out naturally diffident and low. "There is only one thing I don't like in my matrimonial prospects."

"And what is that?" Sir Nicholas asked in some alarm, and it seemed to Jane that Sir Francis, too, was regarding her with an expression of fear, as if not sure what she would mention next.

What did he think? That she would be so foolish as to cast doubts on Anne Boleyn's condemnation? Or perhaps so silly as to mention that she thought the king might not love her so well if she didn't give him a son? She intended to do neither, but awareness of their alarm made her voice lower and more hesitant when she said, "It is that I must share him with the whole country," she said. "Every farmer woman in her cottage has her husband all to herself, but I must share his mind and his love with the whole of England."

Sir Francis said, "You see, milord, what I had to endure from this young lady? At my age, I am condemned to being go-between for two people who could not be more in love were they both children in the first bloom of feeling."

Sir Nicholas laughed. "It is not an enviable plight, my friend." He offered his arm to Jane, in turn. "And yet, I must say, Mistress Jane, that your feelings become you very well and give me, and the rest of the kingdom, hope for a happier match than what we've seen on the throne these last three years."

Jane inclined her head. Without looking she could feel Sir Nicholas's gaze on her, and she would swear he was still concerned. Casting her voice low and aimless, in the tone of a maiden making confidences about her very first love—that tone in which, so many years ago, she had approached Sir Francis and asked him to intercede for her and William with William's family—she contrived to say words that would set Sir Francis at ease without alarming Sir Nicholas or giving him aught to report to the king.

"I've been thinking about my motto," she said. "My device, you know, when I should be queen."

"And what have you thought?" Sir Nicholas asked, in the tone of an older man indulging a maiden's reverie.

"I believe I would like it to be 'Bound to Obey and Serve,'" Jane said softly.

She heard a sharp intake of breath from Sir Francis, but not so sharp that she would have noticed, had she not known what they had talked of and been expecting it. And then Sir Francis said, his voice steady and assured, "That is very good, milady. That is very good indeed."

Thirty-four

❧

ALL morning long Jane had been waiting in the broad parlor of Sir Nicholas's house. She wore a dress of white satin ornamented with ermine, which the king himself had sent to her the day before.

She was sure amid the satin she looked more wan than ever, but since the king meant her to wear white, she dared not disobey.

Edward and Tom and Sir Nicholas and Sir Francis and also several clerks and lawyers were with her. Tom was, as usual, measuring the length of the room by pacing and stopping now and then to exclaim things like, "What can be delaying him?" and "Why would he take so long?"

But to all those, Sir Francis only shrugged and said that sometimes the works of justice took their time, and that there was nothing for it but for them to wait it out and see how it played itself.

By the time the sun had climbed up, high in the sky, Tom was giving voice to thoughts that Jane dared not express. "Will he come?" he asked, wringing his hands together as if he'd been the prospective betrothed. "Did he say for a surety he'd come?"

"He will come, Tom; sit yourself down," Edward said.

But Tom did not sit and continued pacing the room, from one gaily painted window to the other, beneath the magnificently carved wooden ceilings.

In a way, Jane was grateful to Tom for it, for if he should stop pacing, she felt she must start. As it was, she felt as if Tom channeled all her nervous energy and confusion, and she could afford to sit still and quiet upon the bench between Sir Francis and Sir Nicholas.

At this moment Anne Boleyn was walking to the gallows, or had already walked there. At this moment her head was being cut off—that beautiful head with its silky curtain of black hair that had given her power over so many men, including the king himself. That high, uncontrolled laughter would sound no more, nor would the soft, melodious voice that had sung such beautiful harmonies while the deft, thin fingers accompanied it on the lute.

Jane looked down at her own hands which, after her many years of playing at gardening, had grown thicker and a little calloused, and repressed a wish to sigh. In a way it seemed an odd destiny that such a beauty as Anne Boleyn should be cut down and someone like Jane put in her place.

Thoughts of what Sir Francis had told her of Anne's true crime ran through her mind, and she shivered. What Sir Francis did not know, and could not know because he was not a woman nor admitted to the secret talk of women in their reserved rooms when no men are near and no men can hear them, is that Anne Boleyn was truly guilty only of being beautiful.

As Henry had been led, by his life as a king, to believe that everyone and everything must give way to his wishes and his orders because he was king, so had Anne Boleyn been deceived by her long reign of beauty.

She'd gotten used to men doing whatever she wanted because she was beautiful. She'd gotten used to men panting and begging after her like so many well-trained dogs. She did not understand that her beauty faded whenever she was pregnant, or tired, or out of humor. Nor did she understand that to the king, his desires counted for more than even her beauty.

And so she'd been deceived into acting as a beautiful woman always acted to any man she married—as the owner of his soul, the possessor of his heart. And she'd ordered him around and screamed jealously, while taking for herself the right to keep a string of men, hopelessly enthralled by her, dangling from her charms with no hope.

But that was not what King Henry wanted in a woman. Oh, the beauty perhaps, but not beauty's flaws. Because men didn't understand that beauty taught women to command.

Jane folded her hands upon her lap. She wondered how many times the tale had played itself like this. How many times a plainer woman succeeded where the beauty had failed.

And yet she mourned for Anne's beauty and for that voice that must by now be stilled.

She was roused from her reverie by a sound of hooves upon the courtyard outside the main door. And then by the sound of boots down the hallway, approaching the parlor.

The king came in first, wearing yellow but looking pale and shaken, as well as tired from what must be an hour-long ride. For it was at least an hour from any place where the shot of the cannon announcing an execution at Tower Hill could be heard.

He was pale and tired-looking. He came in and stood at the entrance to the parlor, surveying them all. The fingers of his right hand struggled to pull off his thick leather gloves, and they trembled just a little. So did his voice as he said, "She is dead."

Jane understood the tremor—there was regret there, and she understood that, too. She, herself, lamented Anne's lost beauty. She, herself, lamented Anne's voice and Anne's cleverness, gone with that graceful head forever severed from her body.

If Jane, her rival and one who had witnessed Anne's ungracious and cruel treatment of her other rival, Catherine, and the king's oldest daughter Mary, could feel this sorry for Anne Boleyn, how much more would the king not feel, who had been so in love with Anne Boleyn once?

Remembering Sir Francis's words, remembering the little boy she'd glimpsed in the king, sometimes at times of the greatest distress, she approached him and put her hand upon his newly denuded hand. It felt warm to her touch and moist with sweat from being confined within the glove.

The king gave her a surprised look, and she wondered if she was being too daring and said in a low voice, "I've missed you, Your Grace."

"So you have," the king said, and managed a smile. "So you have, Jane, of course. And I have missed you. But after this, we will be betrothed, and you'll have me bound in lawyers' knots, which are sometimes harder than the knots of the Church and God. And then you'll be sure of me."

"Oh, I don't need to be sure of Your Grace," Jane said. "It would never occur to me to doubt your word. Only I miss seeing you and hearing you."

The king grinned, and the sick look of mingled grief and guilt, anger and desolation left his features altogether. He turned towards Tom and Edward. "You see, gentlemen, that I hasten here to cure your lovesick sister's ranting. I imagine how hard it must have been for you to keep her quiet while you were waiting."

"Actually, she waited with complete faith in Your Majesty," Edward said. "It was Tom who paced and moaned."

The king turned his grin on the youngest Seymour. "Ah, Tom. So young and lusty. I wonder how much more nervous you will be when it is your betrothal. I hope I live to see it."

Behind the king, only now having caught up with him, came Cromwell, with a sheaf of papers in his grasp. "I have here," he said, "all the present contracts of betrothal to be read by all and signed by the lady's guardians here present."

The next hour turned very dull indeed. Jane sat beside the king, while the papers made their rounds of the gentlemen, and this and that was discussed, this clause and this point, and that exact meaning.

She was to understand that by those contracts the king had contracted to her a dowry of several castles, dependencies, and parks, including a garden in London, though it was a garden Jane could never recall visiting.

Should she survive him, as the difference in their ages seemed to dictate, these properties would remain to her after the king's death. As queen dowager, she would be able to call upon her rents for support and quite play the tyrant to any younger sons she and the king might have. Only not so much, she thought and checked herself with a reminder that here, unlike in the rural provinces of her childhood and unlike the autocratic widows she'd then met, there would be question of a kingdom, and probably Jane's eldest son would be the king and have more authority than she over any other children. He would dispose their marriages and their lives, using boys and girls alike as pawns in marriages to foreign princes.

The idea was strange, as was the idea that it would matter not how plain her daughters were. It would be their dowry and the possible alliance with England that would see them married off.

In that wise an hour was passed, and then all present signed the betrothal contract. After which, Jane was standing, her hand in the king's, and swearing solemnly that she intended to marry Henry, king of England, very soon, in a formal and binding marriage.

The king swore the like. They both signed a betrothal contract saying this was their will and entered upon with no coercion. King Henry set his seal to it.

And then, somehow, the rest of them vanished, leaving Jane and King Henry alone in the parlor. He took her in his arms and pulled her to him. She felt the soft satin of his coat, the lace beneath her face.

"Ah, Jane," he said, and, bending his head, covered her lips with his, and kissed her deeply.

His mouth tasted of ale and some herbs, as though he'd chewed chance-picked herbs during his ride. Which she suspected he had, as she had often seen him do just that, idly picking up some herbs from the wayside before mounting, and then chewing them all the way during his ride.

Soft yet powerful, his lips covered hers completely, and his tongue pushed into her mouth, the first time ever that another's body penetrated hers.

It was an odd feeling, and oddly pleasurable. As she felt her legs go weak, the king's arms surrounded her and prevented her from falling.

When he pulled away, his eyes looked full of soft amusement. "Easy, Jane," he said. And then, with a small smile. "You know, many farmers, aye, and noblemen, too, consider once the formal betrothal has taken place the couple are as good as married. I could take you upstairs right now, Jane, to your room, and claim my marital rights of your body."

Jane felt too weak to protest, but she felt blood rise to her cheeks as she thought that, betrothed though they were, they were not yet married and that a king might very well be able to break a bond of betrothal that would be inviolable for a lesser man.

"Please, lord," she said. "I've kept my maiden knot intact all my life. And I wish to let it go only upon my wedding night. We are so near, Your Grace."

The king smiled. "So we are," he said soberly and bent again to kiss her, but this time only a chaste kiss upon her forehead. "And so it shall be. This time there shall be no doubts at all about the legitimacy of my issue. When you give me a prince, Jane, I want everyone to know he was born in proper and lawful matrimony."

He stepped away from her. "But because I'm not sure I can control myself that well in your presence, it might be fit if you leave. I've asked your brothers, Edward and Tom, to take you to Wolf Hall, where your lady mother and your worthy father claim themselves desirous of feasting you and, doubtless, making a parade with you before all their neighbors." King Henry smiled. "And meanwhile, I'll arrange everything for you so that you may step into the palace and find it to your taste and everything ready for your comfort as queen."

Jane had already heard from Edward that she was to go back to her parents' home in Wiltshire, and though she feared a little that her influence with the king might weaken during her absence, on the whole she did not think it would. Nor did Tom who was, after all, the one most likely to worry in the family.

On the contrary, Tom seemed to think that her absence would only make the king miss her more.

She curtsied to her new betrothed. "I will miss you, milord," she said, inclining her head to look at her feet in very real modesty and chagrin.

When she raised her head again, the king was looking at her with a wistful smile. "So will I miss you, Jane," he said. "So will I miss you."

Thirty-five

THIS time, not only did Wolf Hall look small and plain, but everything seemed very strange to Jane. Life at Wolf Hall had been turned upside down, not because of the king or some other great man visiting, but because of Jane herself.

She arrived at her parents' doorstep in a sumptuous litter, far grander than the one she had once commanded for an ill-considered expedition into the London streets.

All along the way were the people, alerted by rumor or suspicion or perhaps merely interested in the grand parade making its way down their roads and paths—litter and carriages and several noblemen as escort, mounted on very grand horses—the spectacle breaking the even tenor of their days.

They took off their hats and peered at her, if the curtains chanced to be open enough for them to see her. They gaped, openmouthed at her splendor of silks and jewels. And, to Jane's great relief, no one called her a whore or a concubine, twin epithets that had followed Anne Boleyn's ill-fated time on the throne.

When she got near Wolf Hall, the peasants did come to see her and, doubtless alerted, seemed to know what she was about and that she would soon be their queen. They called out the softest of benedictions that Jane remembered hearing, long ago, when she went out in Queen Catherine's train: "God bless you."

She dipped into her purse and threw a few coins of what the king had given her to distribute as largess, and the children of the villages they crossed followed the litter a while, calling out indistinct good wishes and benediction.

At her parents' doorstep, her mother came out to greet her and gave her curtsy and escorted her, not to her accustomed small room but to a grand room in the new east wing that had been built for the king's visit.

Jane's maids followed her, two young girls that the king had appointed to look after her wardrobe and jewels.

And life slid into a glorious pattern, such as Jane could never have imagined when she lived here. Her parents, who had always been so intimidating and distant, now, without relinquishing their rights to rule her as their daughter, yet treated her as visiting royalty.

It was all, "Jane, would you wish—?" And "Jane, we've contrived something for your amusement."

Each day brought a new delight. Hunts and expeditions, chases and visits, till Jane hardly had any time for her old, accustomed pastime of needlework.

On the morning of the fifth day she spent at her family home, she rose early in the morning and walked about, before her maids or her mother, or anyone were awake.

She went out to the garden, where she was disappointed to see that the roses, on which she had lavished so much care during her time here, had mostly died for lack of care. A few remained, blighted and uncertain, struggling to put forth leaves and flowers that looked deformed or stunted.

Jane badly wanted to pull up the weeds blighting the beds, but she thought if her mother were to catch her with her hands in the dirt, she would be far from pleased. And, on that thought, Jane wandered back inside, through paths where she broke the morning dew–bedecked cobwebs with her face and where memories assaulted her at every turn.

There, there, she'd stood when she'd heard that the Dormers rejected her intention to marry William. And there, she'd run and led William to trip when he pursued her. And there, by the great barn, she'd stood with Tom and Edward, when she had intended to go on a ride with them and, coming in to ask permission, had heard herself called plain.

She went into the house, which was cooler than outside, and walked along the gallery, looking at the portraits of her ancestors, Esturmis and Seymours all, and wondering what they would have thought if they knew one of their own blood would marry the king and—with God's kind benevolence permitting it—mingle their race with that of the kings of England.

And she wondered what they would think if they knew how plain Jane was and that she had attracted a king, despite her plainness.

She wandered into her mother's room and sat at the virginal. It had been a long time since she'd spent time playing, as she could always command more skilled players than herself when she had a need for music.

Slowly, hesitantly, she set her fingers to playing a beginner's melody.

"Oh, there are you are, Jane," her mother's voice said from behind her, and her mother swept in on a waft of scent. She held a bundle of fabrics in her hand. "I looked for you in your room, but you were not there, and your maids did not know where you had gone."

She smiled as she said this, but Jane could recall how she would have been scolded for a similar infraction, many years ago.

"The king has sent fabrics with you," Lady Margery said. "And Edward's wife, Catherine, has brought some drawings of patterns. I have skilled enough seamstresses around here to set to the task so that you will not be utterly disgraced when you go back to London as queen. But will you sit with me and pick which fabrics should go with which gowns?"

Jane sat down and picked over the fabrics. They'd obviously been purchased for Anne Boleyn's household and were in the colors which would have flattered the lady's vivid complexion. Jane, being paler, tried to mitigate the effect of so many rich reds and overpowering greens by insisting that they insert here a pale blue panel and there a pink one, so that the colors nearer her face were lighter and flattered her pale-white complexion, which was her only claim to beauty.

Her mother ventured one or two opinions, but in the main let Jane have her head. Only when Jane discarded a set of patterns as being "too French and too bold," did her mother venture to dissent.

"You know, Jane," the older Seymour lady said, toying with the fabric samples and the drawings of elaborate gowns. "Gentlemen, aye, and gentlemen husbands, too, sometimes like to see their wives display a little bit of flesh. Provided they are assured that such flesh exists for their pleasure only and will never be uncovered to another's touch."

Jane laughed at this. Sharp in her mind was the memory of being nine and of hearing herself being referred to as plain, never likely to catch a husband and likely only to find a place in a convent which didn't ask too much of a donation to take her in.

Seeing her mother look at her, puzzled, and feeling giddy with her own triumph, Jane said, "Come, Mother, I know that I am plain. And surely, you know that I am plain."

Her mother looked puzzled. "You are not plain," she said. "You are one of the fairest girls in our area, and everyone has ever said that you were too great a treasure to be kept here. Why think you we made so much effort to send you to London and to court? We knew you would get a good marriage." She smiled. "Although we never imagined it would be as good as this."

Jane was confused. She knit her brow into a frown. She was sure she hadn't dreamed the cold hall outside and her mother's words . . .

"When I was nine, I was about to go on a horse ride with Edward and Tom," she said. "And I came inside to ask my nurse's permission. As I was passing this room, I heard you and father talking. You had left the door a little open, and I heard you talking about me."

"About you?" her mother asked in astonishment. "When you were nine?"

"Yes." Jane smiled to show her mother that she was not upset, nor did she hold it against her mother. "I heard my father tell you that I was too plain ever to get a good marriage."

Her mother made a sound of disbelief.

"And you agreed with him and said, since I was the oldest girl and steady, I could help you till Dorothy and Elizabeth were married, and then you could send me away with some convent, a small one that would take a small offering."

Jane's mother looked at Jane, openmouthed. She shook her head slowly. "You dreamed it, Jane. It was one of those vivid dreams that children have. For I'm sure neither your father nor I have ever considered you anything but beautiful and intelligent and likely to do us all proud."

Jane opened her mouth to protest. She remembered what she'd heard. She remembered the cold floor beneath her feet and the breeze blowing her worn and too-short dress around her ankles. But she realized, looking at her mother's eyes, that her mother did not remember it. No, not only did not remember it but, faced with a daughter who had the king's ear and his affections and who could, if she so wished, ask him to punish her own family, her mother had replaced her perception of Jane's plainness with the certainty that Jane had always been beautiful and that they'd always expected great things of her.

Jane felt a chill climbing her spine. It was as though she'd ceased to have a mother, or her mother had ceased to be hers in any way that Jane understood.

Later in her room, looking in the mirror, Jane thought she still had protruding eyes, a too-long nose, a receding chin, and too-thin lips. But the woman looking back at Jane would soon be queen. And that was an honor that even Jane's younger self, promising herself with great bravado that she would be greater and more powerful than all her brothers and sisters, could have dreamed of.

But that younger Jane had known so little. She had no idea at all how dangerous honor could be.

Thirty-six

 THE great barn was arrayed as it had been for King Henry's visit. No. More richly.

There were elaborate tapestries hung from small hooks, covering the great wooden walls. And all the animals had been taken out, and the barn cleaned so that there remained only the barest smell of hay and beneath it a very, very faint smell of horse.

Broad tables had been set at the back of the barn, and a vast space left open for dancing, and a group of musicians had been brought in from out of town to provide very superior music.

All the important families in the region filed in, gentlemen and ladies wearing their best. And they all showed their best manners and bowed or curtsied to Jane before dancing and milling around talking.

Jane wore a gown of the most delicate rose, which accentuated her pale and even skin without making her look colorless and dead, like a corpse newly given up by some river—as she feared more vivid colors did.

Her hair had been expertly arranged by the maid the king had sent with her to attend her. It looped in braids behind her head. Bright and shining, it called attention from her too-thin lips and receding chin.

And over the coif with which she'd protected the most of her hair, the maid had created a most ingenious headdress all made of flowering roses. It was cunningly done, and it looked both startling and strangely appropriate for Jane.

The pale roses did not make her look as jewels or harsher-colored velvets did, as if her small face would presently disappear in the midst of all the riot of color. And the maid had carefully tweezed Jane's hairline to make it smooth and emphasize its height, calling attention to that smooth, high forehead that was Jane's one claim to fashionable beauty.

She'd seen William and his wife when they came in. William looked the same, only older.

Jane had expected that as William grew, his frame would fill in with muscle, and he would look sturdier and better proportioned. But this hadn't happened. He retained about him the awkwardness of adolescence, to which was added, strangely, a fast-balding head, a wrinkled face, and a general look of having grown old without having grown up.

He wore, as usual, magnificent clothes, all velvet and silk, and he had by his arm a small, vivacious woman, her thickened form speaking of many births. Jane had heard that Mary Sidney had brought William Dormer no less than six children and that he was prodigiously fond of her.

As William bowed to Jane and Mary curtsied and blushed, Jane looked at her old intended for some sign of remembrance, some sign that he was thinking of the night when Jane had been denied to him. But in his blue eyes she met only wonder as he looked towards her.

Perhaps he had never realized she could look so fine when dressed in the best and with her hair properly arranged by a skilled maid. Perhaps.

Jane watched him while she greeted the rest of the guests. She watched him while she danced with all the important people at the ball. While they paid her high compliments and spoke of her beauty and elegance and how they always knew she was destined for great things, she watched William dance attendance on his round little wife.

Oh, she didn't regret him. How could she? Although her life with him, in these fields, might have been quieter, it would have cost her that knowledge she now had of the greater world of court. And also, she would never have grown to think of the king as a man and a lover. And the king, middle-aged though he might be, yet cut a finer figure of a man than William Dormer.

At last, in her obligation to dance with all the gentlemen present, she found herself on the floor with William Dormer. And as she gave him her hand for a step, she said, "It has been a long time since we met or spoke, Sir William."

He seemed all confused for a moment. That tongue-tied silence she remembered came over him and, though his mouth disposed itself to a hundred different words, he never uttered.

"It has been some years," Jane said. "It was, I think, before your wedding."

His mouth worked some more in silence, at last, for all its labor, managing to disgorge the one word: "Yes."

Another took Jane's hand for a few steps, and then William was at her side again, and Jane said, "Do you ever walk in the fields of a summer morning, Sir William?"

He shook his head no.

"Oh, I beg your pardon," Jane said. "Of course, you never were one much for walking. But do you ride? Into the forest on a summer morning."

William sighed. He frowned, forming new wrinkles on his forehead above the nose that towered over his too-close-together features. "Not very often," he said at last. "I have the responsibility of the estate and many matters to oversee."

Jane allowed him to go through the rest of that set of steps in silence, but when the figures of the dance next threw them together, she said, "And do you, Sir Dormer, ever visit our little hideaway in the hedge?"

She did not know for sure what she expected. Panic, fear, and the paleness of the guilty? Or a sudden shocking redness as he recalled their many hours spent in foolish talk? Or yet, perhaps, a vague look of remembering, the look of a man staring back at a pleasant time in his life.

She got none of these. Instead, Sir William Dormer looked at her in utter confusion. "I do not understand," he said. "I do not know of what you speak."

"Oh, come, come, William," Jane said, in her confusion reverting to the address of their youth. "How can you forget? You met me the first time in the place where the hedge makes a round and encircles a space of moss and roses and running water. How can you not remember?"

She thought, as the words came rushing out of her mouth, that William Dormer might think about how she was now to be queen and meditate on what had befallen the acknowledged lovers of Anne Boleyn.

Though if he had been Jane's lover—as he had not—it would have been before the royal marriage and would only at best render it invalid and never count as infidelity, William

Dormer—if Jane remembered their conversations well—was too cunning and discerning a man not to realize that the displeasure of the king meant death, whether the displeasure was legally treason or no.

But when Jane looked into William's eyes, she saw no fear and no desire to hide what had been for fear it might blight him. No. In his eyes, turned to her, she saw nothing but the blankest of surprise and the most utter confusion.

She thought of asking further, of asking if he remembered coming here and waiting in the dark of night. If he remembered Sir Francis, who had promised to intercede for them with William's parents but had been unable to carry the day for them. Of asking William if he'd hurt himself on that night when he'd thought to envelop Jane in his arms and had chased her down garden paths till she made him fall across an overreaching root.

She thought of asking all this, but looking at his blank, steady gaze realized it would add nothing to her knowledge. He would still not understand nor remember anything between them.

Instead, she spoke tartly, as she said, "You're accounted most fortunate in your choice of wife, Sir William."

"Yes," he said. And smiled. "Yes. It is quite the love story, you know. I met her the first time when we were both scarcely ten, and I was so impressed by her beauty and grace that I decided right then she was the one for me, the woman I would marry. I was fortunate when my parents agreed to secure her for me."

Jane remembered his moaning, his dread of marriage, his complaints about being matched with some Sidney girl.

She wanted to throw his evasions and lies in his face, to call him to admission that he had not only not coveted his wife from the beginning but had not even been sure of which Sidney girl he was to marry until his parents had rushed him into a match, seeking to make Jane's influence vanish.

But looking at him, she realized that he was not that same young man who had courted her, not the William Dormer who'd been afraid of marrying a pretty and lively Sidney girl.

This was a Wiltshire landowner, a gentlemen with a knight's title and little else to his name, who was charged with providing for and looking after a growing brood of children. He would worry about his daughters' dowry and his younger sons' entrance into Church or army or whatever profession was chosen for them. He would scrape and save and make an effort to set aside enough money to give his descendants a proper start in life. And he would worry about his fields and his sheep and the price of wool rising and falling, all of which would affect his rents.

No wonder, then, that he didn't remember his talks with Jane or his interest in her. Their lives were so divided as to be—as it were—in different worlds.

And Jane realized with a start that William was right. What had happened between them had taken place between quite different people: a plain girl and an awkward young man, inexperienced and ignorant and subjected to the whims of their elders. That Jane and that William were as well passed from existence as if they'd been lying at the bottom of their graves.

Their dance came to an end, and he bowed to her. She smiled at him and said, "Thank you for the dance, Sir William."

And she found she had nothing more to say to him. Like her conversation with her mother, this talk with William had only served to show her that the young Jane who'd lived at

Wolf Hall was very different from herself. She could never return to being that plain and unhappy young girl. And that Jane would never know anything of being the queen, which this Jane would become in just a few days.

Thirty-seven

THE queen's closet at Whitehall had been hung with festive cloths where the embroidery depicted weddings and maidens in fields of flowers.

Archbishop Cranmer had arrived earlier and made both Jane and King Henry aware that he'd signed a form of dispensation for relatives close in blood for both of them. Not that their relationship was, in any way, within the forbidden degrees of consanguinity. They rated no nearer than fifth cousins. But the king wanted this marriage to be considered absolutely valid and seen as such by all courts in the world, that their heirs would not suffer any doubt among the world's princes.

The king himself was dressed all in white—stockings of finest silk, and hose, shirt and doublet—all of it embroidered in the same white but in sparkling thread so that he looked like a vision of glory.

And Jane had been dressed in golden velvet, just pale enough not to overwhelm her but to make her hair seem more golden than spun-sugar pale. Before the wedding, ladies' maids had pressed all around her, some of them who had been Queen Anne's maids before and whom the king, in the absence of a queen, had confirmed as members of the new queen's household.

They'd doused Jane with rose water and adorned her with roses, till Jane felt she was not herself at all but rather a doll that all these ladies played with, each vying with the other to make the doll look prettier.

She went into the closet proper, and the king turned and looked at her. He smiled. He looked fond and devoted, but most of all, he looked impatient.

Jane trembled a little. This was a day she thought would never arrive and which had arrived in a much stranger form than young Jane could ever have dreamed of. She looked at the king and thought he was a more resplendent groom—both in looks and rank—than she could ever have hoped for. And if the marriage came at some danger, what of it? Was not a woman who married always subjected to her husband's will and even his whims? In what was Jane different save that, if her husband tired of her, she would be legally put to death and not merely made miserable unto her death in some purlieu or provincial hideout?

The queen's closet looked clean and polished and more festive than ever with the bright cloths upon the walls. Her memories of it, from Queen Anne's reign, were of praying or reading in this space. Nothing more.

But now she stood beside King Henry, and he took her hand. Presently, he was sliding his ring onto her finger and making her his wife.

To the archbishop's question, she promised to take King Henry as her husband, to love and honor and obey. She was bound to do all those before, his being her sovereign. Making him her husband as well did not change much of that promise.

Afterwards there were toasts and a wedding supper. Tom and Edward and Jane's sister-in-law Catherine all attended. But the king and Jane were served alone and quite apart, and Jane found it odd to be called Your Majesty. She realized she would have the title the rest of her life and thought she might as well make herself accustomed to it, but it seemed still passing strange.

All through the food, the courses succeeding each other, Jane kept thinking of what was to follow. Not that she dreaded it. She remembered how her body had responded to the king's kisses, and how her blood had ever heated at his touch. To be in bed with him and let him do what was a husband's privilege made her blush and look down and know not what to say.

It did not help that the king looked on her with a knowing smile, when he saw her blush. The only thing Jane feared was that she knew so little. Her only ideas of what went on in the bedroom between married people was what she had seen between horses and dogs, and sometimes the sheep on Wolf Hall pastures.

In this, she must account herself at a disadvantage, when compared to the children who came from poorer homes, where the entire family slept in one room. She now regretted never having listened to the bawdy conversation of Madge Shelton.

All too soon the night closed in, the guests excused themselves, and the royal musicians exhausted their repertoire of songs of praise relating to their union.

Jane's ladies-in-waiting came and led her to the bedroom.

They helped her out of her attire, but none of them made any comment nor any bawdy jest. It seemed that the ladies the king had retained were all young, much younger than Jane, and all of them looked both hesitant and shy, as if not sure how much joking or jest the new queen might condone. Or not.

They helped Jane onto a silk nightshirt, the cloth sliding, cool and smooth, over her naked body and making her shiver. And then Jane lay down and pulled the covers up over herself, till she was left looking out, half sitting upon a pile of pillows.

Her maids said good night and left. After the door was closed, it opened again, and Jane's heart sped up, thinking it was the king. Instead, one of her maids, a young one whose name Jane couldn't quite remember, came back and kissed Jane on the cheek and wished, "Your Majesty, joy and a fine night and that you might bear a prince for the good of the kingdom."

Then, as though startled and shocked at her own daring, the girl turned a bright red and ran out of the room, pulling the door closed behind herself. And Jane sat in the silence of her room, wondering when the king would come to her and how it would all be. She realized, for the first time, how watched she would be and how everything that took place in this room tonight might mean a wholly different future for everyone out there, from the courtiers to the merest yeoman who tended fields as far away as Derbyshire.

She waited long and wondered what was taking the king so long to come to her. For a moment, a fluttering fear took hold, that he would not come, that he had realized during the cere-mony how plain Jane was, and that he would, presently, have her put away without ever consummating their marriage.

At that moment, it all seemed like a cruel joke and the most horrible of mockeries that could be perpetrated on a young woman. It lent a piquancy of fear to her waiting.

But the waiting took so long that eventually even that fear vanished, and she drowsed into sleepiness.

She was almost wholly asleep, when the door burst open and a great explosion of voices and laughter made her wake with a start. It was then true, she thought. This had all been a joke and now the whole court had come to make mockery of her.

But, blinking, she saw it was far from the whole court, but only the king and a few of his gentlemen, among them Edward and Tom, who looked far the worse for drink, Sir Francis, and Sir Nicholas Carew.

"What, now, wife?" the king asked, with a broad smile at Jane. "Fall you asleep before I come to bed?"

Jane tried to command words and felt herself blush hotly, only to blush more still as Tom said in a bawdy voice, "I wager Your Majesty will soon rouse her."

"Shouldn't it be rather," Sir Francis asked, laughter in his voice, "the king who should be roused by her?"

"Aye," the king said, and winked at Jane. "And she will lie for me."

In confusion, Jane lowered her eyes. The king looked surprised, then smiled. "Gentlemen," he said, "we are making my bride blush. Come, you wastrels, and help me out of these clothes and be gone from my chamber. The only drunken man in this room should be myself."

At that, the gentlemen laughed and hurried to help the king out of his clothes and his great boots. Jane could not see much of him as they crowded around, helping him out of his clothes. But she caught a glimpse of broad shoulders and arms that might be layered with fat but were also thick with muscle. The only blemish on his large but well-shaped legs, once accounted by all the finest legs and calves in Europe, was the white cloth bandage for the wound he had received at the joust and which had not yet healed.

Sometimes, when it was cold or excessively hot, it was said that his wound caused him great pain.

Other than that, he might have been a younger man in years, and his body looked just as Jane might have imagined, save that, with little but her own body for comparison, she'd failed to imagine so much hair. There was russet hair down the broad back, and hair curled in the front. The arms were covered in a downy coat of hair, and the legs in somewhat curlier and coarser fur.

When the gentlemen stepped away from the king, he was wearing a white silken nightshirt, much like Jane's own, save somewhat broader. He pulled back the covers on the bed and lay himself down beside her, reaching for her hand from atop the covers and holding it.

His own hand, so much larger than hers that it engulfed hers completely, was warm and moist and held hers tightly. "Be gone," he told his gentlemen. "Your work is done, for you see, I am very properly in bed with my wife."

They bowed to him, and one by one they left, not without Edward casting his sister a look of concern and hope.

The door closed; Jane did not know what to expect. From what she'd seen between the beasts in the field, she wasn't absolutely sure it wouldn't all happen very quickly and violently. She tensed in expectation of an assault.

But the king said, "Oh, Jane," and squeezed her hand hard, and leaned close and kissed her gently on the forehead and the cheeks, finally capturing her lips and kissing her, at first softly and then as passionately as before.

His mouth tasted of strong liqueur, and Jane thought she must have got drunk from whatever alcohol was left in his breath, for little by little she could feel her passion rise, till she wanted the kisses and waited impatiently for the next one.

And when his hand quested down her body, it raised heated response in sighs and moans. And when he embraced her, she embraced him back, fully willing and fully wanting him.

She had been raised to expect great pain at the taking of her maidenhead. She'd heard women bled, and this had made her expect that it would be like a wound and much to be feared.

But there was no pain at all, and for a moment she feared that the king would think her already debauched and imagine that she'd had lovers before him. It was with relief, as the king called for refreshment to be brought to them, afterwards, that she noted a spreading stain of blood on her nightshirt and the bed.

The king smiled at her and said, "There you have proof you were a true maiden, Jane."

Jane could only incline her head and say, "And now I will be a true wife."

To which the king chuckled and said, "I hope so, Jane."

Wine was brought, and fruit and some sweets, and they partook of them reclined upon the bed. Jane's fears that she had disappointed the king were allayed by his holding her hand and kissing her, now and then, even as he ate. And her fears were further put to rest when, after the food and wine were consumed, he wanted to do it again.

Jane fell asleep almost immediately after, tired by the unusual exertions. She woke in the middle of the night with a sound like quiet sobbing.

She stretched her hand and found the bed empty beside her. Where was the king? Where had he gone? Could he have left to go to his own room? Was that normal, and something she should expect?

She blinked and opened her eyes. The bed was empty, but the king hadn't gone far. He was sitting upon a window seat by the half-open window, looking out on the perfumed night, outside.

The air that drifted through the window was warm, full of the smell of flowers. The sky looked a very deep blue, and the stars upon it sparkled like diamonds among velvet. There was a fine full moon, too, round and casting its pallid light upon the landscape.

If Jane remembered rightly, from that window, the king would see the gardens stretching out and in the distance the river.

Jane wondered what had made the king awaken, and she started to rise upon her elbow, ready to call him back to their bed or to ask if he needed her assistance in anything.

But by the light of the full moon, she noted tracks of tears down the king's face and sparkling tears on his reddish beard. The tears stopped the words she would have said, and she stared, not knowing why a sovereign prince should cry, and on his wedding night yet.

As she looked on, his mouth opened and one word emerged. "Anne."

It was spoken with intensity and passion.

Jane lay back down, turned her back on the king, closed her eyes, and pretended to sleep. But she would lie awake a long time, behind her closed eyelids, wondering why the king called the name of his dead wife. More importantly, she would wonder if the emotion she'd heard in his voice was sadness or fear.

Thirty-eight

❧

THE letter from Lady Mary was openly delivered, while Jane sat with the king in her own parlor. Surrounded by their ladies and gentlemen, the king had been gaming, and Jane had been sitting by the fire, embroidering finely upon a small garment that she hoped would serve for a son—though she had yet to get pregnant.

The messenger in the livery of the king's eldest daughter came in, and knelt, and proffered Jane a sealed paper. Jane saw the king turn from the gaming table to look at her and at the messenger, as though wondering what this could be all about.

With trembling fingers, Jane broke the wax seal on Mary's letter and unfolded the page to find the same decisive black handwriting she'd read once before.

"Your Majesty, my queen, and my right and proper mother," the letter opened. It gave Jane a start for a moment to think that she was indeed, at least where the law was concerned,

mother to this young woman only all of seven years her ju-
nior. "This serves to bring you my most heartfelt congratulations on the occasion of your marriage to my noble and kind
father."

So far all that was proper, but there was still quite a bit of
the letter to go. The next paragraph spoke to the point, "Your
Majesty will remember when we had occasion to correspond
before, how I entreated with you to speak to my father of me,
for I am the most wretched of his subjects and live daily in
pain and fear for my life. You said then that you would endeavor to do for me what you could, should you ever have
such power at your disposal."

The next paragraph showed that the writer preserved a
sense of humor. "I am well aware that royal promises are not
always kept and cannot at any rate be enforced, but I beg Your
Majesty, should it be possible, that she say two words to my father, the king, on my behalf." It was signed "Princess Mary"
but also "Your humble daughter."

Jane turned the paper over and over in her hands, not sure
what to do. On the one hand, she had promised the Lady
Mary that she would give her all assistance, should she one
day be in a position to do so. And, royal or not, Jane did not
presume to go back on her promises.

On the other hand, was she truly in a position to assist?
Clear in her mind were the words of Sir Francis in Sir
Nicholas's garden. Had she truly that power over the king? She
thought of the king's tear-stained face, his calling his late
wife's name during their first night together.

"Madam, what says my rebellious daughter?" King Henry
asked from his table.

Jane had been conscious of his watching her for some time.
She played for time by saying, "She wishes me well on my

wedding. And declares herself my humble daughter and myself her right and proper mother."

King Henry chuckled. "Well, in that at least we see some progress. For I never thought she would accept our marriage, even though the Dowager Princess of Wales be dead."

He looked at Jane in that moment, and she detected a stab of fear behind his eyes. Trembling, not sure how she would be received, she said in a voice a little above a whisper, "Milord, would you consider receiving the Lady Mary at court again?"

The king's face showed astonishment. Blank astonishment so complete that she could not tell whether he was repelled or enticed by the thought. He looked at her, his face a mask of surprise.

"If she submits to your royal will," Jane hastened to say. "Of course. And acknowledges that her mother's marriage to Your Grace was never valid and that she is, indeed, only your natural daughter."

The king frowned. "Are you out of your mind, madam, to be interceding for Lady Mary? Should you not care instead for the children you will bear me and whose right and honor in governance will surely be challenged by Mary?"

Jane lowered her head, but only for time enough to reflect. He'd asked her if she was out of her mind, but he had not in fact said that the request displeased him. Instead he'd mentioned their children's rights at succession, which Jane must invoke as part of her concern. Other than that, she had observed the king liked nothing so well as her showing a due regard for his own happiness and joy.

"Not out of my mind," she said softly. "And duly concerned, of course, for the future of any children I might bear Your Majesty. Which is why I think that, if with proper inducement of being restored to Your Grace's affections, the

Lady Mary will consider properly revoking her claims to the throne, it will save our children much trouble. And us and the country much grief. Besides . . ." She looked up, gazing at him through her pale eyelashes, which must veil most of the expression in her eyes and give her a look of subdued modesty. "Besides, milord, it grieves me to see one of the most precious jewels of this kingdom thus shut away." She saw the king start to open his mouth to retort and forged on. "For bearing Your Majesty's blood, Lady Mary must be much above the common run of women. And also . . ." She hesitated.

"And also, madam? Having spoken so long and on so much, you cannot hesitate now. Tell me your mind, lest I die wondering."

"Also, I find that it is not good or right or meet for Your Majesty to be thus divided from your children. I think it makes Your Grace less happy, and your happiness is my greatest concern."

The king opened his mouth to speak but only sighed, and, having sighed, shook his head slowly. He looked away from Jane and toward the messenger Lady Mary had sent.

"You may tell your mistress from me," King Henry said. "That the king and queen are sensible of her very proper wishes for their happiness, and more wish to believe than credit that Lady Mary is anxious for a reconciliation.

"Let her know that, should her wish be truthful and should she desire to be reunited to our affections, she has only to acknowledge that her mother's marriage to me was never valid, and that Lady Mary was born in bastardy. If she do that and recognize that any children Queen Jane might bear me will have precedence over her in succession, then I am willing to see her face again."

The messenger bowed and received a coin from the king in

reward of his efforts. Before the man straightened and left the room, Jane was getting out of her chair and flowing to kneel at her husband's feet.

"You are too good, my lord," she said. "Too kind and generous and always ready to forgive even those who have long held out against Your Grace."

The king's large hand, heavy and warm, petted the back of her head. "You are a good wife, madam." He reached down and helped her up. "But only, pay attention to my words, you delude yourself in thinking that the Lady Mary will listen to you any more than she listened to me. She is a stubborn woman and very little likely to pay obedience to you any more than she did to me. Your efforts will be for nothing."

Jane being halfway through rising, the king seized her hand and kissed it. "But I wish you to know I do not hold it against you for trying. In this as in all things, I think you seek only my pleasure and comfort, which after my long trouble, I cherish."

Jane bowed in recognition of his compliment. She sat back in her chair and resumed her sewing, thinking only that she had in this way discharged her obligation to Lady Mary and contrived to have no harm come to herself.

But later, in the privacy of her room, she thought she should perhaps send a letter to the Lady Mary, which would increase her likelihood of accepting her father's offer.

With much care and thought, she composed her missive and wrote, "Dear Lady Mary, By the time you receive this you will have heard of your father's reply to my wish. It is perhaps not as much as you expected, and I imagine that the rejection of your respected mother's long-held claims to the rightfulness of her marriage will wound you and cause you to think of rejecting the king's offer out of hand. I beg you to not react immediately and to think. Should I give the king, our sovereign, children, which I hope by the grace of God and my excellent health I soon may, they will be the heirs to the throne. Because my marriage to your father is beyond dispute, and even you yourself acknowledge it to be legal, you must realize that my children will have a claim well before yours. However, if by then you have not admitted the invalidity of your own claims, you might well cause strife in the kingdom and much suffering not just for my children, but for the whole country in general, as factions form and people are killed defending your claim. I beg you to remember that your mother, who is surely with the saints in heaven even now, never wanted that there be an invasion or any strife to enforce her claim. She did not wish to bring suffering on this, her adopted land. How much less should you wish to make this country suffer, when it is the land of your birth. I must beg you to consider of this and also of what I judge is your father's very real wish to receive you into his court and his heart again." She hesitated for a moment, then signed herself, "Your fond and honored mother, Jane Regina."

She sealed the letter and, out in the hallway, called on a messenger who would take it to the Lady Mary in her residence in exile. She could not be sure her letter would do any good, but she was sure that any kindness at all offered to the girl who had been so much mistreated would be better than the endless streams of insults and bullying that Mary had received from Anne Boleyn. And it must have a better result.

Thirty-nine

❧

JANE had been married for several weeks and thought her menses were late, though she could not be sure. The truth was they'd never been very exact, and she feared that with the excitement of her wedding and her removal to court, it must all have been thrown off course.

It was a fine summer day, and the king wished to hunt. He had asked her to join, and she'd dressed in her best hunting attire. But when she came out of her chamber, the king was not waiting. Instead, there was a messenger, telling her the king wished her to meet him in his quarters.

Jane was surprised and a little alarmed, thinking that perhaps the king's leg had been troubling him again, and wondering if this meant they must put off their sport.

Rushing through the hallways, she was followed, as always, by two of her ladies. It seemed as though she could not go anywhere unaccompanied these days, and she wondered if it

were because the king feared for her, honored her, or wanted
to ensure she had no opportunity for dissipation or falling prey
to other men's seductions.

She did not resent him for this. After all, she herself was
sensible to the horror of installing a bastard, and not the
king's true son, on the throne. But on the other hand, she felt
herself very hemmed in and too much in company at all times.
That solitude that she was used to seeking in Savernake Forest, that solitude that had caused the king to once nickname
her Diana, was now all but vanished, and she must learn to be
a creature of the court, always in company with others.

At the king's door, his sentries let her pass, and she went in
to find him in his chamber, fully attired for hunting down to
the heavy leather riding gloves. But instead of picking up his
bow and going out, he was holding a cup of wine.

"And here she is, gentlemen," he said to the chamber full of
his attendants. "Queen Jane, who can perform miracles."

There was a confused murmur of applause and some loud
exclamations of joy, and Jane stood on the threshold, feeling
her cheeks go hotter and wondering what this meant. Had her
maids perhaps, certainly wrongly, informed the king that she
was with child? Why else this loud acclamation and this surprise?

The king put his tankard down and advanced, in two quick
steps, upon her bewildered self. He took her hands in his and
kissed the palm of one and then the other. "Madam," he said.
"Were it not that we are very soundly trying to suppress all such
forms of gross superstitions, I would order this very moment
that a statue of you be made, that it might be venerated in all
the churches as the patron saint of family and good order."

"I don't understand," Jane said.

"Remember, madam," the king said, "that you took it upon

yourself an ungrateful enterprise, these many days ago, when you—to my great astonishment and horror—sought to restore my daughter Mary to my good graces once more?"

Jane, who had almost forgotten the messengers and the exchanged letters, nodded. She could not in any way imagine how this present effusion of joy could have come from her gesture on behalf of Lady Mary.

"Well, after years of trying to get my daughter to concede to my just understanding of her situation in this kingdom, I thought you were a fool for trying the same again, and with little more chance of succeeding than if you were one of the many fools who have long tried to convert lead to gold and continue trying despite all previous failure."

He let go of her, picked up his cup again, and gestured towards one of his valets, who hastened forward with a filled cup that he handed to Jane.

"But you, milady, must work miracles. For this morning, by a messenger who looked tired enough to have ridden here nonstop from my lady daughter's home, I had a letter from Lady Mary. In the letter she professed herself my humble and obedient daughter and asked that I forgive her the many years she held out against my will. She also admitted that my marriage to her mother was not legal and that she, herself, is no more than my natural daughter, though in that, she holds herself the daughter of the greatest and best king in Christendom."

He smiled at Jane. "Is that not fair and well spoken?"

"Very," Jane said, feeling her legs go weak as she realized that her imploring letter must have found its mark and, being kind after so many years of unkindness, had made the poor girl agree to anything at all. "And will my lord forgive her?"

"How can I not?" the king asked. "When she will in all things give way to my will and treat me with respect." He looked at Jane, a very fond look. "It is your example that has worked this change in her," he said. "And by your grace that she has learned to be gracious." He looked around the room. "You see, men, one good wife can transform the whole kingdom, even my stubborn daughter."

Feeling dizzy with relief and joy and sure that having the Princess Mary at court and the whole family united would be the best, not just for the king and his family but for the country as well, Jane put down her cup and started to go on her knees to the king.

The king reached down to lift her up.

"I must thank you," Jane said. And felt tears come to her eyes, such was her relief. "I must thank you on behalf of my poor daughter, whom you have consented to receive."

The king beamed on her. "That you consider her your daughter truly speaks highly of your kind heart, madam, but I must thank you, more than you must thank me, for it is to my family's peace and great joy that you have brought about this reunion."

"Thank your daughter and God that she finally saw the light," Jane said.

The king downed his glass of wine, then looked to her. "And I suppose now we may go hunting," he said. "Unless . . ."

He looked at her suddenly, with a calculating, considering look.

"Your Grace?" she asked, startled.

"Well," the king said. "It has come to my attention, to my great chagrin, that the court is divided. There are those who favor my natural daughter, Lady Elizabeth, and who disdain Mary and accuse her of all inequity, even onto witchcraft and plotting against me with her cousin, the emperor. And there are those who favor my daughter Mary, hold her as a true princess and

Lady Elizabeth as nothing and could not be happy unless I send Lady Elizabeth well away from me and never consider her in anything. Or perhaps coax the mite up a gallows to her death." He looked towards Jane. "And it has occurred to me that since you've shown so much kindness to Mary, you might very well, for all I know, wish me to ban Elizabeth from my sight."

"Oh, no," Jane said. She was horrified and felt sure that her too-transparent countenance must show it. "Can Your Grace really think me so wicked? I must be Elizabeth's mother, now, as I must be Mary's, and in all things the law of God enjoins me to treat my stepdaughters well, poor motherless things. I would not have you send Lady Elizabeth away from court, nor in any way diminish her standing. In fact, after me, your daughter Mary should take precedence over the entire court. And after her, your daughter Elizabeth. For bearing Your Grace's blood they cannot fail to be the most noble women in the land."

The king laughed, a delighted laughter. "Right glad I am," he said, "that I have not to give away any part of my family for your sake, milady." He turned to his companions. "And now let us all go hunt, though I should instead go to the church and spend my day on my knees to thank God for having at last sent me a companion so ready to do my will and so conformed to my nature in all things." He took Jane's hand. "Come, my lady Queen."

They started out the door and down the staircase, when Jane thought she should send Mary proof of her very real gratitude for giving in to Jane's request. "Have you sent word to your daughter already?" she asked. "That you wish to pardon her?"

"Indeed I have," King Henry replied. "And I've also let her know that my queen and myself intend to visit her a week hence." He looked gravely towards Jane. "She has been away from court for so long that I thought it would be easier for her if I should go visit her and we should get reacquainted in the privacy of her own lodgings before she were required to meet with all the curious eyes and wagging tongues at court."

Jane bowed. "Can I send her some proof of my own affection before that? A ring, perhaps, or some other trinket?"

King Henry shrugged. "She might as well know what a kind and understanding mother she has. And learn to be grateful."

Forty

❧

THE year made its round from summer to fall and brought about, in its annual turn, the dinner with the ambassadors from several friendly and inimical countries which had last been attended by Anne Boleyn.

Jane, feeling precarious in her tenure, since her womb had yet to show any fruit of her passionate union with her husband, dressed in her best to attend, followed by her two step-daughters, Mary and Elizabeth, in that order, as being the next most important women in the realm.

The two daughters of the king had been at court for some months, and the king seemed to enjoy their company much. As for Jane, she enjoyed well enough having them in her chambers, where they must spend most of their time.

Lady Mary was, it was true, a proud and silent young woman, now rounding the corner of twenty. Her shifting status and the trouble in the kingdom throughout her life had prevented any suitable match being made for her, nor did she know when there would be hope of one.

This left Mary as loose of purpose and confused of direction as Jane herself had felt, so many years ago in her parents' provincial home in Wiltshire. Like Jane then, Mary now could hope for nothing and expect nothing.

Added to this, Mary was of a great and mystical faith and, like Jane, spent a lot of her time at devotionals and prayer. Jane found her faith all increased by the stubborn refusal of her womb to bear fruit, and the two young women often spent hours in prayer in the queen's closet.

Sullen though she might be to the rest of the world, Mary was only affectionate towards Jane, and Jane, who'd never truly had a female friend, responded.

Lady Elizabeth was something else altogether. She was a pretty child, with a mass of curly red hair and huge dark eyes. Precocious and an early speaker, she had been aware enough to notice when her mother had died and her own estate had been decreased. Lady Elizabeth's nurse had told Jane the story of how the child had asked, "Yesterday milady Princess and to-day only milady Elizabeth. Why is this so?"

Jane wondered what the nurse had answered to that question. She had not asked the woman, being all anxious to change the conversation from Lady Elizabeth and her unfortunate mother. And thereby hinged the trouble that Jane suffered from right now—that Lady Elizabeth, young and innocent though she might be—made for a very uncomfortable presence at court.

Sometimes, while at some sewing or occupied with embroidering, Jane would look up and find the young girl's gaze trained on her, looking at her as if she could see past Jane's face and into Jane's thoughts and feelings.

Jane had often wondered what Elizabeth saw there and if she found in Jane any guilt for Anne Boleyn's death. Oh, Jane felt blameless, herself, but she could imagine that many at court saw her as the motor for Anne Boleyn's fall.

This was how after the dinner, when performers were invited and talk issued up and down the long table, Jane found herself staring down the table, and steadily into the big, heavily fringed eyes of Lady Elizabeth, which were staring back at her.

"Your Majesty is very pensive," Chapuys, ambassador from the Empire, who sat at Jane's right hand, said.

Waking up from her thoughts, Jane looked at the ambassador, a small, dark man who had been one of Queen Catherine's main supporters and friends, but who had, at the last, proved unable to assist her in any material way.

"I beg your pardon, Ambassador," Jane said. "I'm afraid I was miles away in my own thoughts and providing very little entertainment and company for you."

The ambassador smiled, a dark and fugitive smile that Jane associated with Spain and tempers bred in warmer climates. "You were looking at your little daughter-in-law."

Jane startled. She usually referred to the girls as her daughters or by their names, though *daughter-in-law* was indeed the proper term for the children of one's husband by previous wives. "Yes," she said. "Yes. I was looking at Lady Elizabeth. Such an intelligent child and witty already. And growing very well."

The ambassador looked distressed and pressed his lips together. "Her mother . . ." he said.

Jane looked away from the ambassador and found Elizabeth's eyes fixed on her. "What a mother is cannot be held to the child's account," she said.

"But you know," the ambassador said, "they do say blood will tell."

Jane looked at Elizabeth, who stared at her with the same intent and knowing expression Anne Boleyn might display. But Lady Elizabeth was Henry's child and a daughter of England who might one day, if Jane produced no heir, ascend the throne and rule over all.

Jane turned a triumphant smile on the ambassador. "I believe," she said, "that if blood will tell, Lady Elizabeth's will tell very well indeed, for she is the daughter of one of the gentlest and noblest kings in Christendom."

Without turning, she could tell the king had started looking at her. She could hear he had suspended his conversation, and he had that sound to his breathing that he made when he was watching her and perhaps enjoying the performance.

Chapuys must have seen Henry turn to look, because he bowed slightly and said, "Your Majesty is indeed admirable. You must petition the king your husband to let you have the cognomen of Pacific added to your names, for you are indeed a peacemaker."

"Milord . . ." Jane said. "I petition the lord my king for nothing. He gives me all I need and much besides, being quite extravagant to me in his generosity. It would be churlish of me to ask for more."

She felt King Henry's hand on her arm. He leaned over her and spoke, his breath tainted with sweet wine. "Leave my lady, Chapuys. You see she is too well bred to wheedle and beg anything of me."

Jane turned to look at him and found his breathtaking grin close up and turned on her. "However, for once, the old devil has the right of it. For you are a peacemaker, Jane."

And in that moment, whatever might come later, Jane was sure she had succeeded in bringing happiness, if fleeting, to the kingdom's troubled royal household.

Forty-one

"MILADY, please. It came by a messenger, and it says it's urgent."

The lady who had bent over Jane's bed looked apologetic, as Jane opened her eyes. But she pushed a sheet of sealed paper in Jane's face. The seal was good, black sealing wax, and had been impressed with a ring that bore a cross cut on its stone. The type of ring clerics wore.

Jane sat up and looked about her. The king had not shared her bed that night. She thought that it was because he grew tired of his efforts not being rewarded with a prince. Jane, too, felt tired and worried, but she contrived to show nothing.

Too well did she remember Anne Boleyn's rages, and now she understood the despair that fueled them at the refusal of the body to do what was clearly and urgently needed. But Jane would not behave this way. Jane would be faithful and calm and patient. And if the king sought his pleasures elsewhere . . .

She thought of him lying with another woman and felt a sudden stab of jealousy. Not yet sure whether he had married her for an heir, for love, or merely because she was comfortable to live with and he had need of calm after Anne's storms, she did not know. But she had grown to love him, and the thought that he might choose to spend his time in another's arms hurt like a buried spine beneath the smooth surface of the skin—showing nothing but growing to an illness.

But in her mind she heard the king tell Anne, "Endure it as your betters have."

And so should Jane. She sat up and tidied up her hair with her hands, and strived to turn an unruffled look on her lady-in-waiting, as though the king's absence were wholly to be expected and as though she and he were in perfect agreement on this. "A letter came?" she said. "By messenger?"

"Two letters came," another lady said, and came in bearing another folded and sealed sheet of paper.

"The first letter is from the prioress of Clementhorpe, Your Majesty," the first lady said.

And the second lady, approaching fast from Jane's other side, said, "And the second is from your daughter Mary."

Jane took the letter from the prioress first. It started with the usual salutations and praise of her most gentle and wise majesty and then continued, "It is rumored everywhere that Your Grace is a just woman and religious, and I thought it incumbent upon myself to let you know the outrages that are being committed against religious houses, monasteries, nunneries, and abbeys throughout the land."

It went on to list a long description of ravages: plate and decorations stolen, the images of saints taken down and broken, holy relics thrown out and trampled into the ground. And nuns raped, monks wounded or hanged within the portals of their house if they offered the slightest resistence, and all in all such ravages as could be expected of the most savage of armies.

"And all these," the prioress's letter said, "are being committed not by pagan invaders from some backward land, but by English soldiers on English soil.

"I feel that you and our good king cannot possibly know the evil being committed in your name, and I beg you to acquaint the king with it and to prostrate yourself at his feet, as I would, should I have the chance, and ask him to save the nunnery at Clementhorpe.

"Indeed, I know that in many places throughout the land clerics have committed scandals and outrages. But our priory is not guilty of any such, and myself and my nuns have struggled always to live a holy life. We do not deserve to be despoiled and disbanded to go live around the countryside, with no means of support and thrown at the mercy of relatives who thought long to have disposed of us."

Fresh from reading the letter, her mind still in turmoil and not sure what to think of it all, Jane reached for Lady Mary's letter and, breaking the seal, proceeded to read much the same type of news, only this time mentioning nunneries and convents everywhere.

Mary also said that some noblemen from the north had started a Pilgrimage of Grace, which was nothing less than armed rebellion against the Crown. It was said there were fifty thousand soldiers and who knew how many common people marching beneath the banners with a cross and the pictures of Christ crucified.

Jane read the letter again, unable to believe it, though she could easily agree with Mary's statement that these ills had been visited upon them because of the great sin of dissolving monasteries and nunneries.

Yes, Jane could agree with that, and the more she read, the more she agreed with the prioress, too, that the king could not know the great evil being committed in his name.

She rose from the bed, called for her ladies, and insisted they dress her, and quickly. Once decently attired, she picked up the letters and started out of her rooms and towards the king's.

At the door, going out of her rooms, she hesitated. What if the king did know of what was happening? What if he thought Jane was criticizing his decisions?

But Jane had risked her life for less—because she had once given Mary her word of honor that she would help. How could she now refuse to help unfortunates who appealed to her?

And what was more, how could she refuse to hear the imploring cries of God's own servants? No. Did she do so, she would be in peril for her mortal soul. And there was more. Whatever Jane's mother said, hadn't she, herself, once been destined for the convent?

If Jane hadn't strived so hard to fight against fate that had endowed her with such meager charms, she might even now be in one of these convents being disbanded. She might be walking, barefoot and dispossessed, across the country, throwing herself on the compassion of strangers, all to reach her parents' home and the only shelter she could possibly find. And she imagined how she would be received, if she were the daughter who'd been thrown out of a convent with only the clothes on her body and possibly with her honor ruined forever.

A feeling for that other Jane she might have been propelled Jane half-running down the hallway so fast that the inevitable two ladies that accompanied her everywhere had trouble catching up. And when they did, she had already opened the door to the king's quarters and thrown herself in, headlong.

Her husband was at a table, with a map open in front of him. At her entrance, he started and sat straight, and she realized he had been asleep over the map. Possibly, he had been asleep all night.

His skin was creased in the way one's skin got creased when one slept all night over papers and on a hard table.

Jane felt an inrush of relief that he hadn't abandoned her, that he hadn't been bestowing his attentions on another woman.

But then she noticed he was looking at her with a set frown, his eyebrows low over his eyes. "Good morrow, Wife," he said. "What brings you here so early?"

She realized the manner of her entrance looked eerily like those scenes she'd so often watched Anne Boleyn make, when she rushed in on King Henry, hoping to catch him at some infidelity, that she might rant and rave at him some more.

Immediately she fell to her knees, at his feet. "I come to request a boon, milord," she said.

She looked up and saw the king look at her, bewildered. "You, milady?" he asked. "But you never request anything."

"It is not for me," she said, and, trembling, she handed him both letters. "These letters were received by me this morning," she said. "And as Your Grace can read, they tell of horrible outrages against houses of religious worship. Our daughter Mary thinks the rebellion is but a punishment for this. I beg of you, milord, to restore the houses of religious retirement, and I am sure that all the revolt in this kingdom will cease."

The king drew in breath but did not speak. Jane looked up and saw his face, thunderous with anger. She'd never seen it so. He looked at her with a gaze that might as well be of hatred, and the veins pulsed on either side of his forehead.

"Get up," he said without offering her any help to do so. "Get up, madam. You go too far."

Trembling, Jane got up and stood, as the king, too, stood, towering over her, a man in a fury.

"I have suffered you to intrude in domestic matters," he said. "Because those are, properly speaking, the province of woman. And I've allowed you to talk nicely to that insufferable man, Chapuys, who hates me with a deadly hatred, because I thought you might smooth him in some sort of confidence that I could exploit. But in matters of policy, you have no say. This," he said, pointing to the letters he had flung on top of his table, "is why I must have a son, madam. Because in matters of policy all women are doddering fools. You concern yourself with giving me a son, madam. That is your only duty. Not policy."

Trembling before him, Jane could do no more than lower her head. She had often seen Queen Catherine and even Queen Anne talk back to the king when he was in this kind of fury. Indeed, Queen Catherine sparred so well with the king that it was often he who withdrew, tongue-tied and defeated. Even Anne Boleyn, as she then was, had told the king not to debate his wife, for he would never emerge victorious from such a challenge.

But in the end, as Jane had seen, no matter how well his wives answered, or how they seemed to carry all before them with their rational arguments, their replies had served for little else than to infuriate the king further.

He had come away from their arguments raging, and he had set about thinking of ways to humiliate them and bring them down in turn.

Jane was not so foolish as to try a course that she had already seen led only to tragedy. Instead, she lowered her head and trembled and was still.

The king raged on for some more minutes, and then his hand came down, and reached for her chin. He grabbed it between his two fingers and pulled it up, forcing Jane to look up and into his eyes.

"Madam," he said, "if you ever again feel compelled to advise me or reproach me on matters of policy, remember this—I made you queen, and I can unmake you just as quickly as I elevated you. Remember you, milady, the fate of your predecessor."

Jane drew in a sharp breath, surprised, shocked, revolted. That the king meant what he said, she could not doubt. He was looking clearly at her, with full intent and meaning.

But she could not believe that the same man who lay with her in bed and who could kiss her and caress her in the night would be so callous and cold to her in the daytime.

This is how Anne Boleyn must have felt, she thought, and she walked away from the king's quarters feeling that the solid ground under her feet might give way at any moment and leave nothing but a yawning chaos. And the gallows.

Forty-two

❧

LADY Lisle came in, as had been appointed, and Jane sat in her room, ready to receive her.

It was a cold winter day, and there was a good fire in the fireplace. Jane had been embroidering, but now the embroidery lay upon her lap, her colored silks in disarray. The king had never again mentioned his anger at her for interceding for the religious houses.

He would not. She could see that in his mind he would regard what she had said as making no more sense and having no more reason for being than a babe's incoherent babbling. What a child said before he was sure of his words might be offensive or pleasing, but all in all it meant nothing much.

And the king had visited Jane often enough, even if he did not spend every night with her. Perhaps he had a mistress. Jane had heard rumors to that end. Or perhaps he was simply occupied and busy with putting down the rebellion and with disbursing the riches being acquired from the dissolution of the religious houses. She did not know, and she did not dare ask.

What she did know was that Jane was not yet with child, and she was well over half a year married. Perhaps she was barren and would never conceive. Perhaps the same hand that had fashioned her to be unappetizing to the male eye had endowed her with a barren womb. Or perhaps one announced the other. She could not say, and she was tired of praying and crying and trying to force her body to do what her rational will wanted it to.

Now the business of being queen commanded her attention. The two Basset sisters, Anne and Catherine, relatives of Lady Lisle, were applying for positions of ladies-in-waiting at court, just as the young Jane had once been brought in to be interviewed by Queen Catherine.

Looking at her fire, while her hands rested on the embroidery and silk upon her lap, Jane wondered if the two girls had also—as Jane had—spent the night sleepless and fearing being turned away.

Now Lady Lisle came in and bowed low. "Milady, I have brought my cousins, the Bassets, the ones I've spoken to Your Majesty about."

Jane looked up and tried to look alert. "Yes," she said. "I remember you mentioned them to me. Catherine and Anne, you said. As you know the court lost several ladies when . . ." But she could not mention Anne Boleyn nor the ladies who had been dismissed because they had been close to the former lady. "When I became queen, and I'm always willing to give a chance to eager girls from the provinces. You told me Catherine was fifteen and Anne seventeen, did you not?"

"No, milady," Lady Lisle said. She was an elder noblewoman of the martinet type, who had grown thinner and drier with years and who must now be very close to sixty. She stood tall and ramrod straight, in the widow's weeds she'd worn now for a good twenty years, ever since Lord Lisle's death. "Begging your pardon," she essayed a curtsy as though only then remembering that Jane was the queen. "Anne is fifteen and Catherine seventeen, and they are both good, honorable girls, so gifted at music and so graceful at dancing as you've never seen."

Gifted in music. The words set Jane's suspicions to jangling. Oh, not suspicions that the girls meant anything by it, but a feeling, a sense that here was something dangerous.

The king was excessively fond of music, a good musician and composer, himself. And music was the one thing at which Jane could not please him.

Oh, she endeavored, as always, to provide for his enjoyment. She had hired the best musicians and made sure they had the best instruments and that they were always around, ready to play when His Majesty called upon them.

But she, herself, could not play. And if in her chamber there were girls who played exquisitely, would the king's eye not come to rest on them?

Jane was very much sensible that she herself had once been a lady's maid. As had the queen before her been lady-in-waiting and lady's maid to Queen Catherine.

The king, when displeased with his current wife, liked to look within the palace itself. Was it not foolish to furnish him with temptation?

She nodded to Lady Lisle. "And have the girls served?" she asked. "At any court?"

"They have served at the court of France," the worthy lady said. "Where they were accounted great beauties and very witty."

Jane thought of Anne Boleyn, who, likewise, had learned to be a lady-in-waiting at the court of France. And what she'd learned of French style, French fashion, and French manners had served her well when she played for the king.

"Very well," she told Lady Lisle. "Send them in."

The girls came in, sweeping majestically on a trail of perfume and silk and very beautiful outfits indeed, which, nonetheless, left their front and the top of their bosom quite uncovered.

Jane looked at them a long while, in silence. The older one was dark. There was to her features and her dark flashing eyes a hint of Italian, a suspicion of the Spanish. She was ramrod slim but endowed with curving breasts and generous hips. And her lips were large and red and looked soft, the same way her eyes had an imperious look to them, as though she were used to people kneeling at her passage.

Or at least men.

Without looking like Anne Boleyn, she seemed to Jane to have something of Anne Boleyn about her—a sparkling, vital quality, a restlessness, an ambition, which seemed to pour out of her like fire will pour out of the sky in a thunderstorm.

Looking at her, Jane could well imagine her dancing with the same verve and vitality that had animated Anne and which had made the steps of any simple dance an incantation of lust, a spell that wove temptation into the heart of every man present.

She wore a headdress, the cloth at the back of which hid her hair.

Jane suspected that Catherine, like Anne Boleyn, would have a great curtain of silken black hair. "Please, remove your head coverings," she said.

The girls hesitated.

"Remove your head coverings, girls," Lady Lisle said, impatient. "You heard Her Majesty."

The sisters reached up and carefully undid the pins that held their headdresses to their heads. Underneath they wore white coifs, the hair tucked beneath.

"The coifs also," Jane said curtly.

The girls reached up and untied the strings beneath their chins before pulling their coifs free. Their hair sprang loose.

Catherine had indeed a long curtain of black silken hair, straight and perfect, long enough for her to sit upon it if she were not careful. As Jane looked on her, with what Jane very much feared must be a horrified expression, Catherine Basset shook her head, making the black silky curtain sway about her face, and smiled a little and gave Jane an expression of such profound disdain that Jane might be the one applying for Catherine's favor.

Jane set her lips and looked away from the girl and at the younger sister. Anne had softer features, set in a round face. Her pale brown eyes, too, were rounded. And her hair was a dark, curling bronze. By no means an unpleasing woman, she had a look of innocence and stared at Jane with an expression of great awe.

"Would it please you, Mistress Basset, to live at court?" Jane asked the girl.

She curtsied deep and blushed. "It would be my greatest joy, Your Majesty."

Jane nodded and turned back to look at the formidable Lady Lisle. "I'll take Anne as my lady-in-waiting. She can remain here. I will call a servant to show her to her quarters and carry your belongings."

"Their mother," Lady Lisle said, "was most desirous that both her girls should serve together."

Jane narrowed her eyes. Anne was pretty, but Jane could seek to risk it. Catherine had been replaced by a woman who was her opposite. And so had Anne Boleyn. If the king grew impatient with Jane's failure to conceive, he would probably look for someone closer to Anne's type than her own.

Catherine Basset had too much of Anne Boleyn's fire to make altogether a safe companion at these times. And then, Jane thought the girl already had contempt for Jane, herself. Jane would not choose to surround herself with people who despised her. She was not fool enough for that.

She matched her voice to Lady Lisle's tone of dryness. "Their mother might very well think so, if she pleases, but this is my court, and I want Anne to serve me, but not Catherine."

She heard Catherine make a sound of annoyance and would swear the girl stomped her foot beneath her elegant gown.

Jane ignored her and turned her attention to Anne Basset, who was blushing and looking by turns pleased and mortified. Jane judged that Anne had been bullied all her life by her imperious sister and lived in her sister's shadow without daring even to draw breath too loudly.

Now she found herself preferred over Catherine, and the knowledge had to gratify her. But at the same time, she would feel afraid of serving alone at court. And doubtless she would also fear her sister's revenge, should her sister ever have a chance at such.

"Mistress Basset, have you decent clothing, or are all your gowns cut too low in the French fashion?"

"My—my gowns are all like this. I was assured they were in the latest fashion and all that would be favored at court."

"Well, perhaps the French court," Jane said. "At the English court, and in my service you are to be furnished with velvet bonnets and frontlets, and not these ridiculous French hoods. And you must find yourself suitable gowns of black satin and velvet. And you will definitely need cloth or lace chests to fill in at your neckline."

"But Your Majesty," Lady Lisle said in some outrage. "My cousin has brand-new attire, all of the best quality."

"And all of it French," Jane said. Oh, she could well imagine the expense providing new attire for the girl again would be for a provincial household. She remembered, when she'd first come to town, how her parents had groaned at the required apparel and its cost, till Sir Francis had thrown in fabric and the services of a girl to help Jane sew it. "At this court we dress more decently than in France. And we behave more decently, too."

She fixed a steady gaze on Anne, who blushed and nodded frantically. Jane could swear she heard Catherine snigger, but she chose not to pursue it.

"And what's to become of the girl's French attire?" Lady Lisle asked.

"Oh, it can be made into two years' worth of petticoats," Jane said. She rose and called for a servant and directed him to take Anne to the quarters set aside for new ladies-in-waiting to the queen.

"Their mother," Lady Lisle said, as she adjusted her gloves on her long, thin fingers, "will not be pleased."

"I am the queen," Jane said. "I need please no one but myself and my royal husband."

Jane had the satisfaction of seeing the proud Catherine Basset look agog at Jane's stern pronouncement as if the importance of royalty had just dawned on her.

Or perhaps seeing her ambitions slip away from her.

Forty-three

❧

"I heard you displeased Lady Lisle today," the king said. He'd come to Jane's bedroom after Jane had gone to bed. Now, attired for bed in his long nightshirt, he sat on the side of the mattress and looked at her with an inscrutable expression.

Jane stifled her sudden need to take a deep breath and wondered if on this, too, she would be told by the king to mind her own business. She would definitely, if the king had already made up his mind that he would have Catherine Basset in attendance. She remembered the king saying something like that to Anne Boleyn on the subject of Jane.

Maintaining her voice calm and even, she said, "I did, I'm afraid. She brought her two cousins, Anne and Catherine Basset, for me to meet, with the idea of making them both my ladies-in-waiting."

"And you wouldn't have them?" the king asked, raising an eyebrow.

"Oh, I would have Anne. I have nothing against Anne. She seems like a pleasing girl, quiet and somewhat diffident."

"But not Catherine?" the king asked, his voice stern to Jane's ears. "She's not a pleasing girl?"

Jane shook her head. "I found her . . . proud," she said. "She seemed to be in no awe of royalty, and I swear she was laughing at me behind her hand."

The king allowed himself a small smile. "Laughing at royalty is an unpardonable sin," he said. "Though I daresay it's been done and survived."

"I daresay the same, Your Grace. But I do not relish being laughed at. It is my own ladies, and my own household, and I choose to suit myself." She was quiet a long time, looking down at her hands, which she had folded on her lap. "Does Your Grace disagree with my decision? As the motto I chose says, I live to obey and serve Your Grace. Only let me know, and I will call Catherine Basset back to court and make her my lady-in-waiting."

She looked up and found the king staring at her, his expression grave and attentive. She couldn't guess what he was about to say, and she wondered if the Catherine girl had already ingratiated herself to him, if Jane was already in the process of being set aside and did not know it.

But the king only smiled, a small smile. "Wife, I hear Catherine Basset is a beautiful and graceful girl. I think you are jealous of her."

Oh, so this was it. The king was seeking to provoke Jane's jealousy. She knew well what the reply of both the queens before her would have been.

Catherine of Aragon would say she was not jealous, that she could never be jealous of an inferior and that if it pleased the king to amuse himself with filth, then he could do so, and Catherine would not be troubled.

As for Anne, she would scream and rant, call the girl a slut and a bawd and accuse the king of taking his pleasure with her.

Though both of the queens had managed, for some time, to keep the king in awe of them with their temper and their screaming, Jane knew that in the long run it would not work at all. And she did not want to go down the same path. If she must be doomed in the end, through the lack of a male heir or some other lack of her own which sent the king questing for pleasure elsewhere, then let her be lost on her own account alone, and not on account of what she had learned from the queens her predecessors.

Deliberately turning her back on saintly but stubborn Catherine and on proud Boleyn, she bowed her head. "Indeed, I am jealous, milord," she said. "The Basset girl is very beautiful indeed, a dark, proud type, which I must always envy but can never hope to imitate. And I feared Your Highness's eye would be called to her and that Your Highness would leave my side and my bed and go to her."

The king was silent when Jane looked up. She could not read his expression at all.

"Is it wrong, my lord, to be jealous?" she asked. "Is it wrong to wish to keep my husband always to myself? If it is, I will do my best to mend my ways, milord, and to fill the court with the prettiest girls and the ones who don't seem to admire me at all. For though it is my household, it is your court, Your Majesty, and I endeavor in all to serve my husband."

Again she paused, and again she looked at the king. Henry

still did not speak, and Jane did not know what to think of the expression in his eyes.

He looked back at her, his eyelids half-closed, his mouth set in something between a smile and speaking.

"You must know," Jane said, half expecting that at any moment he would leave her room or else tell her that she could not expect to keep him all to herself and that she should learn to suffer his infidelities as her betters had. "You must know that I only feel jealousy because I love Your Grace so well and I count you the best husband, the kindest man a woman can know, and cannot bear the thought of ever being parted from you. And yet," she said, "if Your Grace should wish to send me from court, I would go, such the love I bear Your Majesty."

Now the king spoke, now he moved. He said "Jane," in a fond and gentle tone, and he reached towards her and pulled her to him, enveloping her in his arms, crushing her against his chest.

That night their lovemaking was gentle and prolonged, as loving as it had been on their first night together and yet filled with an unhurried tenderness only possible between those who know each other and are aware of the other's body and its responses.

It lasted long, and it was good, a perfect union of bodies and souls.

And that night, when Jane woke, the king was not awake and by the window.

Outside, snow was falling, soft and thick, and the fire roared in the fireplace, showing that while she'd been asleep some servant must have made their way into the room to stoke the logs. And the king slept silently beside her, his face looking much younger than his real age, relaxed and by the light of the fire.

Jane stared at him a while. At least tonight he wouldn't go to the window and think of Anne Boleyn.

Forty-four

TRINITY Sunday, the bells rang in joyous celebration throughout the land.

In her pew at St. George's Chapel at Windsor, Jane heard the bells peal and felt as though they were bubbling laughter of joy. She, herself, felt like bubbling with laughter. For today, for the first time, she had felt the baby move within her.

This moment, commonly spoken of as the baby quickening in his mother's womb, was the first time she was certain that she was pregnant and the baby alive within her.

She'd told the king, who'd been excellently pleased and who'd told her that it was a sign that this child would be a boy. "For he is surely given by God," the king had said. "If he will quicken on Trinity Sunday."

The priest enjoined them all to pray in thanksgiving for the quickening of the babe in the queen's womb. Throughout the land, everyone, great and small, was praying in thanksgiving for the same reason. Her mother and father in distant Wilt-shire, and William Dormer and his pretty wife Mary all would have learned that the queen was with child and that the baby was moving in her womb.

As they came out of the chapel, she heard the call of the people, outside, begging for a glimpse of her. She went to the balcony, with the king by her side, and stood while the people below wished her long life, health, and happiness.

And then she walked through the court, where all her ladies-in-waiting curtsied low, and where all courtiers seemed to regard her with great respect.

It seemed to her that everywhere she passed, her belly, somewhat thick and showing beneath the extra panel she had added to her skirt, gave her power over those around her. For the first time she understood Anne Boleyn's words, when she had said that her babe would rule over them all.

But Anne Boleyn had been wrong. It was Jane's child who would rule them all. And Anne Boleyn's daughter would scarce be remembered.

That afternoon, in her chambers, the king approached her. "Madam," he said, sitting down on the floor by her feet, as though she'd been the sovereign and he a courtier, as though she'd been his mother and he a child. "I have a request to make of you."

Jane put her hand down and touched the king's shoulder. "Your Majesty requests nothing. He only has to order and I to obey."

The king chuckled and turned a smiling face in her direction. "Perhaps, but it is something you have for some time known I wished and you have yet to do, so I thought perhaps Henry, like a humble lover, should request a boon of his wife."

"Anything you say, milord."

"I wish for you to sit for Master Holbein," King Henry said. "And let him paint your portrait and sketch some miniatures. For I would have a portrait of you to hang beside the ones of my ancestors and so that future generations of kings know whence they come."

Future generations of kings. Jane cringed at the thought of future generations of kings looking on her plainness. She wondered what they would think of the protruding eyes and the too-thin lips.

"I will sit," she said, slowly, "if Your Majesty wishes it. But you must know that my likeness is not such as future kings should relish or would enjoy claiming me for an ancestress."

Henry looked at her, smiling, and looking only faintly disapproving. "I do not have the pleasure of understanding you," he said. "For I can never look at your face without feeling moved with love and admiration. To me your face shows all goodness and sweetness that is woman. Are you saying that your husband is but a fond fool? Or that future kings will have better taste than I?"

Jane realized she was treading on thin ice. She dare neither criticize the king's love nor his taste, and so she was rendered mute, looking only on him.

She had, indeed, known for some time that the king wished her to pose for a dynastic portrait, a picture of herself as queen. And it was only partly the thought of how her face would look down the centuries, to generations yet unborn, that had held her back.

There was more.

There was also the certainty that her position was precarious and that she might at any moment be removed from the throne, from the king's mind, from the memory of the kingdom.

She knew not what had happened to portraits of Anne

Boleyn. Portraits of Queen Catherine had been relegated to distant fastnesses, where the king would not have to stare on the face he'd once loved and then come to hate, when the woman that possessed it had refused to do his bidding.

What would happen to Jane if she failed to provide an heir?

But then . . . what if she provided an heir? And at the thought of this, the babe kicked hard within her womb, and Jane could not help but be absolutely assured he was a boy. But then . . . if she provided an heir, wouldn't her grandchildren, and her great grandchildren, and the generations of kings who would descend from her want to know what she looked like?

As if reading her thoughts, the king turned halfway around and seized her hands and held them. "I never understood why you consider yourself so plain," he said. "Oh, you have not the fire, the intent, which some women have, like that Catherine Basset that you disliked so." His eyes twinkled with humor that indicated he was teasing her. "But to me that never mattered. You have such a sweetness of look and of frame. And you look quite . . . old-fashioned. Like the queens of old, mothers of all good English virtue, who could be counted on to love their husbands and bring up their children right. When I look at you I see you as the portraits of my ancestresses that show good women and kind, devoted to their husbands and their God and more willing to die than to compromise their honor." He looked up at her, earnestly, meaningfully. "Never change Jane," he said.

And, after a moment, "Oh, and make sure to pose for Master Holbein. I cherish your likeness and would like to have it in several miniatures to always carry with me. Don't deny me that."

Confused, filled with a sense of standing at the beginning of a long dynasty of kings who would come from plain Jane's body, from her fertile womb, Jane inclined her head. "I will do what my lord bids me do," she said.

Forty-five

THEY moved to Hampton Court over summer. The palace had been Anne Boleyn's favorite, but now all of Anne's coat of arms, all of her signs and symbols had been removed from stained glass and wood, from plaster and marble.

In their place there stood the symbol that Jane had chosen, a phoenix rising from a castle, the symbol of the new Tudor dynasty that would spring from her.

King Henry hunted and sometimes took expeditions to little towns not too far distant. But he never went more than fifty miles from Queen Jane and stood, he told her, ever ready to come back, should she summon him.

Jane did not summon him. There was no need. The pregnancy went well, and there was nothing lacking. After the first few months, when Jane had felt unsteady and always on the verge of crying, she now felt contented.

She viewed the enlarging of her belly as if it were the ripening of the fruits towards harvest. She was contented and fruitful and ready to deliver the child who would rule over England.

In her moments of silence, spent embroidering the trousseau of the prince that was to come, she dreamed of her child who would look like his father but perhaps have her pale face. He would be a pretty boy with a laughing countenance and grow up into a handsome man, agile and good at riding and hunting and jousting and those other great pursuits of every noble gentleman.

And after him would come another two boys and perhaps two girls who, with Mary and Elizabeth, would give the king, their father, enough material to contract many princely marriages and arrange many firm pacts on the strength of them.

At the end of the summer, she took to her room, beginning the period proper of her confinement. Her court, which had always been quiet, now became very quiet—just her ladies and herself—though the king came back to sleep every night, if he were within riding distance of her.

He was there beside her, in the bed, when her pains overtook her in the middle of a night in October. She'd been so concerned with not delivering too early that her first thought had been that the child could not possibly be born now, that it would be a repeat of Queen Catherine's and Queen Anne's many premature births and tragedies.

But some small sound she made, while trying to stifle the pain, woke the king. He looked at her and smiled wide and said, "It is time, Jane, it is time."

There was no privacy for queens. Oh, there was truly no privacy for any woman. Jane remembered her own mother's lying in and how neighbors would come from all around to help with the birth or to give their opinion of what must be done.

Little Jane herself had been admitted to the birthing room, to run for a bit of claret for her mother, or to fetch some warm water or cold compresses, or other necessities that changed moment to moment as the lady of the house gave birth.

But at least in those cases, all the people in the room had been female and known to the mother. The people who filed into Jane's room were more male than female, and only a few of them more than a distant acquaintance with her.

There were her brothers, of course. But then there were also many great nobles of the kingdom who had vied for the privilege to be present at the birth of their next king and who stood at the foot of the bed, rank on rank, talking and laughing and paying—it seemed to Jane—no attention at all to her.

But the king came, also, and held onto her hand, while midwives and doctors were ushered in, and Jane's maids and ladies-in-waiting bustled around, fetching all those things that Jane had fetched when she'd stood in at her mother's lyings-in.

At first the pains were well spaced and mild and allowed Jane to think on the strangeness that queens must give birth as did prize horses, watched by all so that everyone was sure there had been no replacements and that the issue was truly worth what it purported to be.

But then the pains started coming closer, more violent, till all of Jane's slim and small body shook with them, and it seemed to her no human being, no single, mortal creature could endure this.

She heard herself scream, and in her mind her screams seemed to echo together with the screams of Anne Boleyn and, presumably, of Catherine in the same position.

And labor went on. And on. And on. Jane didn't know how

long the pain had lasted. Nor could she be sure how long she'd be laboring to free her body of the burden upon it.

She knew only that now and then someone pressed a soft cloth against her forehead, mopping up the sweat that had collected there. And that sometimes someone from the foot of the bed said, "You must push harder, Your Majesty, push."

In her mind, she remembered someone telling her mother to push harder. She heard again Anne Boleyn's screams of pain at giving birth. Had dying hurt half so much as this? How much could a severed head hurt compared to this body-splitting torment?

And yet, the child was in her, and the child must come out.

From the distorted sea of her pain, she heard voices. The voices and the faces of those who possessed them all seemed to belong to an indistinct confusion, a mass that she could neither see nor hear clearly enough.

But some of the words were unavoidable. Some words she could not ignore. Like the man who held her pulse with too-cold and dry fingers and said, "She is small, Your Majesty, and the baby is large. I am afraid she will not last."

"She will last," the king said, with assured good humor. "Jane will last and give me many children."

And Jane thought he was only so sure because he could not possibly know how badly Jane hurt or how she felt as if her whole body were being torn apart.

"Push, Your Majesty, push," a voice said from the foot of the bed, and Jane tried, but she could hardly command enough strength to breathe, much less to push this unwieldy burden from within her.

She heard herself whimper. She heard her voice, low and unsteady, say, "I cannot. I cannot. For the love of Jesu, just cut the child out of my belly and let me die in peace."

From either side of the bed rose arguments. That it was against the law of God to sacrifice the mother for the child. And that Jane was not so far gone as she thought.

It seemed to Jane the physicians disagreed, one saying she could do it, and the other saying she couldn't. And Jane must agree with the physician who said Jane would die of this. Because Jane felt her mortal nature slip away and not even the wish of seeing her child could keep her in the world.

"Jane."

She knew that voice. It was the king's voice, clear and imperious. "You swore to obey me in all things. You made your obedience into your badge, your shield of honor. Jane, queen of England, wife of King Henry, I order you to push."

And somehow, from the great love and fear she bore for her sovereign, from her pride in always being obedient, Jane found strength and power. She reached up with desperate hands and found the great wooden bedstead that Anne Boleyn had ordered carved for her, but which she had not lived to use.

Pushing hard against the bedstead, Queen Jane put all her strength into pushing her burden out of her body and into pushing new life into the world.

The end of pain was so abrupt it surprised her, and for a moment she thought she had died and entered heaven. For that was exactly what it felt like, as though she had passed instantly from the torments of hell into paradise.

She heard a baby cry and thought how strange that the baby was here with her, in paradise. Then, blinking her eyes, clearing them of sweat and tears, she saw that she was still in her room in Hampton Court and that none of the ambassadors or dignitaries was looking at her.

Instead, as one of her ladies covered the queen's lower body with a sheet, the people who'd come to watch the new king being born were all looking towards Jane's husband, Henry, who stood by the bed holding a large, rosy child in his arms.

Jane wondered if it were a boy and a girl. The king was smiling. Would he smile for a girl?

She tried to find the voice for a question, but it wouldn't come, and so she must look her query at the king when he turned to look at her.

The king laughed, as if guessing her anxiety, and spoke softly, feelingly. "It's a boy, Jane. It's a boy. England has a prince."

And Jane allowed herself to fall into sweet sleep.

Forty-six

THE next days were a blur. Jane woke to eat, and the rest of the time she slept.

No one would deny her anything. Any food she fancied, anything she wanted, she could have. Quail were brought to her, and sweets and any wine she wished.

The little prince, whom the king had said would be named Edward, after his great-grandfather, was brought in, too, often enough on the arms of the large, sturdy woman who had been made his nurse.

Jane would hold him in her arms, and he would look on her with an intent, adoring gaze that made Jane want to smile and cry at the same time, because here was a male who would never care at all if Jane was plain. To him, she would remain always the most beautiful woman in the world.

She lay in her dim room and tried to get her strength back.

Throughout the land, there was great praise and great joy. People thanked God, and bells rang in celebration.

And Jane realized that this time, if the worst were going to happen, if the king were to die, there would be one heir, an undisputed king. And much as the situation of a boy-king might be precarious, it would not cause armies to rise and march and kill each other in support of now this bastard prince and now another.

She leaned back against her pillows and contemplated that she had done what neither of the queens before her had managed.

That the king was pleased with her, she could not doubt. He often came into her room and sat by her bed, talking of their son and how already the days-old babe showed such strength and spirit that King Henry was sure Edward would make a great king himself, when his time came.

And Jane slept, and woke again.

"If I do not disturb Your Majesty," a timid, girlish voice said.

Opening her eyes, Jane noted that the king was gone from where he had been sitting by the bed, holding her hand. Turning her head the other way, Jane saw that Mary stood by the door, holding little Elizabeth by the hand.

"Elizabeth wanted to see you," she said, "and assure herself we still had a mother."

"You have a mother," Jane said and, with sudden worry, "Lady Mary, you do not resent . . . You do not feel that I have pushed you quite out of the way, by having a son who will reign after his father, do you?"

For some reason at that moment, she couldn't bear the thought of injuring Mary, who was almost her only female friend and certainly the most sincere one.

But Mary reached for her hand and squeezed it. "Do not make yourself uneasy, Your Majesty. It was never my fate to reign. And I'm glad to see the honor go to your son, a worthy prince and conceived in most lawful matrimony. I shall be very contented. What I gained by having Your Majesty as a mother more than compensates for losing the succession, which is why I had no qualms in signing away my legitimacy. Do not trouble yourself, Your Majesty, and rest, for tomorrow will be the baptism, and it will be a long and tedious ceremony. You are the mother of our future king. You have saved the country from great strife. My father the king wants you to be present at the ceremony, that you might be honored as you should."

"I am glad," Jane said. "I am glad you will have a brother to reign after your father and protect us all."

And at that moment little Elizabeth pulled at the bed-clothes and said, in that great precocious voice that sounded too grown-up and full of meaning for her years, "We are all in God's hands, and it is He who chooses who shall reign and who shall not."

Forty-seven

 And then there had been the baptism, a long, tiring ceremony of which Jane remembered no more than this ambassador and then that paying homage to her.

From that on, it had all been a dream.

And now she lay in the great bed at Hampton Court, and she felt as if the bed, the rich curtains, the soft sheets all were on fire.

The wine she'd drunk had only cooled her tongue for a moment, and now that its flavor had started receding there was in its place the parched and sickening taste that ever comes to a mouth with a great fever.

The figures in the room—the king, the priests, the attendant ladies, even the burning fire in the fireplace—all seemed to recede, becoming transparent and immaterial.

Only one person was vivid and solid and material. She

stood by Jane's bed and smiled. Her merry smile curved the corners of lips well-suited for humor and joy. And her dark eyes sparkled with mirth, as they did after she'd just made a mocking comment about anyone or played a particularly clever prank.

She shook her head—which Jane was surprised to see was firmly attached to that slim neck that resembled the stem of an elegant flower. Her great curtain of silky black hair, lose behind her back, swayed with her movement.

And the lips opened, and Anne Boleyn's musical voice said, "Ah, Jane, you see. You struggled so much and tried so hard, and yet you will end up just like me. Was it worth it, then, to be obedient, to do all the king wanted only to die like this?" She laughed, her great, intemperate laughter. "And he never even loved you. Oh, he might tell you all that about your being sweet and kind, but in the end, Henry likes a woman who stands up to him. And he likes beauty." Anne Boleyn's face came very close to Jane's, swimming on a mist of fever that clouded Jane's senses and her thoughts. "And you have no beauty, Jane."

And it was true. Jane had known since she was nine that she had no beauty.

But she reached inside herself, and looked back at the spiteful face smiling maliciously at her. She had no beauty, maybe, but she had wit and kindness and a good understanding. She'd understood the king far better than either of the former queens.

"I've given him a son," she said. "Who do you think he will love and remember?"

Anne Boleyn looked shocked, as if Jane had slapped her, and her face dissolved and changed into the fat, doughy face of Jane's attendant.

"She's fading fast," the woman said, speaking over Jane's head and towards the king, who sat on the other side, holding Jane's hand. Jane could feel the moisture of tears upon her skin, and she turned to look at the king and saw him crying and staring back at her with a doting, loving expression such as she'd never seen on his face when he looked at Anne Boleyn. Or at any of the women with whom he trifled.

It was an expression full of love and adoration. He'd called her his entirely beloved wife before, and that was what his expression said. That she had been, was, and would always be his entirely beloved.

Jane grinned in mockery at the ghost she could no longer see. Into the joust of life, she had come equipped with such paltry weapons as to be inconsequential. The woman's arms of beauty and grace had not been given to her at all, and in their place she'd been given a keen mind and a ready heart—inconsequential lances that seemed to break whenever a man's eyes perceived a more beautiful woman.

And yet with them Jane had achieved what Anne Boleyn, for all her beauty, had failed to manage. Anne had gone to her death forsaken, accused of witchcraft, and dragging down with her all her dearest friends.

But Plain Jane would die the queen, honored and loved, the mother of the future king and King Henry's entirely beloved wife.

Author's Afterword

Writing about Jane Seymour posed its own particular problem. Of all the wives she is perhaps the least documented. Most books and websites take no interest at all in our Jane until the king goes to Whitehall for hunting, when she suddenly bursts upon the historical scene. Part of the problem is that Jane was born before the registration of births was made compulsory in 1538. It is therefore often difficult to pinpoint the date of her birth.

After much reading of contradictory evidence, I decided to go with the assessment of William Seymour in *Ordeal by Ambition: An English Family in the Shadow of the Tudors*. He relied primarily on internal evidence of other events within the family as well as upon what had been written about Jane by contemporaries. On the basis of this, he had Jane as the eldest girl, born after four boys and before another six children.

The story of Jane's romance with William Dormer as well as the part played by Sir Francis Bryan in getting Jane her position at court are also inferred by William Seymour from evidence.

For the marriage's taking place in the queen's closet at Whitehall, I took as evidence the overwhelming majority of books and websites. Though this contradicts a legend that claims she got married at her parents' house, that legend could be based on the memory of a party thrown in honor of the just-engaged Jane. In local lore it would get turned into a wedding feast.

As for Jane's "romance" with Sir Thomas Wyatt, I'll own that it's entirely my responsibility. In the climate of Henry VIII's court it is almost impossible that Jane didn't have at least a platonic attachment before the king's gaze lighted on her. However, if she was, as portrayed by practically everyone, a maid of modest and moderate behavior, no one would know of her inner romantic life, save maybe perhaps the person who was the object of it. To be honest, she might have developed tender feelings for anyone, including someone who left no mark in the pages of history. I, however, had to pick someone who would be interesting to write about. I chose Sir Thomas Wyatt because he introduced the sonnet to England, which makes him a dashing, romantic figure and the perfect foil for our quiet Jane.

Since what I read to research the book often consisted of a paragraph here and a sentence there in other people's biographies, it is impossible to relay a full list. As I've confessed, I relied primarily on *Ordeal by Ambition* by William Seymour. However, for anyone with interest in this era I would also recommend Alison Weir's *Henry VIII: The King and His Court* as well as Weir's *The Six Wives of Henry VIII*. Jane is also given at least cursory treatment in any book about Anne Boleyn.

All in all I found Queen Jane a gentle presence in a rough time and empathized with her choice of the "least evil action." Certainly her behavior stands out as more ethical than the raw ambition of her family and of practically anyone else connected with Henry VIII.